THE DISASTER

Deep beneath the placid waters lurks a hidden menace. Dormant for decades, it will rain death and destruction on an unsuspecting populace.

THE CREATURES

Once docile fish, now man-eating monsters, they are the first victims of the ecological cataclysm—but they won't be the last.

THE LAKE

Some people notice the water looks different. Some people fear their community is endangered. But no one expects the horrifying truth: everyone will die unless the threat is destroyed.

The LAKE

R. KARL LARGENT

LEISURE BOOKS   NEW YORK CITY

A LEISURE BOOK®

June 1993

Published by

Dorchester Publishing Co., Inc.
276 Fifth Avenue
New York, NY 10001

The name ''Leisure Books'' and the stylized ''L'' with design are
trademarks of Dorchester Publishing Co., Inc.

Printed in the United States of America.

ONE

Wednesday A.M., September 1

There is an irony to all of this. After all, I am a writer—not a reporter, mind you, but a story-teller, a novelist—and what was happening had all the elements of a good plot. Perhaps I didn't see it at the time because I was caught up in it. I can assure you however that, if I had realized what was unfolding, I damn sure would have kept a journal of some kind. *The National Inquirer* or *The Star* would have snapped up the story like hotcakes. If I had been alert enough to take a few pictures, it would have been even better. But, I did neither. There is no hour-by-hour chronicle of what happened, and there damn sure aren't any pictures.

The events that took place, recounted to the best of my ability, are not on paper. They are in my head, like a nightmare—and that may be even worse.

The way I remember it, Sam Patton was the

first to talk about it at any length. For Sam, belaboring a subject meant two grunts instead of one. He looked up from whatever he was doing that day and began the conversation. "Hey, Elliott, have you noticed that damn smell over at the far end of the lake?"

I had and I acknowledged as much.

"Smells like something died," he said.

At the time I was engrossed in the sports section of the morning edition of the Fort Janes's newspaper and a cold Bud, and I wasn't paying a whole lot of attention to what Sam was saying. If indeed he was saying anything at all. When writers slip into a downer—a funk out, or a block as it's often called—they tend to crawl inside their own heads and dial out the rest of the world. And inside my own head is a good way of describing exactly where I was that Wednesday afternoon, five days before all hell broke loose in Jericho.

I had just spent the better part of the morning pecking away at my word processor and had nothing to show for it. In addition, I had been forced to sit through two irate phone calls: one from my agent, who wanted to know when I was going to get my ass in gear; and one from my editor, who less than tactfully suggested that I quit screwing off, get back to work and meet a deadline for a change.

All of which I was trying to put out of my head. It was hot and sticky and pisspoor weather for a writer. Writers need cloudy days. On sunny days, they feel as if the world is passing them by while they are cooped up with a blinking cur-

12

sor on a black-and-white monitor listening to the monotone symphony of their keyboard. The locals called that time of year the dog days of summer, but I hadn't seen any of the local mutts enjoying the weather any more than I was.

"Looks hazy down there too," Sam said. "Did you notice? Worst summer we've had in years. No wonder business is off." Then he added, "Thank God the Jubilee is coming up."

I remember looking around Sam's tavern. With the exception of a fat guy and his dishwater blonde girl friend slobbering over two beers and keeping time to a Willie Nelson recording, the place was empty.

Sam was right—August had been miserable. A depressing, energy-sucking low pressure area had settled in over the area some two-and-a-half weeks earlier, and it had taken up permanent residence. Everyone was complaining about the heat and the humidity. To make matters worse, the local weather forecasters were saying that the supersaturated air that blanketed the entire valley was going to hang around into early September. Great, just great, I kept telling myself. The day after Labor Day I was headed back to the Keys empty-handed. My three-month, get-the-book-done sabbatical was over and the only thing I had to show for it was a half-done manuscript and a case of heat rash.

Sam Patton, the proprietor of Patton's Pier, was not exactly an astute observer of human behavior, or he would have noted that my disposition was as deplorable as the weather. He did notice that my bottle was empty though, popped another and set it on the bar in front of me.

"It's strongest over there by the channel leading back up toward the slough," he said. "Ain't seen anybody fishing over there in days. That smell probably runs them all out."

A bartender and small talk. At least he was trying, which was more than I could say.

I turned around on my stool and studied the lake. It looked placid, or maybe I should say stagnant. The writer in me took over and I mentally clicked off: smooth, motionless, calm, quiet—none of which really seemed to describe what I was looking at. There was something else about it—something disquieting or perhaps even disturbing?

It was the dying days of summer, the locals were bracing for the community's biggest weekend of the year, and the lake was all but deserted. At that particular moment there was no breeze and the rental sailboats were still all tied up at the marina. By the same token, there were no water-skiers and not a single jet ski in sight. I had been hanging around Jericho just long enough to know that it was the worst part of the day for fishing and it didn't surprise me that I didn't see any fishing boats. With the exception of a handful of noisy kids splashing in the water up the road at the municipal beach, there just wasn't much activity. "Too hot to fish," I said, trying to be sociable. "You've heard that old line about mad dogs and Englishmen?"

Sam Patton was an ex-jock, which probably explains the blank look he gave me. That line, I had to remind myself, was not very likely to be in his playbook. He grinned and nodded because he thought that was what he was supposed to do when a customer made an attempt at humor, even if it didn't make any sense to him. He studied me for a moment and went back to polishing his beer glasses.

This is as good a time as any to step back for a moment and explain how all of this got started. Ginny Fordice owns a cottage here on the lake and Ginny is my literary agent's partner. She caught her husband, Marvin, an investment broker, playing tangle toes with his secretary one afternoon and promptly lowered the legal noose around his neck. Presto: instant cottage owner as part of the settlement. The sordid scenario would make even more sense if I told you that Ginny and I are friends, and she knew I was having one hell of a time trying to meet a too short deadline on a too long novel. Bottom line: the nice lady offered me her cottage for the summer while she went to Europe, and I jumped at the opportunity for a temporary change in the scenery. The only problem was that I had only half finished a manuscript that was supposed to be completed when I returned to Key West. Blame it on Cyn, I told myself. She's the real culprit behind my lack of progress.

When Sam looked up from his labors again, he was still trying to make small talk. "Know somethin', Elliott, I been thinkin' about that book you said you was writin', and I got a question. If you're writin' about sharks, how come you're here at a freshwater lake? Ain't no sharks here."

"Good question," I said. I usually respond with that phrase on those rare occasions when I actually have an answer, which I seldom do because writers are hardly ever good conversationalists. "It's simple: the cottage is free." I did not bother to add that writers never have any money and free is one of the most cherished words in their vocabulary.

I had learned early on in the summer that vague half answers usually satisfied Sam; on cue, he went back to his chores and I finished my second beer. Two was enough. Lunch break was over and I was halfway off the bar stool when Bert Freeman walked in. Bert was one of the more colorful locals, one of the first people I met after my arrival and one of the guys I played poker with on nights when Cynthia was tied up at the bank. He spotted me, headed straight for the bar, slapped me on the back and crawled up on the stool next to me. "Hear about the fish Hatch caught?" he asked.

I braced myself for another one of Bert's biggest-damn-something-or-other stories and shook my head.

"Biggest damn garfish I ever saw," he proclaimed, "weird looking thing."

Bred, born and raised in the city with more recent stops in Marathon and Key West, I don't know a hell of a lot about inland-lake living, and fish of the freshwater variety is one of them—unless, of course, it happens to be on the menu at the City Club or Tank's down near the White

The Lake

Street fishing pier, where folks from the north eat when they get homesick. "Garfish?" I repeated. Garfish was a new term to me.

"Yeah, garpike. Damn ugly fish."

Locals have a knack of knowing when out-of-towners don't know what they are talking about. The expression on my face was a giveaway. Bert seized the opportunity. He launched into a lengthy, unscientific description of garpike. "Unpleasant-looking bastards, big long snout and a mouth full of razor-sharp teeth."

"Sounds like a lady I used to date," I said.

Bert frowned at me. Still, it was plain to see that my ignorance on the subject of garpikes was enough to inspire him. By the time he had finished I knew I would have to spend a good 30 minutes with *Malcolm's Guide to Freshwater Fish* to get the real facts.

When Bert paused to order another beer, I made my getaway. "See you this evenin', E. G.?" Sam asked as I headed for the door.

"Depends on what Cyn is doing," I said. I could have saved my breath. Bert was already bending Sam Patton's ear with the details of Graham Hatcher's biggest damn catch.

It was a good half-mile trek from Ginny Fordice's cottage to Sam's place, a nice walk on a good day and a pleasant reprieve after spending the morning crouched over a word processor. It was a pleasant experience when it was cool. But it wasn't cool; it was downright hot. And to make matters worse, I had a couple of beers sloshing around in my stomach.

The early September sun was relentless, the temperature had clawed its way into the mid-nineties and there was little or no breeze. The walk back to Ginny's place was certain to be a bummer. It was compounded by the fact that the minute I stepped out of the door of Sam's place I could smell it. For the first time I noticed the odor that far from the slough.

Let me dwell on this so-called odor for a moment. Sam had said more than most about it, but Cynthia and several others had mentioned it over the past couple of days. The first time I noticed it was the day I was headed south around the lake to Herd's Grocery. The top of the car was down and because it is tantamount to incarcerable insanity to drive anything over 15 miles an hour on the lake road, I was plodding along taking in the sights. Bachelors, especially those who have managed to survive 40-odd summers, learn to slow down when the scenery gets interesting. And the scenery three cottages down from Herd's Grocery was spectacular. Both of the scenic vistas had blonde hair, long legs, skimpy bathing suits and great tans, and they were inclined to wave when I drove by. I learned a long time ago that the appreciated appreciate their appreciators.

I was crossing the stone bridge when I noticed the odor. I remember glancing back up the slough because the odor seemed to be coming from that direction. That slough, Bert had been assuring me, was where the big fish were caught. Within moments though, I had passed over the bridge, the odor faded and I promptly forgot about it.

The second time I encountered it, the odor was stronger. Thinking back, that was two days prior to Sam making his astute observation. I had drifted down to the dock, just after sunup, a cup of coffee clutched in my hand, intending to make my ritualistic, start-of-the-day assessment of the climate. I could smell it then: a peculiar, unpleasant smell, but a long way from being what you would call nauseating. There was a slight breeze at the time coming across the lake from the slough, and there appeared to be a hazy patch over the area in the vicinity of the bridge. At the time I remember being all too willing to chalk the odor off to some kind of local atmospheric phenomenon. What the hell, I told myself. I had never been in Jericho in August before. And besides, other than an occasional casual comment or two, no one seemed to be paying much attention to it.

Still in the process of trudging my way back to Ginny's place, I decided to stop in at the Hatchers'—ostensibly to see the big ugly fish, but more to see if Graham Hatcher could supply an off-duty writer with a temporary respite from the heat and something cool to drink. Graham had a reputation for mixing up the best gin and tonics on the lake.

Looking back, I was more than a trifle curious about a fish described as having a long ugly snout and a mouth full of razor-sharp teeth. Even though it wasn't a shark, Bert's description made the creature sound intriguing.

Dolly Hatcher came to the door. She had her usual half-blitzed smile and a frosty pink concoction loaded with ice poised in her gnomelike hand. Dolly looked like an albino version of Aunt Jemimah—same engaging smile, same ample dimensions. It was no more than three o'clock in the afternoon and she was ready to party.

"Elliott!" she said. "Come on in." She turned and called out to her husband. "Graham, come in here. Elliott Grant Wages is here." Some people call me Elliott; others call me E. G. Once there was a girl in Mississippi who used to call me Elliott Grant. But seldom do I hear anyone use my entire name. Dolly was one of the few.

Graham Hatcher bounced into the room with a big grin on his face. He was carrying a drink. "Hey, E. G., are you thirsty?" he asked.

"Thought you would never ask," I said with a slight drawl. Local speech patterns have always been contagious for me. Graham liked the fact that after only three months I sounded more like one of the locals than some folks who had lived around Jericho Lake for years. He intensified his toothy grin and scurried over to a big bar that encompassed most of one wall of the Hatcher's spacious living room. Dolly moved to the couch, planted herself and patted the seat beside her.

"Sit down," she said. "As soon as Graham fixes you a drink he'll show you his fish." I did and she cooed, giggled and fussed until Graham handed me one of his lake-famous compositions.

While I sipped, I thought about the sociologists who contend that when folks live together for a long time they start to look like each other. Dolly and Graham were living proof of those contentions. Graham had a moon face, several chins, a flat sideways kind of nose and squinty, smiling eyes. All of his facial features were bunched right in the middle of his face. Beyond that, a person couldn't tell much about his head because he was always wearing one of those floppy-brimmed, terry-cloth hats that conceal everything else. Rumor had it that he was bald. The rest of him was clearly portly. He was short, but not quite as short as Dolly, who was built like a basketball.

"So you heard about the fish, huh?" Hatcher asked.

"Think about it. If Bert Freeman knows, the whole world knows."

Dolly slapped her leg, laughed, drained her glass and got up to fetch herself a refill.

"I'm afraid the word's out. According to Bert you not only caught the biggest fish he has seen in some time; you also caught the ugliest."

"Yeah," Hatch said, "it's a damn weird looking critter all right. I've been fishing this lake for forty years and I've never seen anything like it." He lumbered out of his chair and motioned for me to follow. "Come on, I'll show it to you."

We stepped out of the Hatcher's air-conditioned retreat into the soggy midday heat and walked across his yard down to the pier. Dolly was right behind us and the Hatcher family dog brought up the rear. Along the way, the round man regaled me with a blow-by-blow description of his conquest.

"Went out early this morning to beat the heat,"

he said, panting, "and slipped over on the east side of the lake. Fished there for several hours. Nothing, not even a nibble. Then I drifted a bit south until I was a couple of hundred yards from the stone bridge, but far enough away from that damn smell not to let it bother me. I cast a couple of times and wham—I mean big wham. That sucker hit my plug and took off with it. But after he took about thirty feet of line, he quit on me, no fight at all. I figured I had tied in to one of those big buffalo fish. By the time I got him up to the boat, I realized what I had. A big, I mean damn big, garpike. The sonofabitch was so big I could hardly heft him into the boat. Can you imagine that? All I was trying to do was scare up enough crappies for Dolly to fix us a little lunch treat and I end up catching this pisser."

I looked back at Dolly. She was beaming with pride. Her man had caught a real pisser.

Graham dropped to his knees, leaned over the side of the pier, wrapped his short, blunt fingers around a heavy leader and pulled his prize out from under the shadows of the dock. For once in his life, Bert Freeman had not overstated his case.

Graham Hatcher's catch was downright hideous. The creature had dull, brown-black eyes encased in a bloated, grotesque looking head. There were a series of red cancerous sores around the wretch's mouth and the serrated rows of razorlike teeth were blackened to the extent that they appeared to be in an advanced state of decay. The head melded away into an elongated tubular-shaped body networked with open lesions and ridged with nodules.

Dolly's dog growled when Hatch hauled the beast out of the water; then it backed away a couple of steps and began to whimper.

"That's a garpike?" I asked.

"Ain't very pretty, is it?" Hatch said, nodding.

At that particular moment, I was reflecting on the night that Cyn and I had declared war on a bottle of Laphroaig and gone skinny-dipping in a spot not far from where Graham Hatcher claimed he had landed his monster fish. Never again, I told myself.

"Tell him how big it is," Dolly said.

"Seventy-four inches. Measured him myself." By then, Hatcher's dog had backed away still farther.

Dolly was all smiles. Her hands were on her hips and I could tell that, in her happy eyes, moon-faced Graham was pure hero. "I've been around this lake all my life," she said, "and I have never seen a garpike that big. The biggest one I saw up until Graham caught this one was thirty inches long and that was at the Fisherman's Jubilee thirty years ago." Dolly took a couple of sips of her drink in toast to her hero.

"Has to be a record," Hatch said. "I'm gonna take it in town later and enter it in the Jubilee fishing contest."

Record or not, I had already decided it was the only garpike I ever wanted to see. "I've seen enough," I said, shaking my head. "Bert was right. But if you ask me, the damn thing looks like some kind of prehistoric monster."

Hatch rotated his catch and began to point

out some of its unusual features. "It is kind of weird. Look at this. See the teeth, the way they are angled out? Then count them. This is a relatively young fish, but for some reason all the teeth appear to be rotted." His cherubic face had broken out in a sweat. He was struggling to hold the beast out of the water. He pointed to the serrations along the body. "See these splits in the skin? I never saw anything like that either. Sounds weird, but it almost looks like the damn thing grew so fast its skin couldn't keep up with it."

I had to agree. That was exactly what it looked like.

Graham Hatcher lowered his lifeless prize back down into the shallow water and it floated into the shadows under the pier.

"Well, what do you think?" Hatch asked.

I was reluctant to tell the old boy what I really thought because at that very moment I wasn't certain that I wasn't the target of an elaborate practical joke. Hatcher, Freeman and Patton were capable of it. What the hell did I know? Maybe all needle-nosed garpikes looked like that one. The local yokels were not above jerking the chain on the tourists. And since they all knew I was leaving right after the Labor Day weekend, I figured the boys might just be having one last elaborate giggle at old Elliott's expense. Either way, it was big and it was ugly, and if it was legitimate, Graham Hatcher had caught himself quite a fish.

We started back up to the house with both Dolly and Graham speculating about how their fish should be mounted. Dolly's dog, however, was having nothing to do with Graham, and I was thinking about all the times I had dipped my precious hide in those same waters. As far as I was concerned, Graham's catch looked thoroughly capable of snapping off toes, fingers and other assorted projecting anatomical parts with consummate ease.

As we worked our way back up to the house, any number of questions had started to meander through my brain. Did mothers with small children know that things like garpike were cruising blissfully around under the surface of that lake? What were all those lesions and the bumps and oversize nodules about? Before I went off half-cocked and started conjuring up questions that didn't need answers, I decided I had better do a little research of my own.

At the door of their cottage, I thanked the corpulent couple for the drink, confirmed that it was indeed one ugly fish, wished Hatch luck in the fishing contest and started across the lawn.

Dolly and Graham Hatcher both smiled and waved. Out of the corner of my eye, I saw the dog again. Its tail was tucked between its legs and it was still whimpering.

Thinking back about it, I doubt that Hatch's garpike upset that pooch any more than it did me.

By the time I had showered and called the public library in Fort Janes, I had managed to learn a thing or two about garpikes or gars: *Genus Lepisosteus*, freshwater ganoid, very hard scales, voracious and aggressive, family Belondiau, up to thirty-six inches in length.

The problem was that Hatcher's big, ugly fish was twice that long and I had come to the conclusion that the locals weren't pulling my leg. Of particular interest were the notes I had jotted down on color. According to the three references the nasal-voiced research assistant at the library read me, gars were green, gray or greenish-brown. None of the three references mentioned anything about the definite pinkish cast of Graham Hatcher's catch. As I thought about it, I vaguely remembered one of those so-called universal laws about species deviation in sharks: mavericks and rogues may and often do depart in size and behavior, but not pigmentation and overall characteristics. Paraphrased, a garpike, like a shark, could deviate pretty far from the standard, but he couldn't change his overall color and shape.

Interest in gars, big or small, waned as the afternoon wore on and the activity on the lake increased. Most of it was occurring across the lake at the city beach and at the marina. It was only Wednesday, but some of the out-of-towners had already started to arrive for the pre-Jubilee festivities. In their honor, I fixed myself a tall drink, rattled the cubes around to chill it down and went out on the deck to catch what little breeze there was.

Two youths with single-masted Butterflies had managed to extricate themselves from the flotilla of anchored pleasure craft clustered around the marina. They were at least 300 yards from shore, tacking back and forth toward the east end of the lake. I watched them for several minutes, then went in to answer the phone. It was Cyn. She was running late. We made some cooing noises, then I hung up and went back out on the deck. By that time, one of the boys had capsized. His buddy was laughing while he tacked back and forth waiting for his friend to right his craft. The outcome was still in doubt when the doorbell rang.

No one answers the door for Harrison Peters. He simply barges in. To his way of thinking, even lovers could disentangle themselves as slow as he moved. Despite his new uniform, he looked worse than usual. His shirt had big circles of perspiration under each arm and his tie was off. "Hey, E. G.," he shouted, "where are you?"

"Out here on the deck."

I could hear the refrigerator door open and close before he waddled out on the deck with a beer. The bottle was half empty before he sat down. "Christ, it's hot."

Harrison Peters was a genuine one-off. He had a ruddy face, full and round, with big shaggy eyebrows that were the same color as his half-white, half-blond hair. Every feature was out of proportion: eyes, nose and ears all too small and everything else too large.

Rumor had it that Peters used to be an engineer for an aerospace company in Fort Janes. Rumor also had it that he pounded knots on his boss in a bar one night and kissed off ten years with the firm by walking out on his job the next morning. Rumor also had it that was when he came home, back to the place where he grew up. And in an effort to keep his unemployed stomach from growling too loud, he took a job filling in for the then ailing Jericho County sheriff. He ran for election when the old boy retired two years later and had served as sheriff ever since, which, in this case, was something like 25 years.

Bachelors, we had hit it off right from the outset. No more than a half-dozen days had passed during the course of the summer without us sharing a beer or two and one of Harrison's caustic observations on life. Harrison Peters was one of the people I knew I was going to miss when I went back to Key West. "It's a goddamn zoo out there, and the damn Jubilee hasn't even started," he said. "Beats me why something like this brings out the worst in people." Peters was in a bitching mood. He both wanted and needed to complain; he did not want or expect responses.

I watched the youngster get his Butterfly righted and set course for the south end of the lake. His buddy was right behind him. True, this was my first Fisherman's Jubilee; and unless Cynthia Wallace, who had already made it a summer to remember, or Ginny Fordice, who had loaned me her cottage in the first place, saw fit to see that I returned, it was also going to be my last one.

Cyn had already regaled me with several stories about how what she called the sleepy and picturesque, village of some 1,200 crusty year-round residents swelled to thousands of madcap, hell-raising partygoers over the course of the three-day holiday. She made it sound like the Jericho County Fisherman's Jubilee was probably a good idea back in the days when the founding fathers wanted to have their own private little taking-out-the-piers party at the end of summer, but it had long since gotten out of hand. The picture Cynthia Wallace, Harrison Peters and others painted sounded more like a sordid orgy, a waterlogged sixties kind of rock festival.

"The damn tourists are starting to raise hell already," Peters said with a grunt. "I had to lock three drunks up earlier this afternoon. They were breaking up furniture down on the pier near the marina."

With that he went back into the house to get himself another beer, and as he did, a ski boat roared by pulling two skinny, bikini-clad waterskiers. The girls were laughing; the driver was drinking a beer.

By the time the sheriff came back, looked out at the lake, sagged back down in his chair and began sucking on his beer, he had changed the subject. "Did you smell that damn stink down by the bridge?"

I nodded, decided that wasn't enough of a response and said, "Un-huh, even Sam Patton was complaining about it down at his end of the lake."

"Everyone is bitching," Harrison said. "What the hell do they think I can do about it? Pass out gas masks?"

"In a town as small as Jericho, people have two choices," I said. "First they tell the sheriff;

then if that doesn't work, they take their troubles to Jesus."

Harrison grunted.

As far as I was concerned, it was simply an unpleasant odor, worth no more than a casual mention. But the locals were making a big thing out of it. I felt like telling them that the smell was nothing compared to August in the city during a garbage strike, an experience I remembered from my graduate days.

"Maybe I ought to drive over to George Lancer's place and talk to his hired hand," Harrison said. "Could be a dead calf or something. He's been having all kinds of problems with his pastures and livestock lately. You know, body gases, all this heat, them damn carcasses swell up, lay in the sun for a few days, the gases build up and they explode. Smells like hell when they do."

Harrison's description was just a tad too much for me. My stomach was giving me fair warning of the impending revolt and I went in the house on the pretext of getting a refill. I was hoping the interlude would change the subject again. It didn't. When I returned he was still grousing about the smell.

"Or maybe it's that damn plant," Peters said.

"What damn plant?" When the Jericho County sheriff was in one of his moods I kept my questions simple. It allowed him to vent his frustrations quicker and to get on to other complaints.

"That Bartel plant," he said.

"Bartel?"

"Yeah, that Bartel plant over on the backside of the slough near Montana Hills." He didn't elaborate but he did get to his feet. The bitching session was almost over. "Guess I better head over to the fairgrounds and see where they're setting up the rides. Gotta make sure those clowns all have their permits."

Just as Harrison Peters never waited to be invited in, he seldom bothered to bid his host or hostess farewell either. Harrison Peters never seemed to have the time nor the inclination to indulge in the social graces. I knew he was gone when I heard the door slam behind him.

When I looked around, the two Butterflies were gone too.

Wednesday P.M., September 1

In order to get to Cyn's place from Ginny's, I had two choices: turn east or west. The shortest way, due south, is directly across the lake. I turned east to avoid the line of tourist traffic streaming into Jericho.

Peters was right. A string of cars a half mile long had already started winding its way into the village. The fishing faithful loved these little shindigs.

The eastern route took me past Herd's Grocery, Graham Hatcher's place and Patton's Pier. Sam's parking lot was crowded. When I got to the bridge I slowed down and rolled down the window. Harrison was right on both scores. The odor was worse where the slough bled down into the lake and it was beginning to smell not just unpleasant but as if, to use Peter's words, something had died.

I stopped the car, got out and looked back

across the lake in the direction of Jericho. For the first time I really noticed it. Even now I'm not quite certain how to describe what I saw— a thin veil of fog, a mist, a cloud that seemed to be hovering close to the surface of the water. It wasn't opaque. In fact, looking at the distant village of Jericho through it, there was a kind of shimmering, gossamer quality to it. I made a mental note to check into whatever it was, but that well-intentioned thought was promptly forgotten when I pulled into Cyn's long, tree-lined drive a few minutes later.

Men like to fantasize about women, but they are never fully prepared for an encounter with a woman like Cynthia Wallace. She had black hair, rich green eyes that flirted and invited, a somewhat puggish nose, dimples, and a knock-out tan. And all that beauty only enhanced her tight, five-foot-six-inch body. If that isn't enough to race a man's engine, I'll throw in the fact that she owned a bank.

A banker's daughter by birth, she had forfeited a stodgy vice-presidency with First Bank of Boston and returned home to run the Bank of Fort Janes when her father died. Added to all of that was the fact that she was rapidly approaching what I've always considered to be a woman's prime years, the forties. Among her other baggage was an M.B.A. from Boston University and two failed marriages. Her education, her banking experience and her former mates all occurred back east in a convoluted past that I was never quite able to piece together into a coherent picture.

She lived in Wallace House, a posh and opulent spread on the south shore of the lake. The sprawling estate encompassed three acres, lots of trees, three gardens, a small abandoned stable and 1,400 feet of prime lake frontage. She had a housekeeper, Mrs. Fern, and a mongrel dog named Basketcase. The former was never around and the latter was always underfoot. I had met Cynthia Wallace at a booksigning shortly after my arrival, when the locals were still laboring under the impression that I was a celebrity.

I parked at the back of the house and found a note taped to the rear door. It informed me that she was down on the dock. To get there I had to walk through the house, down stairs leading to the patio, across the garden and several hundred feet of carefully manicured lawn. She was sitting in the gazebo at the end of her pier. On the white metal tea table in front of her was an open briefcase, a stack of papers, a laptop computer and a pitcher of something icy.

"How did it go today?" she asked, looking up.

"The funk fungus is still amongst us," I said, referring to my lack of progress on the overdue manuscript.

She shook her head, probably remembering the night I said there was no such thing as writer's block, proclaiming it to be merely a lack of discipline. But when she handed me a drink, I noticed that her hand was shaking. "Forgive me," she said. "I'm a little strung out."

"Tough day?"

"Damn Bartel."

34

The Lake

I propped my feet up on the chair next to me and allowed as how that was the second time I had heard the name Bartel taken in vain in the last hour. "Just who is this Bartel?"

"You know," she said, "the Bartel Toy Corporation. The ones that built the plant over near Montana Mills near the end of the slough."

"So we've got a toymaker in the neighborhood, huh? I hadn't heard about it."

"I'm not surprised. They built that plant over a year ago, and outside of a handful of people going in and out of there every morning, no one ever hears about it. It sure as hell didn't turn out to be the boost to the local economy that everyone hoped it would be."

"So what's the problem?"

"The problem is every time something goes wrong around here, people blame it on Bartel."

I felt like I was playing the old parlor game of 20 Questions. "Like what?"

Cyn put her papers down and pushed her sunglasses up on her pretty forehead. There were little beads of sweat on her pug nose. "George Lancer is just the latest."

I had no idea who George Lancer was or what the lady was talking about. Then I remembered Harrison Peters speculating about the possibility of the smell being a dead calf on Lancer's farm.

"Today," she said, "Millie Lancer stopped by to explain why they missed their last two payments on their mortgage."

"Tie it together. I'm still in the dark."

"The Lancers think that the Bartel plant is

doing something that is causing their milk production to drop off."

"Is it?"

Cyn furrowed her lovely brow. "Hell, Elliott, I don't know. What do I know about dairy herds? According to Millie Lancer, the pastures adjacent to the Bartel plant have all gone sour. The cows won't graze it, they have to keep the herd confined, their feed bills are up and they aren't making any money. No money, no mortgage payments. So it becomes my problem as well. They want me to talk to Bartel's superintendent, a fellow by the name of Roger Blackmonn."

"Sounds like a reasonable request."

Cyn's face twisted into an unbecoming scowl. "Now just what the hell am I supposed to say to him? 'Your neighbors are pissed because their cows won't graze in the pasture next to your plant?'"

"Let's jump in the car and drive over there," I said. I wasn't really curious and I didn't have a thing for dairy cows; I simply wanted Cyn's mood to brighten.

"That's part of the problem, Elliott. You can never get through to anyone over there. All calls are answered by the company's central switchboard in New York. I've driven over there twice in the last two days. There is never anyone around, no cars parked in the lot—not to mention the fact that we never see any trucks going in and out of there. They made a big deal about the county putting in a rail spur, but to the best of my knowledge there has never been a rail car moved in or out."

The Lake

"Well, if you're really intent on talking to someone, you can always sit outside and wait for someone to show up or leave. When you see them get in their car, you can run over and throw that awe-inspiring body of yours in front of their car and refuse to move until someone from Bartel agrees to talk to you." The lady's mood was such that I felt compelled to follow my tongue-in-cheek suggestion with a smile so that she would know I was kidding.

Cyn finally allowed a small smile to creep over her face and shrugged. "I guess it's either that or tell the Lancers I can't help them. My father, rest his soul, wouldn't like that one bit."

"All right," I said, starting to feel better myself, "now that we know what we're going to do about George Lancer's problem, what can I do to change your mood?"

Cyn reached out to take my hand. The tenseness was starting to dissipate. She endowed me with one of her blue-chip smiles and said, "Well for starters, you can take me to dinner."

One of the side benefits of using Ginny Fordice's cottage was the silver Carrera I discovered tucked away in her garage. It took a couple of days but I finally ferreted the keys out of their hiding place in a kitchen cupboard and had been driving it ever since. I mention this only because it was a perfect top-down kind of night. We drove to Cyn's club in Fort Janes and had a romantic candlelight dinner tucked away in a remote corner of the club's tea porch.

Dating one of the local power brokers has

its advantages. Banker Wallace was assured of impeccable service wherever she went. It was one of those little things that I had gotten used to, and I was going to miss it when I went back to Key West. As for our relationship, we both accepted the fact that our days were numbered. The summer was almost over. Still, there seemed to be some kind of unspoken agreement not to talk about it. We finished dinner, danced to a couple of mellow Grover Washington recordings and, because Thursday was a workday for Cynthia, started back to Jericho a little after ten.

On the way back, the lady had me take a circuitous route on back roads that eventually took us past the Bartel plant. There wasn't all that much to see; a large, somewhat-imposing monolithic structure was for the most part concealed by darkness. What little I could see was courtesy of a slip of moon that wasn't bright enough to illuminate any detail. At first glance, the only thing that seemed out of the ordinary was a 12-foot-high woven-wire security fence, topped with barbed wire. It looked like overkill considering the peaceful nature of the Jericho countryside. The more I thought about it, the more curious it seemed. This was not Detroit, where 12-foot-high security fences were nothing more than a mild nuisance to someone who wanted to get in bad enough. Cyn was right. There wasn't a soul, a car or, strangest of all, a security light anywhere to be seen.

We sat there for several minutes until the lady asked me if I had seen enough. I had, so we drove on, stopping at Patton's Pier when she offered to buy me a nightcap.

The place was jammed. Fully half the faces I had never seen before. The Jubilee goers were already out in force.

Graham and Dolly Hatcher had the biggest table, surrounded by slack-jawed revelers listening over and over to Bert's saga of the biggest damn fish. Dolly had even given the creature a name: the Giant Gar. Graham saw us enter and looked a little disappointed when we opted not to join the throng of adulators. I assured Cyn I had already paid the beast its due homage.

Sam, sweating profusely, was careening around the smoke-filled bar with all the subtlety of an ape in heat. He found us a table across the room from the Hatcher group, took our order and departed. Within seconds, Bert Freeman had spotted Cyn, plunked himself down at the table with us and started giving her the lurid details of Hatcher's big catch. In truth, I still hadn't decided whether Bert's unbridled endorsement added to or detracted from Hatcher's accomplishment. After all, this was the same man who had pronounced the new Jericho County fire engine the biggest damn fire truck he had ever seen; he had passed similar judgments on Cyn's restored Chris Craft and several other local happenings. They were, I will admit, all notably impressive, but hardly the biggest damn whatever.

Cyn turned to look at me. "You say you've seen it?"

I had learned never to appear smug if I was in

on something big before she was. "Yup," I said casually.

"Why didn't you tell me?" she demanded, and it was only then I realized she was baiting Freeman.

"Suppose I told you that looking at that big, ugly fish wasn't exactly the highlight of my day. The fact of the matter is it doesn't even look like a fish. It looks more like a big, pink, bloated worm, full of holes and cracks with lots of rotting teeth."

Cyn wrinkled her pug nose. "Don't be gross. I get the picture."

Bert was still looking at Cyn. "Sorry for screwing up your story, Bert," I said. But even with all of that, I wasn't convinced I had given the lady a wholly adequate description of Hatcher's fish.

Sam hustled back with the refreshments, a Long Island Iced Tea for Cyn, a scotch and water for me. Bert left and the conversation turned to the possibility of slipping into Fort Janes for the weekend to get away from the Jubilee madness. I like to think Cyn was on the verge of saying yes when I looked up and saw Harrison Peters approaching the table. He was still wearing the same sweat-soaked shirt and he still appeared agitated. But this time his face was creased into an even deeper frown than usual.

"E. G.," he said, "I got a problem." That was obvious. He was ignoring Cyn—and no man on the sunny side of senility ignores a woman who looks like Cynthia Wallace.

This time however there was a sense of urgency about Harrison Peters that transcended even his usual lack of boyish charm. "What's the problem?" I asked.

Harrison's half-mast eyes darted around the room and he led me away from the table. When he was certain that no one could overhear us, he motioned toward the lake. "Remember those two kids on the Butterflies we were watching from your front porch?"

"Yeah. What about it?"

"Something happened."

"What do you mean?"

Peters was measuring his words. "We found the body of one of them about an hour ago, wedged into the pilings at Becker Herd's pier. The other one is still missing."

I looked at the sheriff. "You think they both drowned?" Even as I was asking the question I knew that there was more to it than a simple drowning. The expression on Peters's face was the expression of a man who had encountered something extraordinary. "Are they locals or kids that came into town for the Jubilee?"

"They aren't locals," Harrison said.

At that particular moment I couldn't see why Harrison Peters was telling me all of this. Sure, we were friends, but Peters had deputies and a whole cadre of support people. "Is there a reason you're telling me all of this?"

Peters's eyes were hard. The quirky smile was gone. "Keep your voice down," he whispered. "Becker Herd is the one who found the body. He went out to lock up his gas pumps on the pier and saw something in the water. When he realized what it was, he called my office. After we got a look at the situation, I told him to help Mackey take the body into the coroner's office and keep it quiet until I could talk to you."

"What the hell are you talking about, Harrison? A drowning is a drowning. With all of the lakes around here and all of the tourists, surely you've had drownings before?"

The look on Harrison Peters's face was one that I hadn't seen before. "No damn it, E. G., this one we keep the lid on until we get some more information. A drowning is one thing. Bleeding to death is something else altogether."

"Bled to death?"

Peters's eyes narrowed and he glanced around the room to make certain no one could overhear him. Somehow he managed to lower his voice even further. "The kid's goddamn arm was chewed off right up to the shoulder."

I left the Carrera for Cyn and rode into the village with Harrison Peters. We headed for the offices of Dr. Marion Hoppkins in a single-story brick building on Lake Street. It was late enough in the evening and early enough in the pre-Jubilee celebration that the crowd had pretty well thinned out for the night. A discreet little brass sign on the door to Hoppkins's office indicated he was not only an M.D., but the Jericho County coroner as well.

The waiting room was dark, but the hall leading to the rear of the building was well lit and I could hear voices. Peters led me down the hall into a room where three men were clustered around an examining table. There was a stainless-steel table in the middle of the room with a bright light overhead. On the table was a rubber sheet; under the sheet was a clumpish, irregular shape.

Two of the men were Peters's deputies. One of them, an older man, occupied himself filling out forms. The other was talking to Hoppkins. Peters introduced me and instructed the younger of his two assistants—the one called Mackey—to tell me what happened.

Cletus Mackey was a tall, rawboned man. He had sun-leathered features: wide-set, squinty eyes; parched skin and a small, tight mouth.

"Got this call from Becker Herd," he said, "a little after nine o'clock. He said he was in the process of closing up for the night. Said he had gone down to the dock to lock up his gas pumps and looked down in the water checking for fuel line leaks. He said the water was kind of funny looking and that he thought he saw something moving—not a fish, but somethin' else. He went back up to the store, got his flashlight and his grappling hook—the one he uses to draw boats closer to the dock when he's fueling them. He came back down and poked around in the water until he saw what it was."

The old man poring over the paperwork looked up. "The boy's name is Abner Barker, from Fort Janes, seventeen years old." He laid a waterlogged wallet plus a handful of soggy contents taken from it on the table in front of Peters. The sheriff sorted through the things the teenage boy had no doubt thought were important: a comb, his driver's license, a Shell credit card with his father's name on it, seven dollars and a foil-sealed condom. Peters looked through the contents a second time, then up at Hoppkins. "Show Elliott the body," he said.

Marion Hoppkins appeared to be mired somewhere in his mid to late sixties. He was a slight man with a few strands of gray-white hair carefully combed over the top of his head. He was wearing a pair of half glasses, old-fashioned hobby jeans and a white knit shirt with traces of food stains on the front where the garment stretched over his paunchy little stomach. He pulled back the rubber sheet and my stomach did a fast one-eighty.

I had seen hundreds of photographs of shark attacks, but I had never actually seen a real victim. And even though I knew it was impossible to have a shark attack in a freshwater lake, this was a real-life attack of some kind, and it was a hell of a lot worse than looking at any picture.

The pungent, sticky aroma of mutilated flesh quickly got to me. I had to look away, swallow hard and breathe deeply.

Hoppkins was using a pencil to point out the damage. "You can see what happened. The bone you see here is the humerus, or at least what's left of it. From the way it's fragmented, you can see that it wasn't snapped off cleanly like it would be if he had been run over by the prop of an outboard. I know it sounds weird, but if you ask me, I'd say it looks like it was chewed off."

"Chewed off?" I said.

"Yes, as opposed to bitten off cleanly," Hoppkins said. He moved the tip of the pencil to

44

where the head of the remaining humerus connected to a network of shredded muscles and locked into the glenoid cavity under the clavicle. "This area right here shows excessive trauma. Every ligament, every tendon, even the bicep brachii tendon has been severely mutilated. Again, like it was, I don't know any other way to say it besides gnawed off."

A weary Harrison Peters looked up and rubbed his forehead. "See why I wanted you to take a look at this, Elliott? What the hell is there out there in that lake that could chew a kid's arm off?"

"Well, we know it wasn't a shark," I said, "unless you've found some rare kind of freshwater species, and then I'd have to ask how it got there. Sharks prefer cold water. It's usually sharks and cold water, sharks and salt water. Sometimes there are sharks in river waters that feed into salt water, but not a lake like this one."

Hoppkins pulled the rubber sheet back up over the body. "Well, Mr. Wages, whatever it was, it had to be big and powerful and aggressive. I was a young sailor on the *McHenry* when we picked up some of the survivors of the *Indianapolis*. Some of those guys looked a lot like this boy here. Take my word for it, this kid went through hell before he died."

"Exactly how did you retrieve the body?" Harrison asked, looking at Mackey.

Cletus Mackey stepped away from the examining table and stuffed his hands down in his pockets like a schoolboy. "The body was wedged in the pilings under Becker's pier. I used the grappling hook."

"Could the hook have done any of this?" I asked.

Both Hoppkins and Harrison said it couldn't have. Hoppkins put his index finger to his mouth. "It appears that one of two things happened. Either the lad was attacked and dragged into the area where whatever it was chewed the arm off, or he swam into the pilings under Becker's pier figuring that maze of timbers would give him some protection. Then the thing got him by the arm and tried to pull him out into open water. The way all those muscles and tendons ruptured and shredded indicates there was a great deal of pressure on them before they let go."

Peters looked back at the sheet-shrouded remains of Abner Barker and pursed his lips. Then he turned to Mackey again. "Any word on the other boy?"

Mackey shook his head. "I checked around down at the marina. Neither one of the two single masts these kids rented have been turned in. Charley Cooter at the marina figures the boys probably ran into some girls in a ski boat and forgot all about sailing. He thinks they beached the boats somewhere and took off with the girls. Says it happens all the time. The boys wouldn't lose that much; they only had to put down a ten dollar deposit. Charley wants me to take a cruise around the lake to see if I can spot his boats. He says he needs them for the upcoming holiday."

The Lake

"Did you say anything about the Barker boy?" Peters asked.

Mackey shook his head. "All he was concerned about was his boats."

Peters face colored. "Screw Cooter and his boats. We've got bigger problems. What about the other boy?"

"No sign of him," Mackey said. "His name is Tom Kinder; he's from Fort Janes too."

Peters looked around the room. "Anyone here notified the boys' parents yet?"

Hoppkins stepped forward. "Mayor Chesterton was here. He wants us to hold off until we know what happened out there tonight."

Peters's eyes flashed with anger. "What the hell right has Chesterton got interfering in this?"

Hoppkins had already started to lead the entourage back up the hall. "He says he doesn't want to get everyone all stirred up until we know what happened out there tonight. He thinks people might start getting alarmed and stay away from the Jubilee."

"Alarmed, my ass!" Peters said. "Screw the damn Jubilee! Doesn't he realize that a boy was killed out there tonight?"

As we walked back to Harrison Peters's patrol car, I was thinking about the parents of Abner Barker. This was going to be one Labor Day weekend they would never forget. And maybe they weren't the only ones.

Thursday A.M., September 2

The sun was stabbing through my bedroom window when I finally woke up; it was almost nine o'clock. I reached over to Cyn's side of the bed but she was gone.

After informing the lady that I was going with Harrison Peters the night before, she had bestowed one of those I'm-not-really-pleased-about-that pecks on my cheek and announced that she would meet me at my place. Her last words were an inviting, "Wake me up when you get there."

At that juncture, neither of us anticipated that it would be almost three o'clock in the morning before I had the chance to haul my aching frame back to Ginny's cottage. At that hour it was pointless to wake the lady out of a sound sleep; it took all the strength I could muster just to undress and slip between the sheets.

Still groggy, I brewed some coffee, staggered

into the living room and plunked myself down in an easy chair, where I could keep one eye on the lake and use the other to go over my hastily scribbled notes from the session in Hoppkins's office. In addition, I had picked up a spare copy of Mackey's statement as well.

The deputy's report estimated that the accident had occurred sometime between seven and eight o'clock. Becker Herd had made his gruesome discovery at approximately nine o'clock. I read the sketchy report several times, looked over my own notes, finished my coffee and went in to take a shower. The image of the Barker boy's body stretched out on that stainless-steel examining table was etched in my mind.

Perhaps because most of my novels focus on the subject of my fellow man's encounters with the bizarre and supernatural, I was intrigued as much as I was sickened by the Abner Barker incident. Still I had no theories. By the time we had driven back to Ginny's cottage, I could tell that Harrison Peters was disappointed that I did not have a fast fix or even the hint of a quick solution to his problem. All in all, I hadn't been very much help.

It was not a total loss. I had come out of the session in Hoppkins's office with a hunch or two, and all I needed was a little time to play them out. Peters had already informed me that he intended to bring the state police into the investigation, standard procedure since the lakes are actually state property. In addition, he had his hands full with the tourists streaming into town for the upcoming three-day-long celebration. If I could come up with a fact or two that would aid in the investigation, so much the better.

I put on some shorts, a golf shirt, and a pair of deck shoes, then crawled into Ginny's Porsche and headed for the village. Sleepy Jericho had taken on a carnival atmosphere overnight; the streets were jammed.

The State Department of Conservation exhibit was crammed into a tight little area between the Jericho Chamber of Commerce tent and the mobile unit of a Fort Janes's rock station giving away free balloons. WKMG's motto was blatantly misleading. It called itself the good music station.

There were some 15 or so 300-gallon galvanized livestock tanks crammed under a canopy shelter with a tangle of green plastic hoses and a bank of hissing air pumps to keep each of the displays aerated. Above each tank was a carefully lettered poster board designed to give the only mildly curious tourists more information than they wanted to know about blue gills, crappies and red ears. The entire affair was presided over by a cherub-faced young man wearing a green conservation department uniform. His name was stitched on the flap over his pocket.

"Okay, Chester, tell me everything you know about garpikes," I said.

Chester stumbled around for a moment and finally led me to the gar display. There were five of the ugly little critters in the tank, the largest of which was no more than 25 inches max. All of a sudden I was even more impressed with Hatcher's catch.

"I expected something bigger," I said and Chester looked hurt.

"Actually," he said, stammering slightly, "these are excellent examples of the species, family Belondiau. They don't get much larger than that around here."

I leaned over the tank to study the disagreeable looking beasts and Chester's face lit up. "Oh, I get it. You heard about that rogue gar some guy caught out here on Jericho Lake yesterday."

I nodded to let him know he was on the right track.

"I heard about it. Did you see it? Is it as big as everyone says it is?"

"Biggest damn garfish I ever saw," I said and smiled.

Chester looked duly contrite for not having a bigger gar to display, but he was unwilling to go down without a fight. "What you saw was a rogue or a freak. My district supervisor says the chances of anyone catching one that big are about a million to one."

"That's good enough for me," I said. District supervisors are supposed to know that kind of thing, I consoled myself. I took one last look at the green-brown, needle-nosed creatures and headed back to the car. I had just shot one of my theories full of holes: Bert Freeman really did know a big fish when he saw one.

Since I make my living spinning dark yarns, I've learned to leave my imagination remain unbridled. But with Chester's assurance that Graham Hatcher's catch was one in a million, plus the information I had obtained previously from the librarian in Fort Janes, I had to admit that the chances of there being more than one of those giant creatures in Jericho Lake was highly unlikely. On the other hand, there was always the long-shot possibility that there were two or more of those monsters swimming around out there. And if they were, I had a possible, albeit unlikely, explanation for what had happened to Abner Barker.

I drove around the lake, thought about calling Cyn and apologizing, discarded the idea and headed toward Herd's Grocery.

In the parking lot at Becker Herd's place, I spotted three state police cruisers and a crowd of curiosity seekers gathered to watch the proceedings. It gave them something to do until the carnival rides fired up. I got out of the car, stood at the back of the throng and saw that they had recovered one of Charley Cooter's sailboats. It had a gaping hole in the side. A mental image of Abner Barker's blood-drained body flashed across my brain and I had to wonder what kind of terrifying thing the boy had encountered in his final minutes. So far, only one word came to mind that described the whole affair—bizarre—and bizarre was right down my alley.

I went back to the car and decided to look into the other matter that had piqued my curiosity, the Bartel plant. At the bridge, overlooking the channel back to the slough, I stopped just long enough to check out the odor. If anything, it was a little stronger. On the other hand, the shimmering, hazy phenomenon that had been hovering over the surface of the lake the previous afternoon did not seem to be quite as evident.

When I passed Patton's Pier, my resolve weakened, but I fought it and took the T-road leading to Montana Mills instead. Heading west, the area to my left was mostly marshlands, brackish backwaters that constituted the slough. To my right was scrubland, an area polluted by rusting mobile homes, lean-tos, junk cars and an assortment of other man-made castoffs: tires, abandoned refrigerators and broken swing sets. A foundered pony looked up from his tedium and watched me pass. He was standing in the sparse shade of a scraggly birch and a twisted jack pine.

I rounded a corner and there sat Bartel Corporation's Plant Number 55. It looked even more imposing and less active in the glare of harsh sunlight.

From what I could see, it appeared to be a straightforward, no-nonsense structure, mostly concrete and curtain wall construction. An unobtrusive gray in color, no shrubbery or plants of any kind. There was a single pedestrian gate and a larger one that could accommodate trucks. The rail spur was empty. It was Thursday, the fourth day of the work week, and there wasn't one car parked in the lot. A single Ford pickup truck was parked at the side entrance. A logo, probably the Bartel logo, I figured, was painted on the door. I was too far away to be certain.

After ten minutes of recording my observations on my small Radio Shack tape recorder, I got out of the car and walked over to the security fence. The pedestrian gate was padlocked. There were large no trespassing signs at 100-foot intervals all along the fence. I walked back to the property line to the east and crawled over the stock fence. If I understood what Cyn was telling me, the field east of the Bartel plant belonged to George Lancer. No more than three steps into it, I realized why Lancer's dairy herd was not grazing there. With each step I could hear the sound of brittle, dried grass snapping underfoot, yet it looked green and lush. I slipped my foot out of my deck shoe and examined the sole. It was green all right, but the green came off on my hand. The damn grass had been sprayed. Lancer's pasture was nothing more than dead bunch grass and weeds, artificially colored to give the appearance of healthy pasture. Immediately, two questions came to mind: why hadn't Lancer uncovered this fact himself? and who had painted the ground? There was a burning sensation in my nostrils, and all of a sudden, I felt a little light-headed. I figured it was nothing more than too much midday heat, turned around and headed back to the car.

That's when I saw him. He was standing in the shadows at the rear of the Bartel building, watching my every move.

With my usual flair for tense situations, I gave him what was intended to look like a casual wave of the hand and said, "A little warm, isn't it?"

He didn't respond. He probably figured I was a mental case, tromping around in the 90-degree heat with humidity heavy enough to drown fish. Either that, or he recognized me as a fake tourist wandering around in a fake field with fake grass.

I crawled back over Lancer's fence and headed for the car. I hadn't learned very much. In fact, all I had really accomplished was the gathering of a few more questions. Why the hell didn't the Bartel factory have any employees? And why was a field, in the middle of nowhere, painted green?

The lunch crowd had already started to clear out by the time I had driven back to Sam's place, but Bert Freeman and his cronies were still holding court. I sat down next to Harrison Peters, across the table from Becker Herd. It was the first time I had seen Becker Herd in days, primarily because that's the way I planned it.

Becker Herd is a lecherous old widower—dirty hair, dirty fingernails and dirty mind. In his dirty little store he sells everything from overpriced candy-coated peanuts to cheap sweatshirts. Becker Herd survived on the tourist trade. On top of everything else, he was a motor mouth. On this occasion though, he wasn't doing the talking. He and everyone else were all listening to Harrison Peters explain the saga that was unfolding down at Herd's store.

Peters, more articulate than the others, explained what the police had found in the Barker boy's rented boat. "It has an eighteen-inch-diameter hole in the hull, looks like it was gouged out with something sharp."

"Any sign of the other boy?" I asked.

Harrison shook his head. "No sign of him or his boat."

"I can't see what all the fuss is about," Herd said. "It's plain to see what happened. The damn kid got in the way of one of those ski boats. A prop took off that arm and he drifted in under my pier where he died."

"I don't think so," Peters said, "and neither does that young fellow that the state police brought in."

"Yeah," Freeman said, looking around the table, "I heard they brought in some kind of expert. Who is he?"

"He's from Carmi Institute, heads up the Environmental Studies Department. He's having the Institute send down some more equipment."

"What the hell is he looking for?" Herd snickered. "The kid's arm." The comment fell flat and I made a mental note: suspicion confirmed, Becker Herd was an asshole.

"What kind of equipment?" Freeman asked.

"Seems the Institute has some kind of special barge they use in situations like this. They can measure the depth and temperature of the water, the activity and volume of the springs, the density of the lake bottom, sediment rates, flow characteristics, that sort of thing. Plus, it enables them to get a good idea of what is going on down on the bottom. I understand it even has a freshwater, remote-controlled submersible with video."

"Bullshit." Herd snorted. "If you ask me, it's a bunch of bullshit, a waste of taxpayer's money. All we have to do is put a damn speed limit on those ski boats and quit letting the kids drive them and this kind of thing won't happen."

"The Barker boy rented a Butterfly," Freeman said.

"Exactly my point. Ain't no way a sailboat can get out of the way of one of them ski boats. It's a wonder it doesn't happen more often."

"Maybe it's a good thing that they are going to check the lake," Freeman said. "That fish Hatcher caught yesterday didn't look none too healthy to me."

I decided it was as good a time as any to lay the results of some of my research on them. "After Hatch showed me that garpike yesterday, I did a little research."

Becker Herd slapped the table and laughed. "Researched what—a damn garpike?"

"Exactly. I called the Fort Janes's library. They plugged into their data bank and connected me with the Center for Maritime Studies. I learned a lot about garpikes in those ten minutes. This morning I double-checked that information with the Great Lakes Center at Copper Harbor. Then I went down to the DNR exhibit. Bert is right. There is very little similarity between the fish that Graham Hatcher caught yesterday and your run-of-the-mill garpike."

Becker Herd was still snorting when Sam Patton sat down at the table. His arrival gave me what I was looking for—an opportunity to change the subject. "Do any of you guys know anything about that Bartel plant over at Montana Mills?" I asked.

Harrison Peters gave me a sideways look.

Patton pulled his cigar out of his mouth. "You mean other than the fact it's been a big damn disappointment? If you wanna get the real skinny on the Bartel situation, you gotta talk to Felix Chesterton. He worked his ass off to get them to put their plant here in Jericho."

"But it's in Montana Mills. What happened?"

"I'll tell you what happened," Herd snapped. "That girlfriend of yours cut his balls off. She and George Lancer cut a deal with the Bartel people at the last minute and got the plant located in Montana Mills on land Lancer and your girlfriend's daddy held a joint option on."

"Cynthia Wallace?" I said, making certain Becker Herd and I were talking about the same girlfriend.

"Hell, yes. Chesterton had the deal all wrapped up. Suddenly Cynthia's daddy, old Foster Wallace, gets killed in that accident, she comes home to run the bank and, before we knew what was happening, that damn Bartel plant ends up in Montana Mills."

I reflected back to my conversation with Cyn the previous afternoon concerning George Lancer's money problems. She had said nothing about being involved with Bartel other than the fact that her bank handled Bartel's local accounts.

I sagged back in my chair. "Tell me more."

"Cost a bunch of us sittin' at this table a heap of money," Herd said. "We formed us a company and bought two hundred acres of scrubland east of town. Bartel wanted it. Then your girlfriend screwed up the deal. We were left holding the bag on that worthless land. Skip Perkins had to file for bankruptcy."

"Then to top it off," Patton added, "two years have gone by and I don't think anyone at this table can name a single person from Jericho that ever got a job over there."

I looked around the table, and they were all mute; apparently no one could.

Bringing up the subject of the Bartel plant had the effect of dumping cold water on the conversation. Freeman quickly lost interest, got up and drifted off to another table. Patton went back to the bar and two men at the end of the table fell into their own conversation. Harrison Peters looked at me and shook his head; a knowing little smile was toying with the corners of his mouth.

"Looks like I hit a raw nerve," I said.

Harrison Peters nodded. "Before you go off half-cocked, I want to talk to you."

"About Abner Barker?"

"Nope. The Bartel Company."

"You too, huh?"

"You saw the way they reacted," Peters said. "Bartel is a sensitive subject around here. I guess I'm one of the few that didn't get hung out to dry when Bartel bought the land in Montana Mills. I know for a fact that both Freeman and Herd are still hurting financially."

"Tell me if I got it right. Herd and his cronies bought that scrubland for a song and had a sweet deal put together where they would have made a personal bundle. The disappointment lingers, right?"

Peters, perhaps out of some kind of misplaced loyalty to his old friends, wouldn't confirm my little scenario, but he didn't deny it either. Instead he gave me another one of his crooked, half smiles. "I'll make you a deal, Elliott," he said. "You scratch my back and I'll scratch yours. You do a little digging around into what's going on over at that Bartel plant for me and I'll tell you everything I know about it—the night before you head south."

It was Harrison Peters's way of letting me know there was more to the story than the grousing I heard around the table at Patton's. "You've got yourself a deal, Harrison," I said. "Now, what do you want to know about the Bartel facility?"

"I've got my hands full with the Jubilee and the Barker kid thing. But I think you and I are thinking along the same lines, Elliott. There is something strange about that plant over at Montana Mills, and I want to know what's going on over there."

The request wasn't eloquent—it didn't have to be. A friend is a friend and Harrison Peters fell into that category. We shook hands. "It's a deal," I said.

Peters pushed his sweat-soaked hat back on his head. "The guy who is supposed to be running that operation is a fellow by the name of

The Lake

Roger Blackmonn. He carries the title of super-intendent, but he never seems to be around. I've tried every way I know to get in touch with him. He doesn't return calls and he doesn't answer mail. I can't even be certain he knows we're try-ing to get in touch with him. As far as I know he hasn't complied with any of the requests for fire code or safety code inspections. He's damn near a nonentity. I even checked with the Bureau of Motor Vehicles; no record of a driver's license and no car registered."

"All of which could be explained by claiming he was an out-of-state resident."

"Maybe," Peters said. "But to the best of my knowledge, Cynthia Wallace is the only one around here who has ever met the guy."

With that, Peters was gone, and I was trying to figure out the best place to start. A phone call to an old stockbroker buddy in New York seemed like as good a place as any. Then I wanted to talk to George Lancer.

Thursday P.M., September 2

On the way back to Ginny's cottage, I decided to stop by Graham and Dolly Hatcher's place to have another look at the giant gar. Now that I had seen a normal one, I wanted to do a little comparing. I pulled into the driveway and noticed that the house was closed up and the drapes drawn.

Dolly answered on the first knock. She looked upset and worried; this time there was no wide-eyed, ear-to-ear Jemimah smile. "Elliott," she said a little vacantly, as though she had difficulty recognizing me. She stepped aside in an unspoken invitation to enter. The room was dark and stuffy. "Did you hear about Graham?"

I shook my head. "What about Graham?"

Dolly walked across the room and turned on a soft, unobtrusive light on a table in the corner of the room. When she did, I realized that her husband was stretched out on the couch with a sheet covering him. "Dr. Hoppkins just left," she said. "He says that Graham has had a violent reaction to something."

Violent wasn't the word for it. Graham Hatcher's eyes were swollen, his face was bloated and covered with patchy red blotches. From the distorted shape that hovered under the sheet I could tell that his stomach was distended and he was chilled even though Dolly had turned off the air-conditioning and the room was unpleasantly warm. He rolled his head slowly toward me and tried to speak. His lips were twice their normal size. He was incoherent and the few words that managed to slip sideways out of his mouth were detached and slurred.

I looked at Dolly. "What the hell happened to him?"

Dolly Hatcher put her finger to her lips, led me into the kitchen and closed the door. She poured me a cup of coffee and sat down at the table. All of the color had drained out of her face. "Everything was okay this morning," she said. "Graham got up, dressed and told me he was going to take the garpike into town to have it mounted. I went back to sleep. When I woke up again, I realized he had been gone over two hours, so I decided to check on him. That's when I found him lying on the pier. He looks worse now than when I found him."

"What did Hoppkins say?"

Dolly shrugged her shoulders. "He doesn't know what to think. He took a blood sample and called in a prescription for something that would make Graham more comfortable. They'll be delivering it any minute. I thought maybe it was the deliveryman when you came. He said he would be back later this afternoon."

I went back into the room where Graham Hatcher was lying and tried to get a better look at him. I focused on his hands, where I figured he had handled the fish. Both hands looked as though they had been severely burned. The fingers were twice their usual size and the skin was blackened. There were several elongated lesions where the skin appeared to have split open similar to the skin on the garpike he had caught. "What did Hoppkins say about this?"

Dolly bent over and examined her husband's hands. There was a look of horrified astonishment on her face. When she looked at me, the tears were welling up in her eyes. "His hands didn't look like this when Marion was here," she said. "All this has happened within the last hour." She reached for her husband's hands and I stopped her.

"Better not," I said, without knowing why.

Dolly began to cry. "What should I do?"

"Call Hoppkins. Tell him what is happening. If this is some kind of toxic reaction, Hoppkins needs to know about it."

"But his medicine isn't here yet," Dolly said.

"I wasn't thinking of the medicine," I said. I put my arm around her shoulder. "Look, Dolly, is there anything I can do to help? Do you want me to stay with you until you hear from Hoppkins?"

Dolly shook her head. She was doing her best

to hold her act together. "I called my sister. She's on her way over now. She should be here any minute."

When Dolly headed for the telephone to call Hoppkins, I slipped out the door and went down to the pier. I was playing a hunch. The over-size gar was right where it had been the day before, floating in the shadowed waters under Hatch's pier. But there was a decided difference: the creature did not look nearly as imposing as it had 24 hours earlier. That's because there wasn't that much left of it. Large chunks of flesh on the rotting, tubular body had flaked away to expose portions of its skeletal structure. Plus, the smaller fish it had once terrorized had been feasting. The eyes had been chewed out and most of the triangular black teeth were missing. The water around the creature had a sickly pinkish cast to it. I realized that if the carcass continued to deteriorate at the same accelerated rate, there wouldn't be anything left of the beast in another 24 hours.

While I was still standing on the pier, thinking about my next move, another car pulled into the Hatcher driveway and a woman got out. She looked a lot like Dolly Hatcher.

Thinking Dolly probably had all the help she could handle, I headed for the Carrera, promising myself I would call to check on Graham's progress later that evening.

Maybe I felt so bad about Graham Hatcher because he reminded me of someone out of my past. Now there's a subject I seldom dwell on—

the checkered past of Elliott Grant Wages.

After three years of trudging around in the rice fields and shit trenches of a place known as Vietnam, I came home to court my one true love. Her name was Lucy Brandon. The only problem was that I wasn't her true love. She had spent the war years on the tennis courts of the local country club and married a guy who owned a Ford dealership. The inevitable phone call and clandestine meeting didn't turn out quite as I hoped it would. She showed up for our little tryst six months pregnant.

There was no reason to hang around after that. I went back to school, got a degree, gathered up a few other documents that I thought would validate my life and took off for parts unknown. I spent the next ten years of my life thumbing my way around the Caribbean. Then one night, with nothing better to do, I picked up a pencil to write down my impression of a Jamaican sunset.

That's how it all started.

Okay, so why am I telling you this now? I suppose it's because I always feel compelled to explain why research is a turn on. Sure it's a learning process, but it's more than that. It's a feeling of connectedness—me and the past, me and knowledge, me and little-known facts.

I headed for Ginny's place and did a little telephone homework. There were three calls, all designed to shed light on the Bartel mystery. None of my sources, however, had any information on the Montana Mills's Bartel facility. Then I called Ellery Tweet. I don't call Tweet unless my back is up against the wall. Ellery keeps score of who owes who a favor; and I was already two down in the owe column.

Ellery is a financial analyst for one of New York's more prestigious banks and he has access to information that most people don't even know exists. He listened, reminded me that I still hadn't paid him the bottle of scotch I owed him from my last request and promised to call me back as soon as he had something.

Even without Tweet's input, I had four full pages of chicken scratches on a yellow legal tablet, and it was time to try to make some sense out of them.

The Bartel Group was a New York based, privately held holding company—which is another way of saying it was a great big umbrella for any sin a guy by the name of Randolph Bartel II wanted to commit. Randolph was the only son of Brewster Bartel, a reclusive inventor who had disappeared in a boating accident some 20 years earlier.

Randolph had powered the Bartel Group out of the toy industry and into a variety of more lucrative ventures that included shipping, resorts and mining. They still made toys, but they had lots of other interests as well, none of which shed any light on Plant 55 in Montana Mills.

As a last resort, I tried the direct approach and called Bartel's corporate offices on Sixty-Seventh Street in New York. My call was intercepted by some sort of electronic device with a voice like a Barbie doll that told me to punch a coded number depending on whether my call should be directed to the sales department, public relations, engineering or a handful of other choices. I opted for public relations, then I was informed that all lines were busy and told to hold while they pumped my ear full of bland music. Twenty minutes later I hung up; apparently Bartel did not want to relate to its public.

After waiting over an hour, with no calls from either Tweet or the folks at Bartel, I plugged in my answering machine and decided to launch the second phase of my investigation. I still had two hours before I had to deal with the fact that Cynthia Wallace was upset with me and play the role of her contrite lover. Two hours was enough time to take a tour of the slough. I grabbed a pair of binoculars, a camera, and my S907 voice recorder, stuffed them in a fishing creel I had found in Ginny's garage and borrowed her neighbor's flat-bottomed aluminum fishing boat. I even propped two casting rods in the bow of the boat to add effect. Any fisherman worth his salt would have known I was a shill, but I figured the casual observer, at a distance, might not notice.

Ten minutes later I was creeping along at an exhilarating two knots through the channel between Jericho Lake and the slough. Once again, the aroma was evident and strongest near the stone bridge. The miragelike shimmer on the other hand seemed to have diminished and was farther away from shore than it had been in days. I stayed as far away from both of them as I could.

When I got back into the slough, there was

a bass boat anchored at the far end. The occupants were talking, drinking beer and doing very little fishing. I knew why: it was the wrong time of day to fish. Bert Freeman had told me as much shortly after I had arrived at Jericho at the start of the summer.

I maneuvered my sham operation into the shade of an overhanging willow next to a little grassy strip that jutted out into the water. It was both shade and cover. The cattails and the moon willows added just the right touch. I stood up, made a couple of casts, sat down and pretended to change plugs. Then I hauled out the binoculars.

My position was due north and directly across approximately 500 yards of water from the back of the Bartel plant. I scanned from the eastern fence line to the western boundary. There were no doors and no windows. There was, however, a large observation deck on what would have been equivalent to the third level, if in fact the plant was constructed in levels. On that deck there was a variety of equipment, none of which was distinguishable because of the green canvas shrouds that covered each piece.

I went back to studying the grounds. Through the tinted glass of the binocular lens, the variation in ground color was even more apparent. Three big deciduous trees at the back of the property were completely defoliated and the stand of yellow pine along the shoreline looked just about as bad. Already I was conjuring up visions of some uncaring industrial giant spewing vast amounts of toxic waste into the slough feeding

Jericho Lake. I put the glasses down and recorded that irritating thought on my voice recorder.

When I picked up the glasses again, I realized
I had been discovered. Two men were standing
on the observation deck. They had binoculars
and they watched me watching them. At 500
yards, it was a standoff. I resisted the impulse
to give them a cheery wave and kept scanning.
The one in the business suit appeared to be
doing most of the talking. The bulky one in
what looked to be coveralls of some sort was
nodding. The distance was too great to pick
up subtle detail and I figured that it was likely
we could pass on the street without recognizing
each other.

With practiced casualness, I laid the glasses
down, picked up my Zebco and made a couple
of casts. If there was even a remote chance that
I could create some doubt in their mind about
my real intentions, I wanted to do it. Then, with
an overly animated shrug, I fired up the Johnson
and headed for the channel that would take me
back to Jericho Lake. All the while, I was wondering just how much Cyn would be willing to
reveal about her relationship with the mysteri-
ous Bartel Group.

There was a sticky, uncompromising stiffness
over dinner that evening, despite the fact it was
Cyn's favorite restaurant. The lady was having
trouble understanding why I would choose to
spend time with Harrison Peters looking at
the mutilated remains of a teenager instead of
spending a little sack time with her, especially

in view of the fact that, as she put it, we had so little time left.

"We could have had a lovely evening," she said, twisting the dagger a little deeper.

"I'll make up for it," I said, trying to set the stage for the upcoming holiday. It was the only option I had. As far as I was concerned, the fun menu at Jericho Lake was limited without the Cynthia Wallace entree. I reached across the table, captured her hand and she cooperated. Neither one of us was involved because it was one of those I-love-your-brains thing. The Wallace-Wages relationship had thus far been based on good old-fashioned girl-boy lust.

"You do look exceptional tonight," I said.

"You're doing better."

The thaw had started. I knew exactly where the exchange was taking us, but it was aborted by the shadow that fell across our table.

It was Harrison Peters and that time he had taken his hat off.

Cynlookedupathimandscowled.Herhandtensed.

"Look, Elliott, I'm sorry to have to bother you two again, but something has come up." He pulled out a chair and sat down.

Cyn pushed herself away from the table. "I think I'll go powder my nose," she hissed. When she crossed the dining room, every male under the age of 80 turned to watch her.

"Hope I didn't interrupt something," Harrison said.

Before I could impress upon him that he was screwing up what had otherwise been a lovely evening, a waiter was standing at the table with a folded piece of paper in his hand. He handed it to me and beat a hasty retreat. I knew exactly what to expect. The handwriting was an uptight scribble.

You've got five minutes to get rid of that old fart. If you don't, you sleep alone tonight.

"Problem?" Peters asked.

"Yeah," I said, putting the note in my pocket, "a problem. Now before you completely mess up my life, tell me what's on your mind and then get the hell out of here. In case you hadn't noticed, the lady is slightly pissed."

Peters had an impossible-to-read expression on his face. I couldn't tell whether he did not understand or whether he just plain did not care. He fumbled through his pockets until he found his own piece of paper. It was folded neatly. He laid it on the table with the explanation that Deputy Mackey had just given it to him. It was a Sheriff's Department memo:

HARRISON:
HAD TWO CALLS FROM THE BARTEL PLANT IN MONTANA MILLS. BLACK-MONN IS COMPLAINING THAT TWICE WITHIN THE LAST 12 HOURS THEY'VE HAD SOMEONE SNOOPING AROUND THEIR PLANT. HE WANTS YOU TO CHECK IT OUT AND SAYS TO REMIND YOU THAT PLANT 55 IS A HIGH RISK SECURITY OPERATION.
                                    CLETUS MACKEY

The Lake

I handed the piece of paper back to Peters. "He doesn't have a legitimate bitch. I wasn't even on his property."

"Just exactly where were you?"

"The first time I was on Lancer's property. The second time I was across the slough looking at the place through binoculars. I knew they saw me both times."

"That's good enough for me," Peters said. "I just wanted to know how far you had gone. So much for Blackmonn's complaint. You've already proved there really is a Blackmonn. Now, what else did you find out?"

I took a quick survey of the dining room. Cyn was nowhere in sight. "Not tonight," I said, "I'll tell you tomorrow."

Peters leaned back in his chair. He looked tired. "Okay," he said, "tomorrow."

The words were barely out of Harrison Peters's mouth before I was on my feet in search of what I knew was one upset lady. By the time I got to the bar, I knew it was too late. My search ended in the parking lot. Her Lincoln Continental was gone. I heard footsteps behind me, turned around and the waiter handed me another note. The handwriting alone was enough to tell me that the lady had come completely unwrapped.

Since you find our local sheriff so damned fascinating, why don't you try sleeping with him instead?

I looked at the perplexed waiter. "Did the lady have anything else to say?"

"She said to look at your watch," he said.

I did. It had been exactly seven minutes. Then I heard a fatigued laugh coming from another part of the club's parking lot. It was Harrison Peters.

"She'll get over it," he said. "She used to twist old Felix's tail too."

"Felix Chesterton?"

"Yup," Peters drawled. "Cynthia Wallace and Felix Chesterton used to be quite an item, but that was long before you hit the scene."

I was still standing in the middle of the parking lot with my mouth hanging open when Peters opened the door to his cruiser and offered me a ride home.

We were on the south side of the lake, headed for Ginny Fordice's cottage, and I was mentally formulating a plan to get back in the good graces of Cynthia Wallace when the call came through. Harrison picked up his mic and depressed the transmit button. "Unit fourteen," he said.

"Sheriff, I'm at the Hatcher place, cottage 247, on Jericho Lake. I think you better get over here." I recognized Cletus Mackey's voice.

Peters gave me a sideways glance, turned on his siren and threw the tan-over-cream cruiser into high gear. We arrived at the Hatcher place in a matter of minutes. Mackey's patrol car was sitting in the driveway and there were several people milling around on the lawn in front of the house. Dolly was the only one I recognized. She was being consoled by two women in housecoats.

The Lake

Peters got out of the car and elbowed his way through the crowd. I was right behind him. Cletus Mackey was standing in the middle of the Hatcher's living room with a stunned, sick look on his face.

Graham Hatcher's grotesquely distorted body was sprawled out in the middle of the room and the top of his head was missing. Fragments of it were all over the room, on the ceiling, the walls, everywhere. Beside him on the floor was a .38 revolver.

I froze. It was all I could do to maintain my equilibrium. Harrison Peters wasn't handling it much better. He studied the body of Hatcher, then looked at Mackey. "What the hell happened?"

Cletus Mackey's voice was hollow. He avoided looking at Peters; his mouth formed words, but no sound came out.

"I think I saw most of it, Sheriff," a man's voice said. I turned around and saw a young man standing in the doorway. He was tall, with a prominent brow and brooding, yet slightly effeminate, features. The contradiction was a deep, monotone voice. Harrison Peters recognized him.

"This is Dr. Ira Leonard, E. G., the young man I told you about. He is the one heading up the Carmi investigation down at Becker Herd's place."

Ira Leonard stepped into the room and glanced around. He was wearing a pair of cutoff jeans, a sweatshirt with no sleeves and the Carmi Institute logo stenciled across his chest.

"I was walking by on my way to get something to eat when I saw this lady come running out of the house. She was hysterical. She said her husband had a gun and that he was threatening to shoot her. At about that same time, he appeared in the doorway, aimed at us, squeezed off a couple of rounds and then put the gun barrel in his mouth. You can figure the rest."

Harrison Peters headed for the door and Dolly Hatcher. I finally had the things churning inside me well enough under control that I could take a more critical look at what was left of Dolly's husband. He was wearing nothing more than a pair of white boxer shorts and his body was covered with what appeared to be open sores and boils. The areas through the chest, around the meaty part of his heavy thighs and along his upper arms were twice their normal size, giving the impression that they had actually split open because the flesh was no longer capable of containing the swelling that had taken place. Hatcher's flesh had taken on the same sickly pink tinge as that of his trophy gar floating under the pier in front of the house.

I studied the scene for several minutes and then went outside where Peters was talking to Dolly Hatcher. Cletus Mackey had moved most of the throng of neighbors and curiosity seekers out of earshot. A sobbing Dolly was still being supported by one of the ladies in a housecoat and Ira Leonard was listening intently. She was telling Peters what had happened. Her description was punctuated by gulps for air and shrill wails.

"He'd been getting worse all day. I kept waiting for Dr. Hoppkins to come back. I tried to call his office. They couldn't find him.

"Graham kept getting worse. He was swelling so bad and he was screaming, he said he couldn't breathe. And then he got very angry. He started saying things like I wasn't doing anything to help him.

"I went out into the kitchen to get him something to drink. And while I was out of the room he must have got out of bed and taken his revolver out of the gun cabinet.

"He said he was going to kill me for making him suffer. I ran out the door, he shot at me twice and then . . ."

Peters looked to Ira Leonard and then Cletus Mackey. Both men were nodding. He put his arm around Dolly's shoulder and escorted her over to Mackey's cruiser. Then he instructed the deputy to take her to the hospital in Fort Janes and have her admitted for observation. It was only after Mackey's cruiser backed out of the driveway that the crowd began to disperse.

"Anything I can do, Sheriff?" Ira Leonard asked.

Peters shook his head. "Not tonight. Tomorrow though, stop by the office to make a statement. In the meantime I'm going to try to locate Doc Hoppkins and tell him what happened."

Thirty minutes later, the ambulance arrived and Hatcher's body was removed. After closing up the house Harrison drove me back to Ginny's cottage.

Inside, I fixed myself a stiff scotch and water and ambled upstairs to the bedroom wondering if I could sleep. I knew it was going to be a long time before I could get the grim picture of Graham Hatcher sprawled out on the floor of his living room with the top of his head blown off out of my mind.

I opened the door to the bedroom and found Cyn waiting. She was curled up in the middle of the bed. "I had a chance to think it over," she said softly, "and I cooled off." She pulled back the covers and forced a very insincere smile. There was still a trace of hostility, even though I knew how hard she was trying not to let it show. "So, what was so all-fired important with our sheriff this time?"

The story of Graham Hatcher poured out. There were questions I couldn't answer. There were periods of silence, uncomfortable and strained, and finally there was the darkness. Like me, Cyn was quiet, and finally we drifted off to sleep.

Friday A.M., September 3

When I finally did spiral into the escape world of sleep, my subconscious was populated by people with names like Ellery Tweet and Ira Leonard and Dolly Hatcher. None of the seemingly endless string of dreams made any sense. They were nothing more than fragments, pieces chopped up with no continuity. For the most part they were unpleasant and stressful. Then I rolled over and felt Cyn's body next to mine, her tousled head nestled in the crook of my arm. Her long legs were entwined in mine and she was making a low throaty sound—the kind of sound men really like to hear out of a woman.

I remember disengaging myself and looking at the clock. It was a few minutes after seven. The window was open and the curtains had been pulled back to take full advantage of the fact that Ginny's summer place enjoyed one of the best views on the lake. A shallow morning fog still hovered over the lake. Gray-black objects slipped in and out of that halfworld like tiny boats in a water-bug universe.

There was something both enchanting and disturbing about the scene. I propped myself up on my elbow to watch.

"A penny for your thoughts?" Cyn whispered.

"A lady named Cynthia Wallace." I lied. It was what she wanted to hear and it served no purpose to describe the scene in the Hatcher living room again.

As I think back about it now, it was the consummate setting for lovers, the soft gray of morning before a pink, cool sunrise. Normally it would have been feel-good time, but the Hatcher incident still held center stage in my thoughts.

Cyn rolled toward me and revealed a sleepy face, artfully sculptured, even more beautiful without makeup. Then she stretched. "A day off," she said, "how are we going to spend it?"

"Coffee, cuddle and the morning paper. Then we drive into Fort Janes and get away from the Jubilee crowd. How does that sound?"

She stretched and purred. "Wonderful. But it's your turn to make the coffee."

I got out of bed and meandered into the kitchen, able for the moment to put the Hatcher incident out of my mind. The objective was coffee and the Fort Janes's morning paper. The former was easy, the latter a little more complicated. When the coffee was done, I carried a cup back in to her. She had her back propped against the headboard with her knees drawn up. The way she had the sheet arranged I knew she had not intended for it to conceal everything. After her first sip she asked what I had accomplished the day before.

"On the novel, zilch. On Bartel, not much more than that."

Cyn arched her eyebrows. "Bartel?"

"Yeah, Harrison Peters asked me to dig around and see what I could come up with."

"Why the sudden interest in Bartel?"

"Actually, you're the one who started it when you told me about this guy named Lancer with the unhappy cows."

The lady smiled, shook her head and took another sip of coffee. "It isn't working out quite like we all thought it would," she said.

For some reason, I had the distinct feeling that was all Cyn intended to say, that anything beyond that was as carefully guarded as the ground on the other side of the Bartel security fence. Which is probably the reason I jumped in with both feet. "This guy, Blackmonn, is the real riddle. No one seems to know him."

Cyn gave a funny little twist to her mouth.

"Have you met him?" I asked.

All traces of the lady's good humor faded. "Ta da," she said musically. "Now I get it. You've been talking to the locals, and they told you George Lancer and I snookered the Bartel deal out of Jericho at the last minute and sold them the land on the slough over near Montana Mills. Right?"

"Did you snooker them?"

She pulled the sheet up around her throat. "No, Mr. Wages, I didn't snooker them." Her voice was icy. "The Jericho boys outfoxed themselves. Your buddies Herd, Hatcher, Hoppkins and Felix Chesterton just got a little too greedy. They bought up several old farms and some scrubland on the outskirts of the village, ramrodded a rezoning ordinance through and jacked the price up just a little too high. My father and George Lancer offered the Bartel people an alternative—less money, more acreage—and they took it. Your buddies were left holding the bag; they paid too much for those farms. Bad judgment, bad business."

"So why do they think you're the culprit?"

"When Daddy died right in the middle of the negotiations, I came home from Boston and put the deal to bed. In the process I had a couple of clauses inserted for the Fort Janes Bank. I wanted to handle the local financing and pick up a couple of the Bartel service accounts. In retrospect it wasn't worth the effort. Bartel has been a very big disappointment."

The lady's story was believable—at least believable enough that I bought it. It was all too easy to conjure up visions of the good old boys over at Patton's Pier licking their chops as they tried to squeeze the last nickel out of the slickers from the big city. Still, call it intuition or skepticism, I had the distinct feeling that Cyn had only told me part of the story.

I went back into the kitchen to get refills, and when I returned, Cyn was slipping into a white bikini. "Want to flip a coin to see who goes to get the paper?" she asked.

Getting the paper needs an explanation. Actually, it is a cumbersome ritual that is part of the Jericho Lake summer life-style. The morning edition of the Fort Janes Journal isn't delivered to the cottages around the lake; it is stacked on the pier over at Becker Herd's store. As a consequence, there is a daily parade of small craft up to the old man's dock, where the locals dutifully drop their quarters into a glass jar, pick up a paper and motor back to their homes. At first I thought this was a clever marketing ruse by the newspaper, then I discovered it was Becker Herd's idea. The old lech dreamed up the entire scheme. Every day he would prop himself in a lawn chair on shore behind his store and ogle the parade of bathing-suit-clad cuties as they made their purchases.

We climbed into Cyn's Woody, a 1940-vintage completely restored Chris Craft, and the lady began punching buttons, venting and tweaking the balky beast until it coughed to life. She seemed satisfied when the periodic grunts made the transition into one continuous growl and eased us away from the dock.

On the old ten scale, Cyn flirted with a perfect score—for Elliott Wages's tastes. Between her fantastic tan, long legs and sassy demeanor, she kept my libido in a constant state of agitation. And as we cruised across the lake, if it hadn't been for the faint trace of the bad odor up by the stone bridge, I would have had to give that particular Friday morning a perfect score too.

As we approached the Herd Grocery, I saw Becker perched in his folding chair watching the proceedings. Two teenyboppers in front of us, complete with crash-dive bodies and skimpy suits that called attention to them, were purchasing a paper. They were doing a little extra cavorting for Becker's benefit. They even waved at the old geezer and giggled as they pulled away.

We were next and there were a couple of boats behind us. Cyn was at the controls of the Woody, and she cozied us up to the pier, throttled down, stood up and leaned over to put the coins in Becker's jar. His smutty grin managed to find its way through several chins and a set of hanging jowls. Cyn was making his day.

She handed me the paper, and just as she did, I felt a sudden thump against the wooden hull of the boat. It prodded us gently against the scuff pad on Becker's pier.

Cyn looked at me, a questioning expression on her face.

Before I could respond, a second jolt slammed us broadside into the pier and I heard the sickening sound of splintering wood. Cyn let out a scream and pitched forward. Her head ricocheted off of the dash, her legs went out from under her, scissoring wildly as she toppled over the side into the water. I reeled backward, landing on my back, wedged in the corner by the engine cowling. I was still lying there in a stunned stupor when I saw a hideous monstrosity catapult out of the water. In less time than it took to mentally record it, it was there and gone.

The Lake

The bow jackknifed upward and I felt myself spinning up and backward again. That time I tumbled into the water. The next thing I knew I was spiraling down. The water was all confusion, bubbles and colors and funny sounds. Then I realized something was pulling me down; my ankle had become entangled in one of the towlines. Beneath me was Cyn's pride and joy, bow down, gaping hole in the side. The towline was attached to a cleat on the transom and I was going down with it.

Already my lungs were hurting.

I tried to claw my way back up, but the line held me taut.

I started gulping for air involuntarily and the water gushed in, forcing its way past my mouth and slamming into my chest. I didn't want to panic, but I already had. There was nothing between me and the surface except one tangled piece of nylon and a good 20 feet of water. My fingers no longer worked and the rope seemed to be getting tighter.

Then I saw a shape, a shadow coming directly at me. My mouth opened involuntarily to scream, and the water gushed in again. I could feel myself choking and I knew I was checking out.

They were all round and white and amorphous: funny-looking things floating in space. Whatever they were, they were playing a kind of game with me, hide and seek maybe. One by one, those balloons, those opaque marbles slowly began to distinguish themselves. That was when I realized they were faces: concerned, worried, curious, scared and relieved. They were all looking down at me. Some of them even had voices.

"Looks like he's starting to come around," one whispered.

"That was a close call," another said.

The biggest balloon wanted to know if I was all right.

"Better tell him to lay still," a concerned voice said.

I rubbed my burning eyes. There was a terrible taste in my mouth, as if I had thrown up. I squeezed my eyes shut and opened them again. The faces came into focus and I recognized Cyn.

"For God's sake, Elliott, are you alright?"

I wanted to reestablish contact, but my chest felt as if someone was standing on it. I bobbed my head, motioning for her to put her ear down close to my mouth. When she did, I told her how sexy she looked.

She looked sheepishly up at those who surrounded us, her face flushed. Then she didn't whisper; she sounded angry. "Damn it, Elliott, you scared the hell out of us."

I moved my head, attaching names to faces: Becker Herd, Bert and Candy Freeman, Chester from the DNR exhibit, and a handful of others I didn't recognize.

"Damn good thing Atley Truman happened by," Becker wheezed. "He saw what was happenin', Wages, and he jumped in after you."

When I looked around, only one other person besides Cyn was wet, a freckle-faced kid in a boy scout uniform. Another boy, same uniform, shorter and fatter than Atley, was bone-dry. He looked at his buddy with unadulterated admiration. I shoved myself up on my elbows and tried to clear my head enough to express my thanks to young Atley. By then I could see that we had drawn quite a crowd; the boat traffic onlookers were backed up and there was a line of spectators gawking from the shoreline.

"Well, Atley Truman," I said, "I'm indebted."

He held out a scarred and pitted scout knife for my inspection. "I cut the line with this," he said and started to leave.

"Wait a minute."

"I gotta go," he said. "I'm supposed to be down at the church mowin' the grass. If my mom finds out I was over at Herd's lookin' at comic books I'll be in big trouble."

Cyn gave him a hug, which embarrassed Atley, and he took off at a dead run in the direction of the church. When I got to my feet, the crowd realized that the show was over and began to disperse.

Cyn took the cue to start crying again, slumped down on the pier bench and stared off into space. "I was scared to death. Do you know how close you came to dying?"

I wanted to console Cyn, but I wanted to talk to Bert and Candy Freeman even more. They had been in line to get a paper. They were right behind us when whatever happened happened, and they had seen everything. Bert was still staring down in the waters at the end of the pier. We could see the remnants of Cyn's Woody lying in about three-plus fathoms of Jericho Lake water. There was a huge hole in the starboard side of the hull.

"Damnedest thing I ever saw," Bert said.

"What did you see?" I asked.

For once Bert Freeman was speechless; he shrugged his shoulders. "I don't know what I saw, Elliott," he said. "It all happened so quick."

"But you saw something, Bert, I know you did. Just tell me what you think you saw no matter how weird it sounds."

I was pushing him because I knew that the longer he had a chance to think about it the more his mind was likely to reject it as being totally out of the realm of reality.

He took off his hat and used it to mop his forehead. He looked at his wife Candy, who was now consoling Cynthia. He had the look of a man who didn't want anyone to overhear what he was about to tell me.

"You're gonna think I'm outta my mind, E. G." Already the self-doubt was creeping into his voice.

"I don't care how it sounds. I want to know what you think you saw."

"Well, when you was pullin' in toward Herd's pier, we was some thirty or forty yards off of your stern and I commented to Candy that I didn't know Cyn's Chris Craft had twin screws."

"It doesn't." I said, "One prop."

"Well, it was damn sure leavin' two wakes," Freeman said. Then he gave me one of those I-can't-help-it-if-that's-what-I-saw looks.

"Then what?"

The Lake

"Well, Cyn had just handed you the paper, and that's when all hell broke loose."

"Damn it, Bert, what did you see?" He was starting to procrastinate. The longer it went, the more he doubted himself.

"I couldn't see real good because of the glare," he said, stalling.

Bert Freeman's eyes were doing everything they could to avoid mine. He lowered his voice again. "Well that's when I saw this thing." The word *thing* barely escaped his lips.

"Damn it, Bert, describe it."

His eyes were pleading with me not to press him.

"Was it a fish or a man or what?"

"God, Elliott, don't tell anybody I told you this, but I swear to God, it looked like an enormous garpike." At that point his voice was barely audible.

"How big?"

"Biggest damn one I ever saw."

"Not good enough. Was it bigger than the one Graham Hatcher caught?"

"A hell of a lot bigger."

It took us a while to get our act together. We sat on Cyn's porch overlooking the lake, keeping the conversation to a minimum. The phone had not stopped ringing; some of the calls were even for me, like the one from Harrison Peters.

When he called to inform me that they were getting ready to bring Cyn's boat up, I told him that I was on my way. The research barge from Carmi Institute was being used to winch it up. I figured that Cyn was already discouraged enough without seeing her beloved Woody dredged from the depths with a gaping hole in the side. So I suggested that she get some rest and I headed for Becker Herd's place.

The barge, the *C. I. Harrington*, was turning out to be a genuine tourist attraction. Jubilee early birds with nothing better to do until the festivities started were quick to lock onto anything that looked as if it might occupy their interest for an hour or so.

On the way to Herd's grocery, I turned on the radio in the Carrera and caught the end of a Fort Janes newscast that was talking about the suicide of Graham Hatcher. It described him as a longtime resident of Jericho County and a former state senator; I hadn't known the latter.

I parked in the small lot across the road from the grocery and elbowed my way through the crowd to Herd's pier, where the barge was anchored. Peters, Ira Leonard and two young men in wet suits were arranging a collection of complicated electronic gear along the starboard side of the barge. Dr. Leonard introduced himself again and Peters explained that I was the one who had been aboard the craft when the incident happened.

Leonard wasn't the type to smile a lot. He studied me for a moment, inquired if I was all right and went about his chores. After a pair of twin Honda portable generators were taken aboard and fired up, he picked up a dirty towel, wiped off his hands and started toward us.

The Lake

"Now, Mr. Wages, suppose you tell me everything that happened this morning: when, where, how, everything you can think of. I apologize for the little delay, but your mayor was here just before you came and he insisted that I do everything I could to keep this whole operation as low-key as possible."

Peters snorted and Leonard, squinting into the glare of the sun, tried to find us a place to talk. He settled on a stretch of shoreline next to the grocery where the onlookers were restrained by a security fence.

"Where do you want me to start?"

"At the beginning."

Which is exactly what I did, carefully covering every detail from the first time Cyn jazzed the engine through the time when we pulled up alongside of Becker Herd's dock, finishing at the point where I blacked out in 20 feet of water with a piece of nylon towline wrapped around my ankle. Leonard listened while he chewed on a blade of grass and watched the two men hooking up the gear on the barge.

"How big was the creature?" he asked when I tried to describe the thing that I saw swimming at me before I blacked out.

"Hell, I don't know. Big."

"Could it have been this Atley Truman boy coming to your rescue?"

The question stopped me.

"Can you tell me about its color or configuration?" he asked.

I wasn't certain. I felt like telling him that I was too damn busy trying to save my hide to take notes.

Leonard twisted around in the grass and looked at me. He wasn't smiling. "You said you felt something bump into the boat. Can you describe the sensation? Was it strong? Did you have any particular recollection as to strength or speed?"

The roles were reversed, and I found myself in Bert Freeman's shoes. It was my turn to describe something that defied both logic and the laws of nature. "I had the impression," I said, choosing my words carefully, "not so much of speed, but of brute strength. There was a definite sensation of massiveness."

Leonard nodded. Instead of responding, he turned his attention back to the labors of his assistants. One of them had connected a salvage hook to Cyn's boat and they were winching it up. Her once-proud package of polished teak and mahogany peeked through the surface of the water, dangling unceremoniously from a hoist cable. The exposed hull confirmed the size of the substantial hole in the craft's underbelly.

I followed Leonard out to the barge along with Harrison Peters, and the three of us stared at Cyn's mortally wounded pride and joy in stunned awe. At full stop, what Bert Freeman had described as a big garfish had somehow managed to puncture a three-foot hole clear through the sturdy hull.

Peters let out a chiseled whistle. "What the hell could have caused that?"

Leonard traced the tips of his fingers around the splintered perimeter of the hole. He shook his head. "Without running a few lab tests on a cross section I can't tell whether the force of the blow came from the interior or the exterior. Could it have been an explosion—an accumulation of gas fumes building up inside the engine well?"

"If that was the case, the whole damn thing would have blown up," Peters said.

Leonard shrugged, a little sheepishly. "Boats aren't my specialty, Sheriff. Theories are."

Peters examined the engine well. "Looks okay to me. Dry it out and I imagine we could fire it up."

"Still think it was a giant garpike?" Leonard asked.

I was stunned. It had never occurred to me that someone might not believe me.

"I'm not completely convinced that something didn't set off a small chain of gas explosions. Were either you or Ms. Wallace smoking?"

I looked at Peters and turned to the man from Carmi. "Damn it, Leonard, neither of us were smoking. We were hit. H-i-t, hit. There was no explosion. Something in that lake hit us. It was big and it was ugly. I don't know what it was, but I sure as hell have my suspicions. Why the hell don't you talk to Bert Freeman? He saw it too."

"I tried to," Leonard said. "Mr. Freeman wasn't willing to talk about what he had seen."

Harrison Peters confirmed what Leonard was saying. "We tried talking to him, Elliott, but he was too stoned to help us."

93

"Stoned?"

"Yeah, stoned. Both he and Candy got into the sauce a little early today. When Ira tried to talk to him, he said he wasn't feeling good and he didn't want to talk about it."

By the time I got back to the cottage, Cyn had departed. She left a note on the bathroom mirror saying she would be ready for me to pick her up at 6:30.

I'm expected to attend the opening ceremonies of the Jubilee. After that we can get on to more exciting things.

I glanced at my watch and decided that if I hustled there would be time to buy the lady a drink before the festivities began. I showered, dressed, hopped in the Carrera and drove to Cyn's place.

On the way, I passed the Carmi barge. Leonard, his two graduate assistants and two others were hard at work. The barge was positioned some 300 yards offshore, east of the bridge, not far from the channel to the slough and the place where the unpleasant odor was the strongest. If they worked through the night as Leonard indicated they would, the Jubilee officials and Chesterton, in particular, weren't going to be too thrilled.

Along the way, I took out my voice recorder and reminded myself of several questions I wanted to ask Peters. One: had they located Abner Barker's sailing buddy? Two: had he located Doc Hoppkins—and if so what had he learned? Three: what was the diagnosis on Graham Hatcher? As an afterthought, I made another note reminding myself to call Ellery Tweet back and see if he had come up with anything further on Bartel.

By the time I negotiated the long winding drive to Cyn's spread, I discovered she had company; a black de Ville with local license plates was parked next to her Lincoln. I found Cyn and her guest on the patio with Mrs. Fern pouring refreshments. A large, athletic-looking man was sitting opposite Cyn. Their faces were flushed and it was obvious that the conversation had been less than cordial.

When Cyn saw me, she smiled. Her introductions were strained.

"Elliott, I'd like you to meet Felix Chesterton." As an afterthought, she added, "Felix is the mayor of Jericho."

Chesterton set his drink down, unfolded from his chair and stood up. He was formidable: tall, tanned and trim with a thick crop of silver-gray hair. She could have told me that Chesterton was a professional model and I would have believed her. "Pleased to meet you, Wages," he said. "I've read some of your novels."

He didn't say he liked what he had read. So I immediately wrote him off as being fatally flawed despite his immaculately tailored Panama suit.

"Elliott plans to leave right after Labor Day to return to Key West," Cyn said.

R. Karl Largent

"How unfortunate," Chesterton said. There was just enough sarcasm in his voice for me to know how he felt about that little tidbit of information. He extended his hand, exerted a trifle too much pressure to be sincere and said, "Well, Wages, I'd like to hang around and hear all about your little episode over at Becker Herd's place this morning, but I really have to be going. Duty calls." He looked at his watch and then at Cyn. "You will make it for the opening ceremonies, won't you?"

"I intend to," she said coldly.

The big man departed and a slightly nervous Cyn held her breath until she heard his car door slam. Then she slumped back down in her chair and stared out at the lake.

"What was that all about?"

The lady didn't look at me. "Felix Chesterton is a pompous son of a bitch!"

When a relationship goes sour, it stays that way. Cyn had never talked about Chesterton and I wasn't about to ask. It was none of my business.

"Can you believe it?"

"Believe what?"

"Felix just informed me that the Jericho town council intends to file a lawsuit against the Bartel Corporation."

"On what grounds?"

"Pollution. It's a cease-and-desist order. They are going to demand that Bartel cease operations until Bartel can show proof that they aren't polluting the environment. Felix thinks Bartel is behind the odor over near the slough. He says all the merchants are complaining."

Enough other things had been happening that I had not had an opportunity to talk to Cyn about my two excursions to Montana Mills and the discovery of the painted grass and defoliated trees. And that moment did not seem to be the time or place to start. "Maybe that smell is caused by Bartel's pollution," I said.

Cyn erupted. "Bullshit, Elliott, that's what it is. Pure small-town, red-neck bullshit. This is nothing more than the Jericho good old boys' club way of trying to get back at Bartel for building their plant in Montana Mills instead of buying that land from them."

"I would think you would be concerned too. After all, Lancer is involved in this as well."

"George and Millie Lancer will be taken care of," Cyn said.

I wasn't quite sure what Cyn meant by that remark, but I did not feel inclined to ruin what was left of the evening with a protracted debate on the merits of the Jericho merchants' complaints. Neither could I resist saying, "You have to admit that there is something strange going on over there."

"Just because it looks strange doesn't necessarily mean that they are up to something nefarious."

It struck me that Banker Wallace was being uncharacteristically uptight about the subject. "Look, Cyn," I said, trying to keep my voice even, "I've been over there doing a little poking around. I don't know what's going on yet, but

R. Karl Largent

I'll flat guarantee you there is something strange about that Bartel setup."

The lady glared back at me and I read something in those cool eyes that I had never seen before. It was an unspoken message, broadcast clear and simple and loud: this is none of your affair, Elliott Grant Wages.

Friday P.M., September 3

The Jericho Fisherman's Jubilee got off to a rousing start without Cynthia Wallace. The proceedings were well underway by the time the lady was able to get her attitude adjusted and put on a happy face for the revelers. She donned a pale yellow tennis outfit that only further enhanced all those marvelous things Mother Nature had endowed her with, and we plowed our way through the crowds, rides and exhibits. Throughout the evening though, it was obvious that her conversation with Felix Chesterton was uppermost in her mind.

The entire concept of the Jubilee was a celebration—or a wake—depending on how you wanted to look at it. Labor Day was the end of the summer. On Tuesday, crews would swarm over Jericho and begin the tedious process of closing up the cottages for the winter. Windows would be boarded up, piers taken in, pipes drained and lawn furniture tucked away until the following spring. The marina workers would spend the next several weeks putting the big boys' toys in storage and a skeleton crew would be assigned the task of washing hulls, fogging motors and lining up the low-slung growlers in storage sheds. Jericho was destined to go into a comatose state until the next appointed time for fun.

Not everyone had stayed around to reap the benefits of the partiers at the Jubilee. Some of the more chic shops along Lake and Market Streets had already abandoned the scene. A store with gilt lettering indicating it was Marlin's of Naples, Florida, Paris, France and Jericho had already pulled up stakes and headed for winter quarters. The trendy House of Hamilton had a discreet little sign over its closed door that invited their patrons to visit their boutique in Key West. And the owners of some of the more pretentious estates along Lake Shore Drive had likewise evacuated, preferring not to rub shoulders with carnival people and rowdy beer-drinking fishermen.

Cyn put on a plastic smile and did a marvelous Jekyll-Hyde act. She shook hands with the locals, urged them to have fun and gave the tourists a similar treatment. The tourists received a slight variation though; they were invited to come back and stay longer the next time. For the most part she appeared to be pulling it off.

Avoiding the Ferris wheel, the merry-go-round, and the Thing, we listened to a tiny tot complain because her mother bought tickets that entitled her to ride a frog instead of a swan on a kiddie ride. We capped off our tour of frenzied fun when Cyn introduced me to the candidates in the Young Republican booth. I found it difficult to take those people seriously, with their fake straw hats, silly armbands and fixed, one-dimensional, uncaring smiles.

With that behind us, I offered to buy the lady a nightcap at the Dockside, a quiet little bistro a mile down the road from Patton's Pier.

I managed to get the lady situated, buy her a drink and grace her with my best I'm-having-fun smile before I started. "Okay, it's time to level with old E. G. What is this thing with Chesterton all about?"

The lady glared at me for a moment, shrugged her shoulders, stirred the ice in her drink and allowed the plastic smile to disappear. The body language indicated hard times ahead. "I don't want to talk about him."

"You've been wound tighter than a golf ball since Chesterton left."

She scowled at me. "If you're having such a miserable time, Mr. Wages, why don't you take me home."

I started to get up and she stopped me. "I don't think you really want to know."

"Try me?" I said.

That did it. She pushed herself away from the table. "Take me home."

We rode the three miles in silence, and when she got out of the car, she slammed the door hard enough to impress upon me the gravity with which she viewed my insensitivity. I was in no mood to play games and I overrevved the Porsche as I roared back down the drive heading for Ginny's place and a chance to lick my wounds. There were three days left before the Labor Day weekend concluded the summer, and it was beginning to look as if the highlight of the summer was already history.

When I passed Becker Herd's place, I saw that the Carmi barge had docked and Harrison Peters was standing on the pier talking to Ira Leonard. Since several others, all young men, were milling around as well, I decided to stop. I figured it was as good a time as any to see if Leonard and his crew had made any progress. When Peters saw me coming down the hill toward the barge, he looked relieved.

"Glad you stopped, E. G. Ira here was just starting to give me a rundown."

Leonard reached out and dropped a blackened, triangular object in my hand. It was about the size of a 50-cent piece. "Sorry, Elliott," he said, "chalk it off to academic skepticism."

I rolled the object over in my hand. It looked like a charred guitar pick. "What is it?"

"Best bet is that it's a gar tooth. The biggest one I have ever seen. One of my graduate assistants identified it. The blackened area is an advanced stage of decay."

What Leonard had just handed me was a double-edged sword. There was a certain sense of relief in knowing that I had not been hallucinating. At the same time, there was an even more disturbing feeling, since I knew for sure that Graham Hatcher had not caught the only giant gar in Jericho Lake. There was another one of those ugly bastards swimming around out there, and it was hostile enough to attack a 22-foot speedboat. If it would attack a craft that size, I had to ask myself, what else would it attack?

"You can tell Ms. Wallace I dug that out of the hull of her boat," Leonard said.

I was still rolling the object over and over in my hand when Peters said, "Tell him what else you came up with."

Leonard brought his clipboard up so that the light on Herd's pier illuminated the data. "It's all very preliminary of course," he said, "but so far we have been able to confirm that there are significant temperature variations at various locations around the lake. The surface temperature, as the result of the last several days being in the nineties, is relatively constant. But the variations in temperature are wholly inconsistent with what we would expect to find when we measure at the six- and twelve-foot levels."

Harrison Peters did not have the look of a man who intended to ask why. So I did.

"Jericho Lake is a crater lake, formed by glacial deposits," Ira said. "It covers approximately seven thousand acres and has two basins. Max depth, from our latest soundings, in the east basin indicate it's about one hundred and forty feet deep. The west basin isn't quite that deep. The bottom of the lake is composed mostly of stone with a higher concentration of sediment in the east basin. The DNR charts indicate that there are about eighty springs feeding the lake as well as the slough. Just from what we were able to learn today, I would estimate that there are at least twice that number of springs and a great deal more sediment impact from that slough activity over there than the DNR thought."

"The east basin is the one closest to the slough, right?"

Ira Leonard looked at the area where the bridge connected the slough and the lake. "Exactly. The higher sediment accumulation is the result of the east basin being directly in the path of the flow pattern. We ran core samples and I'm on my way back to Carmi now to run some lab tests. I should have a pretty good profile of what is going on down there by tomorrow morning."

"So what do you think all of this is going to tell us?" I asked.

Leonard appeared to be only slightly agitated by my layman's impatience. I did not have the academic's mind set for patiently sifting through empirical data.

"It will tell us, Mr. Wages, what kind of equipment we need to round up to find a solution to the problem. I brought six of my graduate assistants down with me. I'm having two of them work the barge each twelve-hour shift. I have had the two not scheduled for barge duty searching through the slough over there to see if we can discover some more obvious reason for the peculiar odor. So far we haven't uncovered anything. We had a meeting earlier this evening. Collectively, our opinion is that the odor is not coming from the slough. As for your mirage—

that hazy area that seems to come and go—
it's probably nothing more than the result of
thermal activity. At the moment I see no reason to suspect that we're dealing with anything
more than a phenomenon that results from the
string of unusually hot days we've been having
over the past ten days to two weeks. But just to
be certain, I've told Bake and Simpson to take
air samples of that mist cloud when it reforms
tonight."

Always the writer, even worse, the incurably
curious writer, I had to ask, "Couldn't it be asso-
ciated with the odor?"

Leonard acknowledged the possibility. "Yes,
but we won't know for sure until we measure
the density and composition of the air in that
mist cloud. The gear that we have with us now
won't tell us everything we need to know; it's
too primitive. We need a GN-4Y analyzer that
will break it down into minute particles. I'll be
bringing one back with me tomorrow."

Peters was as anxious as I was. "You've seen
enough of these lakes to make an educated guess,
Doc. What do you think it is?"

"I don't think I should speculate," Leonard
said. "One of my assistants has an interesting
theory though. He thinks it is entirely possible
that the elevated temperatures we discovered in
the basin today could cause a system imbalance
that doesn't allow the trapped gases to escape."

"Trapped gases?" I said. "Is there any danger?"

Leonard shook his head. "Unlikely. Show me a
freshwater lake and I'll find you traces of trapped

gas. It's part of the ecocycle. Theoretically the slough carries a constant stream of nutrients and sediment into the lake, and most of these are going to settle in the closest low spot."

"The east basin?" Peters said.

"Right, Sheriff. Then, inconsistent weather or unusual temperature variations play havoc with the decomposition cycle. It's happening all the time in every freshwater lake. If that is the case, we'll find a way to burp it." Leonard laughed to emphasize the fact that he had made a small joke. From the way it came off, I had the distinct feeling Ira Leonard did not attempt humor very often.

Fortunately, the good doctor had reduced his theory to simple enough terms that even I was beginning to understand. "And that," I said, "could result in mutating life forms so that we get something like the giant garpike, right?"

Leonard laughed, more of a strained release of tension than an acknowledgment of a wrong conclusion. "On the contrary, Mr. Wages, a condition such as the one I've just described would tend to destroy most life forms."

At that point I realized we were right back where we were when the conversation started—no answers, not even a workable theory as to why Jericho Lake was suddenly host to at least two, and perhaps more, giant and, in one case, very aggressive garpike. When I looked disappointed that he had shot a hole in my theory, Leonard defended himself.

"You will recall, Mr. Wages, that Carmi was

called in to see if we could determine what was causing the unpleasant odor. My colleagues and I are with the department of environmental studies. Giant garpike, I'm afraid, are a little out of our line."

I stood beside Peters while Leonard went back out on the barge, unrolled the lake charts and showed his assistants where to anticipate the mist cloud. There was some animated conversation and when he came back, he had his truck keys in his hand.

"I'll see you gentlemen in the morning. In the meantime, keep your fingers crossed. If we can determine what's down there, we can probably find a way to make that nasty little odor of yours go away. Then your mayor can start smiling again."

Leonard departed, the Carmi barge chugged away from the pier and I walked back to the parking lot with Harrison Peters. He started asking questions before I could.

"What have you been able to learn about Bartel?"

"Nothing so far. It's a holiday weekend. It may be Tuesday before I learn anything."

"But you'll be gone by then."

"I'll call you before I go. I may be gone, Harrison, but that Bartel plant will still be there and you'll still need answers. Now, what about Abner Barker's buddy?"

"The state police gave up the search and the dragging operation until they know for certain he didn't leave the lake with some friends. Like you said, it's the holiday and they've got their hands full with other matters."

"What about Graham Hatcher?"

"Autopsy is tomorrow."

"And Doc Hoppkins?"

"Haven't located him. I called his wife twice today; she hasn't heard from him either."

"Isn't that a bit unusual?"

Peters pushed his hat back on his head. He had the look of a man who was reluctant to talk about something. Finally he said, "Not for Hoppy. He gets into the sauce every now and then and disappears for a couple of days. That's what cost him his job back east. They couldn't depend on him. He came back to Jericho to get his act together. Most everyone around here accepts Marion Hoppkins for what he is, and most of the time he's a pretty good combination coroner and doctor."

I had just uncovered another wrinkle in the closely woven social fabric of Jericho. For the most part, I had to hand it to them; with the exception of Becker Herd, they kept their laundry problems to themselves. After three months of close proximity to the principals involved, I was just beginning to discover some of the untidies that had been swept under the carpet: the Bartel situation, the Wallace-Chesterton relationship, and now, the local medic with a chronic drinking problem.

"I understand you and Felix Chesterton finally ran into each other." Peters grinned.

"I didn't realize we were avoiding each other."

"That's not the way the locals had it pegged." Peters winked. "Guess it had to happen. Chesterton just plain ran out of places to hide."

"I don't have any quarrel with Chesterton."

"No," Peters said. "But he sure has one with you. When you started sleeping with Cynthia Wallace, you took all the air out of his financial balloon. He was hoping to get her back till you came along."

The fact that Harrison Peters's remark caught me off stride must have been apparent because he said quickly, "If he could have married that banker lady, his problems would have been over."

I was still standing in Herd's parking lot when Peters drove away. Despite the late hour, the night was hot and humid and getting stickier by the minute.

All the way to Cyn's place, I knew I should be heading in the other direction—but the *I* in Elliott stands for impulsive and the wisdom gained in 43 summers was not enough to offset what was obviously a major chink in the armor of Elliott Wages. I knocked on the door, sent Basketcase into a barking fit and roused Mrs. Fern out of a sound sleep. She didn't even try to stop me.

I found Cyn on the deck outside her bedroom. She was still wearing her little yellow tennis outfit. She didn't seem too surprised that I had come back. She looked at me, but she did not say anything.

"I just talked to Peters. He gave me his version of the Felix Chesterton-Cynthia Wallace relationship. Now I want yours."

The lady's face was hidden in cloud shadows, but there was enough moonlight to betray a definite sag in her shoulders. "You don't give up, do you?"

"I think I have a right to know what's going on."

She waited awhile before answering. "It goes deeper than Bartel and real estate," she said, "and deeper than one of those boy-girl things, Elliott. Felix and I go back all the way to college days. He was always a little too ambitious and a little too greedy for my father. And Daddy never stopped warning me that Felix was clearly more interested in the Wallace money than he was me. To make my father happy, I called the whole thing off. I went on to graduate school and Felix came back to Jericho. When my father died in that automobile crash and I came back, it flared up again. I was in love with him—enough so that I asked him to marry me."

"You asked him?"

"This is the nineties, Elliott. Women do that sort of thing these days."

"And he declined?"

"That's a nice way of putting it. Felix had made some money—enough that I didn't look all that attractive to him considering his political ambitions. He intends to run for governor some day and a two-time loser at the altar wouldn't look good on his arm. Gossip bothers Felix."

"So who broke it off?"

Cyn was not cut out for confessions. She braced herself with a long drink of whatever she had been consoling herself with and avoided eye

110

contact. "Who knows?" she said. "Does it really matter who buries a dead body?"

"I suppose I can guess the rest. Not long after that the Bartel deal crystalized and when you and Lancer swung the deal in favor of the property over on the Montana Mills slough, Felix baby took a first-class financial bath."

She nodded. "He thought I did it to get even with him."

"Did you?"

Cyn didn't answer.

"So when I showed up, contrite but destitute Felix was trying to mend his fences with you and I got in the way, right?"

"I let you get in the way," she said. The tone of her voice indicated she had regained some of her eroded self-esteem and that she had said just about all she intended to say about the subject. She looked away toward the lake.

I had that old feeling again. Maybe bachelors hear too many confessions. Confessions have a way of taking something out of a relationship. It doesn't seem to make any difference whether I'm making them or hearing them; things are never quite the same. We lapsed into an uncomfortable silence, both feeling terribly human and a little too vulnerable—and maybe a little sorry for what the first frost does to the rosebud.

Finally, Cyn dozed off, I fixed myself a drink and sat there feeling like a bastard for forcing the truth out of her. Did I feel any better knowing what I knew? The truth is only time would tell.

R. Karl Largent

*   *   *

It was almost midnight when I checked my watch and decided to leave. I went into the house, got a sheet, tucked it around Cyn and took one long last look at the lake. I was giving serious consideration to going back to Ginny's cottage, throwing my meager belongings in a bag and catching a ride into Fort Janes, where I could take the first flight out in the morning.

That was when I noticed it. I scanned the entire lake once, then a second time; the Carmi barge was nowhere in sight. "Where the hell is it?"

Cyn came out of her stupor. "Where is what?"

"The Carmi barge—it's gone."

"Maybe it went in for some reason."

"I heard Leonard tell them what to do just before he left. He wanted night readings on that misty area."

Cyn dug out her binoculars, handed them to me and I scanned the lake three times. The lake was deserted. I didn't tell Cyn, but I had an uneasy feeling in the pit of my stomach. It's a feeling I've learned never to ignore.

"Maybe they turned off the lights on the barge for some reason," she said.

"That doesn't make any sense. You can't record data in the dark."

I could tell by her voice she was scared and confused. Even without the missing barge it was a clumsy time for both of us. When I started for the door she wanted to know if I was coming back.

"I don't know," I said. It was the only answer

112

I could give her. I wanted to tell her that if there was ever going to be anything between Cynthia Wallace and E. G. Wages, it was going to start with honesty.

I skipped down the back steps, ran to the car, crawled in and raced down the drive. By the time I hit the lake road, I was in third gear. By the time I pulled into Becker Herd's parking lot I already had the answer to my first question: the Carmi barge was not docked at Herd's pier.

It took even less time to get to the end of the pier, and I was again using Cyn's binoculars to make another sweep of the lake. At the same time I was aware of footsteps on the pier behind me. I wheeled around and threw the beam of my flashlight into the flushed face of Bert Freeman.

"Damn it, Bert, don't sneak up on me like that."

Freeman was clenching a pine two-by-four in his hand. He looked relieved when he saw it was me. "Jesus, Elliott, I thought you might be one of them damn tourists trying to steal some of Becker's gas."

"What the hell did you think you were going to do with that?"

Bert Freeman had a sheepish look on his face. He was blinking into the beam of my flashlight. "I ain't sure," he said. "Me and Candy couldn't sleep and decided to take a little walk. I saw somebody down on Becker's dock and thought I'd better check it out. This chunk of wood was the only thing I could find." He looked at the light and the binoculars, then out at the lake. "What the hell are you doing down here?"

It didn't take long to tell Bert about my suspicions. As I did, he started scanning the lake too.

"How long would it take you to go back and get your deck boat?" I knew he had one. Candy Freeman was notorious for screaming around the lake with her two teenage grandsons in Jericho's longest running ski show.

"Ten minutes," he said.

"Get it," I said. "Something tells me we better find out where that barge is."

Bert protested but he went to get it anyway. Ten minutes later I saw the bow light knifing through the darkness toward Herd's pier. He cut back and waited for the wash to settle. When he was close enough, I jumped in.

"Where to?" Bert asked.

"Take us over by the bridge where the slough feeds in."

Bert did.

When we were less than 50 yards offshore south of the bridge, I began playing the beam of his halogen spotlight back and forth across the water. It did not take long for a note of exasperation to creep into Bert's voice. "What the hell are you looking for, Elliott? It's obvious they ain't here."

"Better start circling," I said. "Make each pass a little closer to that foggy area. Maybe we can see a little better when we get closer to it." For some reason, I was as much aware of the mirage-like fog as I was the increasing odor.

"There's that damn smell again," Bert said.

We maneuvered closer until the drifting cloud

of mist looked almost opaque and twice as big as it had been earlier in the day. It hovered above the water, clawed a good 20 feet or so into the air and covered an area that I estimated to be somewhere in the neighborhood of a couple of hundred square yards. It gave the impression of being an alien darkness in an already dark world.

"That shit is thick," Bert said. "I ain't goin' in that stuff."

"Cut the engine!" I wasn't in the mood to listen to his bitching.

Bert Freeman shut his motor down and the bow settled in the water. We sat there for several minutes while I listened. "You don't think they're in there in that damn fog, do you?"

I held my finger up to my lips. "Keep it down."

"Hell, Elliott, if they was in there, you could hear their generator."

Bert was quiet for several minutes, but it did not take him long to get restless again. "Do you realize how big this lake is, Elliott? Hell fire, they could be anywhere. Maybe they went over to the marina to get a cup of coffee."

I reminded him that the marina closed at midnight.

Bert stirred restlessly in the bow while I played the light back and forth over the water. "How deep do you figure the water is here?"

"Thirty, maybe forty feet," he said. "We're close to the trench that runs between the slough and the first basin. I've heard tell it might be as much as eighty foot deep in places along through here."

Bert had just struggled to his feet when I saw something emerging from that cloud of mist. It seemed to be drifting toward us. I threw the beam of the halogen at it and realized it was the Carmi barge.

I dove for the panel, hit the starter button, heard the big Mercury catch and jammed the throttle forward.

We made it, but I had seen enough to know that the sight of the Carmi barge coming out of that mist would haunt my dreams for years to come.

Saturday A.M., September 4

The first gray traces of dawn groped their way into the world around Becker Herd's pier to reveal what was left of the Carmi barge. It sat there like some great and terrible monolith—motionless, implacable and sinister. Bert and I had anchored the barge some 50 yards from where I was standing on the dock; it was a mute, slime-covered symbol of something gone drastically wrong.

When the *C. I. Harrington* emerged from the cloud of mist it was a ghost ship. Except that there were no ghosts. The fresh-scrubbed faces and bodies of Ira Leonard's graduate assistants were nowhere to be found.

After Bert and I had managed to get out of the derelict's way, we circled it, waited until it cleared the vapor cloud, then threw a ski rope over the bow. We towed it to a point far enough away from Herd's pier so that the gawkers couldn't get a good look at it, but close enough for the state police investigation that was going to be necessary to determine what had happened.

From the phone in front of Herd's grocery, Bert had roused Harrison Peters out of a sound sleep and informed him what had happened. We put another call through to Carmi Institute and Ira Leonard. After that, the system worked. The state police post in Fort Janes was notified, and Charley Marlboro, the deputy commander, arrived in the early hours of the morning to take charge of the investigation. The first thing Marlboro ordered Peters to do was round up two local divers to assist in the search for the bodies. They were standing by. At seven o'clock in the morning, everyone was waiting for Marlboro to give the signal to close off the area and begin the search. But the signal still wasn't given—if for no other reason than the deputy commander was involved in a heated argument with Felix Chesterton.

Peters, leaning against the flagpole on the end of Herd's pier, lit a cigar and stared out at the lake. Others, like Mackey, passed the time assessing the prospects for the new day. "Gonna be another blisterer," Cletus said.

"Maybe the damn heat will hold the crowd down," Peters said. There was little conviction in his voice.

A panel truck stopped on the road in front of Herd's store and a man and a woman got out. The call letters of a Fort Janes television station were emblazoned on the side of the truck.

The Lake

The man carried a bulky camera, the woman some electronic gear and a microphone. I wondered what Chesterton would say when he saw them. As far as he was concerned, they were in Jericho at the right time but for the wrong reason.

"Not a trace of them, huh?" Peters asked again. I shook my head. The same questions were asked over and over: Where the hell could they have gone? What the hell was the oily stuff on the barge? Everyone had questions. No one had answers.

The oily stuff everyone kept referring to was a black, sootlike coating that appeared to cover the entire barge. It was slippery and noisome according to Mackey, who thus far was the only one to venture out to inspect the barge at close range.

Peters had asked both Bert Freeman and me to wait around until the search began. From my vantage point on the pier I kept an eye on the vapor cloud from which the barge had emerged. As the darkness eroded into dawn, we had come to the coolest part of the night and at that point the cloud appeared to have spread until it covered most of the southeastern third of the lake. Tentacles of the vapor cloud had crept to within 30 or 40 feet of the shoreline near the bridge and actually enveloped the pier in front of Bert and Candy Freeman's cottage. In the first light of dawn the cloud was gray and opaque and ominous.

"What the hell do you suppose it is?" Peters asked.

"Beats me," Freeman said, "but I'll tell you one thing, Harrison, I sure as hell ain't goin' near it."

One of the divers walked out on the pier toward Peters just as Candy Freeman arrived with fresh coffee. "What's the deal, Harrison? Do you want us to search for those two or not? Arty and me have been waiting out here four hours already."

Peters shook his head. "The state police are calling the shots now. As soon as Marlboro gets through talking to Chesterton, we'll rope the area off and get started." The diver grunted, lit a cigarette and headed back to shore.

Meanwhile, Marlboro and Chesterton's discussion had become animated. "Think Chesterton is stonewalling it?" I asked.

Peters shrugged. "Can't blame him, Elliott. This Jubilee is like manna from heaven for the merchants; I can understand Chesterton's reluctance. The town council will hold his feet to the fire if he allows Marlboro to close the lake. So far we haven't supplied any answers. My guess is he won't close it down until he's certain he doesn't have any alternative."

"I think you'll find some of your answers at Bartel."

Peters looked at me. "You think they're causing it?"

"What else is different around here this year?"

Peters was still thinking my question over when Marlboro broke off his conversation with Chesterton and started out on the pier. He was a tall man with a crooked nose and the shoulders of a linebacker. He headed straight for Peters. "Get ready to close her down, Sheriff. I want the entire south end of the lake cordoned off. We'll close the lake road and route traffic along the north shore."

"Like hell you will!" Chesterton said.

Charley Marlboro was one of the few men in the crowd tall enough to stand eye to eye with Felix Chesterton. "If I say we close it down, Chesterton, we close it down. In case you've forgotten, this lake is state property. Your authority stops at the edge of that road up there."

Chesterton backed away; he was smart enough to know he had to change his tactics. The stridency in his voice dissipated and he turned to Peters. "All I said is, before he closed the lake, I wanted to talk to the city attorney and find out what our liability is to the vendors and the people that set up the rides. If we get hit with a fistful of lawsuits, it could bankrupt this town."

Ira Leonard stepped forward. "Look, Mayor Chesterton, I appreciate what you're saying. But I think you should consider your obligation to the people coming in for the Jubilee as well. As it stands now, we are telling you this lake isn't safe. It's true we don't know what we're dealing with yet—but I can assure you, you haven't seen lawsuits like you'll see if someone finds out that we knew there was a problem and didn't close this lake down."

"He's right, Felix," Peters said. "We've already got one death on our hands and the Kinder boy is still not accounted for. Now Dr. Leonard here has two students missing. We could have a real disaster on our hands if we let people use this lake today."

"Sheriff Peters is right, Mayor. If we close it down maybe we can find out what's going on down there," Leonard said.

"That is exactly my point, Dr. Leonard. You don't know. At the moment, we have no confirmation of anything other than the fact that a very unpleasant odor exists. And that odor is a long way from where the Jubilee activities are taking place."

"Did you see what was left of the Barker boy?" I asked.

"Stay out of this, Wages." Chesterton snarled. "A kid gets run over by a speedboat. It's too damn bad, but it happens. If not this lake, then any one of several in the area—James, Crooked, even Snow."

"Do I have to remind you that there are two men missing from that barge?" Leonard said.

"What happened to them?" Chesterton demanded.

"We don't know yet," Leonard said.

A smile spread over Chesterton's face. "Gentlemen, I think I just made my point."

"What about Cynthia Wallace's boat?" I asked.

Chesterton wheeled around and stared at me. "The way I hear it, Wages, she ran into the goddamned pier."

Marlboro stepped between us. "Okay, you've got your two hours, Mayor. But unless I find something to defuse this situation, I intend to order Sheriff Peters here to close down the lake at nine o'clock this morning."

"We'll see about that," Chesterton said.

Chesterton departed and Marlboro called the divers down, ordering them to continue the search. "Wages," he said, "you were there last night. You go with them."

My heart wasn't in it, but I agreed.

There is a streak of countryboy common sense that runs through Wages males, and it was telling me I should extricate myself from the soap opera unfolding in Jericho and get back to my own business. I hadn't written a salable word in days and there would be hell to pay when I had to call my editor and request another extension.

Instead, I wheeled out of Herd's parking lot and took the lake road toward the stone bridge across the mouth of the slough. The odor was stronger than before, but the vapor cloud appeared to be diminishing again. I made a mental note that the vapor cloud, whatever it was, seemed to be more apparent in the darkness hours and less obvious in the daylight—or was it just less noticeable?

By the time I pulled into the Bartel plant I had put my theory on the vapor cloud aside and was concentrating on what I intended to ask Blackmonn, assuming I was able to locate him. To my astonishment, the pedestrian gate wasn't locked; and when I tried the front door, it wasn't locked either. The Bartel people were either being very cavalier about their security or someone had screwed up.

The front door opened into a spartan lobby and another door opened into a long corridor with a low ceiling. There were small trail-tracer lights along the wall but other than that, no lighting. I could not recall seeing a corridor quite like it: no windows, no wall hangings, no carpet—colorless, featureless and odorless—pure sterility. There was a constant, low-pitched, monotonous hum, and I knew I was being tracked by some kind of concealed surveillance device.

The hall led to another door and it opened as easily as the previous one. This one led out onto a balcony that overlooked a large cavernous area. If the floor hadn't been covered with water, I would have guessed it to be a warehouse or storage area of some sort. There were two concrete causeways extending toward what I assumed was the rear of the building. Overhead there was a network of steel grids that extended out over a bathtub-sized metal object sitting in the water. It was tethered to the overhead grids by steel cables. Tiny red, green and white blinking lights did little to illuminate the area. There was not enough lighting for me to make out any detail. I stood there for several minutes wondering what was going on and what I had gotten myself into when I felt something hard snuggle into the small of my back.

"You are trespassing," a man said. "Lean over, put your hands on the railing and spread your legs." I followed instructions and a hand danced up and down my body, patted my chest and hips and finished off with a quick excursion up and down the inside of my legs. "Now, you may turn around."

I did and had to look down. My captor couldn't have been more than five and a half feet tall. He was nearly bald, had a narrow, pinched face and a funny, squeaky voice. He looked out of place in a white lab coat. The only thing that kept him from being laughable was the fact that his hand was deftly coiled around a very serious looking semiautomatic.

"What do you want here?" he asked.

"I want to talk to Superintendent Blackmonn."

I think he was surprised I actually had a name. If he was the one who had been monitoring my progress on the surveillance system, he doubt-less had me pegged as some kind of vagrant. I looked pretty tacky after my nightlong ordeal of crawling around on boats and barges in Jericho Lake. I was not what Cyn would have termed presentable.

"You have an appointment?" he asked in a low hiss. By then I was beginning to catch on to his accent; it had definite Balkan overtones.

"Hell no, I don't have an appointment. How could I? No one ever answers the phones around here."

My snarl hadn't intimidated him in the least. He stepped back, groped along the wall until his hand found a small access panel, opened it and pressed a button. A green light came on.

"I have the security breach in custody," he said. "He tells me he is attempting to locate Superintendent Blackmonn."

There was a pause. Then a man's voice came over the intercom. "Do you believe him?"

The man in the lab coat didn't mince words. "No."

"Then escort him to the front gate."

"Wait a minute," I said, talking around the little man. "My name is Wages, Elliott Grant Wages. The sheriff of Jericho sent me over here to talk to Mr. Blackmonn. They've got a problem in the village and the sheriff seems to think Mr. Blackmonn may be able to help us."

My pushiness worked. There was another pause and the intercom voice said, "Dr. Mueller, please escort the gentleman to the third level security office. I will meet you there."

Mueller looked disappointed. I had the distinct impression he didn't get many opportunities to bully people and his latest opportunity was being cut short. He made a sideways get-moving motion with his semiautomatic and pressed another button. A door leading to a stairway opened. He was gracious enough to point the way with the barrel. "Up," he said. Unlike the corridor, the stairway was lighted.

By the time we got to the top of the stairs, I realized Mueller was even smaller than I had estimated. He couldn't have weighed more than 100 pounds. The thin, nearly transparent skin stretched over his skull supported a crop of lifeless, dull brown hair around the ears with a few strands just long enough to be draped across the top of his head. He pointed to another door. "In there."

126

The Lake

When I opened it another man was standing there. He was average height, average weight, average everything—but dressed like he had just stepped out of the pages of *GQ*. "I am Roger Blackmonn," he said. He was wearing a vested seersucker suit and standing in the middle of a plush office overflowing with the accoutrements of status. He studied me for a moment, walked around behind his desk and took a seat. "That will be all, Dr. Mueller."

After Mueller closed the door, Blackmonn motioned for me to have a seat. "Well, Mr. Wages, what can I do for you?"

While Blackmonn opened a gold cigarette case, tapped out a filterless cigarette and put it in a holder, I explained that I had been sent by Jericho County Sheriff Harrison Peters.

Blackmonn assessed me for several minutes and I got the impression a small light went on inside his head. "Now I recognize you, Mr. Wages. You are the gentleman from the sham fishing boat, correct? The man who was pretending to fish while you talked into a recording device and tried to survey our facilities with your binoculars."

"You had better binoculars than I did. I would never have recognized you."

Blackmonn wasn't the kind of man who laughed. His smile did all the work, and it was crooked as though it needed practice. "You alluded to a problem. If there is a problem in our little community, Mr. Wages, Bartel is most anxious to be of assistance. All of our satellite facilities are encouraged to be good neighbors in those communities where they set up shop. Mr. Randolph Bartel II, our chairman, believes in strong community participation on the part of Bartel executives."

I was starting to relax. Blackmonn wasn't at all what I had anticipated. "That surprises me. The folks in Jericho claim they haven't seen or heard much from you."

Blackmonn sobered momentarily, then regained his composure. "Unfortunately," he said, "they are right. It is a situation I hope to remedy in the next several months." He put out his cigarette. "We have had, how shall I put it, start-up problems, Mr. Wages. But things are starting to come around."

"Would those start-up problems have anything to do with a toxic substance being dumped into the slough?"

The accusation didn't faze him in the least. "Toxic problems, Mr. Wages? Hardly. This facility is a fully contained, totally self-sufficient plant. We are even capable of generating our own electricity, disposing of our own waste products, and when we are fully operational, nothing except product will leave these four walls."

"That seems to be the question on everyone's mind, Blackmonn. Just exactly what does this facility do?"

"I'm afraid that I am not at liberty to discuss the Montana Mills mission with non-unit personnel, Mr. Wages. But I can assure you, we produce nothing that could be considered toxic in any way, shape or form."

The Lake

"The people of Jericho are convinced that something coming from the slough is contaminating their lake. There are unpleasant odors and, more recently, vapor clouds forming over certain parts of the lake."

Blackmonn leaned back in his chair. The crooked smile was working overtime. "And you would like me to give Jericho authorities assurances that we are not the culprit, correct?"

"They want more than assurances, they want proof." I knew I was pushing, but surprisingly enough, Blackmonn was allowing himself to be pushed.

He forced another smile. "I will be happy to look into the matter," he said evenly.

"When?"

"I have been out of town for the better part of the past two weeks, Mr. Wages. I would like the opportunity to talk to my staff."

"When?" I repeated.

Blackmonn looked at his calendar. "Next week . . . perhaps Thursday?"

I leaned forward in my chair. "I like tomorrow better."

Blackmonn deliberated for a moment. "Very well, since you seem to feel the matter is so urgent, tomorrow it will be then. Say nine o'clock? I will meet you in the parking lot outside the security gate." He recognized the questioning look on my face. "I say parking lot, Mr. Wages, because we have a very strict security charter here. You were fortunate today. You may not be that fortunate again."

Before I could come back at him, Blackmonn had pushed a button on his desk. "Dr. Mueller, will you be so kind as to show Mr. Wages out?"

Mueller appeared and hustled me to the door. In the harsh light of the sun he looked even worse. He waited until I crawled into the Carrera, then locked the gate. He must have figured that one security breach was enough.

On the way back to Jericho, one thought kept bouncing around in my sleep-starved brain: I had seen nothing that would make me believe Roger Blackmonn was running a toy company.

Instead of hunting up Harrison Peters, I headed straight for Ginny's place. In retrospect, I wasn't surprised to discover Cyn waiting for me. She gave me a hug, muttered something about our big weekend slipping away from us and trudged into the house with me. "I'm sorry about last night," she said. She sounded sincere.

"It wasn't your fault. I was doing the pushing."

"It could have been different," she said softly.

"Let's talk about it later."

She stopped me, turned me around and studied me hard. "Are we going to pretend it didn't happen?"

"I think the people around here do too much pretending something isn't happening."

She looked hurt. It had come out sounding different from the way I intended. "Meaning?" she asked. Cyn was trying hard to make the best of a bad situation.

The Lake

"Look, Cyn, I'm tired, I'm hungry, I need a shower. I haven't had any sleep. Neither my mouth nor my brain is working right. Suppose you give me ten minutes to get my head screwed on straight while you rustle up some breakfast?"

She smiled and headed for the kitchen while I went through what were my normal male morning rituals. Ten minutes later we were devouring hot coffee and scrambled eggs and I was starting to feel like a human being again. All the while, she had an expression on her face that vacillated somewhere between hurt, confusion and concern.

Finally I broached the subject again. "If you know something about that Bartel outfit that would shed some light on what's happening around here, now is the time to spit it out."

She wrinkled her nose. "I don't like that word."

"And I don't like cover-ups."

"Do you think I'm covering something up?"

"Not knowingly, but Bartel definitely is hiding something. And it occurs to me that during all those meetings with the Bartel people, when you were wrapping up the deal on the Montana Mills site, something might have been said to give you some indication of what they intended to do with that facility."

The pretty lady pushed her plate away and her face furrowed into a very unbecoming frown. She was shaking her head. "I talked to Randolph Bartel only once on the telephone. He's the founder's son. Outside of the fact that

131

he is very articulate and soft-spoken, there isn't much more I can tell you."

"What about Blackmonn?"

"Contrary to what everyone thinks, I've never met the man. Honest, Elliott, if I thought I knew anything that would help you, I would tell you."

I was ready to throw up my hands in exasperation when the phone rang. "Wages here."

"Where the hell have you been?" Ellery Tweet said. "I've been trying to get in touch with you for twenty-four hours."

I was in no mood for small talk. "What did you find out, Tweet?"

Ellery Tweet could take longer to get to the point than Harrison Peters. After 30 seconds of hemming and hawing and shuffling papers, he still hadn't said anything. Finally he dialed his voice a notch lower and said, "Bartel is a legitimate toy company all right. But since they are privately held, it's a little tougher to get the kind of information you want."

From the way he was hedging, I couldn't tell whether Ellery Tweet was trying to set me up for a bigger payoff or he was giving me the straight skinny.

"On the surface, their skirts appear to be clean, Elliott. On the other hand, I did learn something that may interest you."

"Let's have it."

"Two and a half years ago, our friends at Bartel, one of America's oldest toy companies, were awarded a research and development contract with the Department of Defense."

"The DOD?" I said. "What the hell would a toy company have to offer the DOD?"

"Beats me," Ellery said. "They were awarded a cost plus contract with a completion date of mid-next year. No penalty clauses and an open end on the completion date if the research looks promising."

"How much?"

"Four hundred million." Tweet let the number fall on the table and rattle around like an empty dinner plate. I let out a whistle.

"The fact of the matter is, Elliott, it's really not all that big of a contract as far as the DOD goes. And I probably wouldn't even have paid any attention to it if the code name hadn't caught my eye. It's called The Jericho Project."

I rocked back on my heels. Tweet had found the hole in the security net. My head was spinning. "Okay, Mr. Tweet, now comes the sixty-four dollar question. What the hell is The Jericho Project?"

Tweet was silent for a moment. "I don't know for certain, E. G. But in the early stages of development, most of these research programs are funded under a code name with a location designation. What that usually means is that if the research stage is promising, Uncle Sugar will invest major-league money in the production phase."

I had the same heady feeling I used to have when I imagined I had just won first prize in the peek under Dolly Parton's blouse contest. "Okay, where do I find out what this contract is all about?"

Tweet was silent again, as though he was thinking. Then he rattled off a phone number. "That's where I would start. It's your old friend, Benny Placeman."

"You know him too?"

Ellery Tweet laughed. "Hell yes, Elliott. Where do you think people in my line of business get their information?"

I mumbled some what were probably wholly inadequate thank-yous and hung up, wondering if I had enough leeway on my American Express card to send Ellery and Mrs. Tweet out to dinner at one of New York's finest. Then I dialed the number of Benny Placeman. He wasn't there but his secretary took my number and promised to have him call back.

Through it all, Cyn had waited patiently, on occasion turning her gaze toward the lake. When I finally hung up, I felt she deserved an explanation.

"What's the population of this county?" I asked.

"Summer or winter?"

"They are different, right?"

The lady laughed. "About twenty thousand most of the year; in the summer it's almost one hundred and fifty thousand. A good ninety percent of the homes on the lakes around here are summer homes only."

"The rest of the year it's pretty slow and pretty isolated, right?"

"Exactly. In the middle of the off-season you could shoot a gun off in Jericho and no one would hear it."

134

The Lake

I sat down at the table, poured myself another cup of coffee and told the lady what I thought. "Theory: Bartel's last minute decision to locate that plant in Montana Mills had nothing to do with your old friend Felix and his buddies trying to gouge them with elevated land values. I think the real reason they settled on the Montana Mills site is because it is even more out of the way than Jericho."

Cyn was still trying to figure out how I came to that conclusion when I saw Harrison Peters's cruiser turn into the driveway.

Saturday P.M., September 4

Harrison Peters crawled out of his car and leaned against the door. "Chesterton was able to convince someone in the governor's office that we didn't have enough hard evidence to call for a quarantine. The son of a bitch has clout. Marlboro is fit to be tied."

"What happened?"

"Bottom line: until either Marlboro or that bunch from Carmi can prove that there really is a risk, they won't let Marlboro shut it down."

I looked past the weary sheriff at the increasing activity on the lake. Most of it was centered around the marina area and the Jericho municipal beach. Other than that, there was only a handful of boats, most of them in the casting tournament, clustered in a small group at the far end of the lake, a long way away from where Leonard and the divers were working. "Maybe we'll get lucky," I said.

Peters's cigar was little more than a soggy stub. He examined it, decided he could get a few more puffs out of it and took out his lighter. "Were you able to get in touch with anyone over at Bartel?"

"Blackmonn himself. Pompous, but underneath it all he seems like a decent sort."

"Could he shed any light on our little problem?"

"No, but he said he would look into it. I'm to meet him in the company parking lot tomorrow morning at nine o'clock."

Peters nodded, grimaced at the taste of his cigar and threw it away. "I'm headed over to tell Leonard and his men that the lake stays open. Want to ride along?"

"I'm waiting for a phone call. I just may have a little more ammunition to fire at Roger Blackmonn tomorrow morning, especially if that call comes through."

Harrison Peters looked like a man who was too tired to care whether I received a call or not. He slumped back into his cruiser and headed back down the driveway. Even before he turned on to the road, Cyn was telling me that I had a call.

It was Ellery Tweet again. "Just uncovered this," he said. I was trying to recall whether I had ever heard that much enthusiasm in his voice before. "Get out your pencil, Elliott, this will put a knot in your tail."

Cyn was standing at the window, watching me.

"I found a former Bartel employee with an ax

to grind, a former toy designer fired by no less than Randolph Bartel himself."

"Can we believe him?"

"Judge for yourself, Elliott. Here's what he told me. Six years ago, Randolph Bartel heard about an obscure British research firm called Steltrack in Liverpool. It seems a couple of their lab types were working on a development project to find a way to encapsulate and stabilize a fused energy system known as CFUS-POLCON-PRIEMON. It's a dry system and it's been around for years. But up until the boys from Britain found a way to handle it, nobody even wanted to look at it."

"Why?"

"Two reasons. One, it has never been stable enough for anyone to depend on it. And two, the theory was that, even if it could be stabilized, there wasn't any way to contain and control it. Sorta like the universal solvent, what the hell do you store it in?" Ellery was laughing. It was an old joke.

I was frantically scratching notes and repeating CFUS-POLCON-PRIEMON over and over to capture it.

"Somehow, Bartel got wind of this breakthrough and sent my contact over to work out some sort of licensing arrangement with Steltrack. When they couldn't come to a mutual agreement, Bartel resorted to the old American power play and bought the company."

"Works every time," I said, "but I don't see the connection."

Ellery rifled through more papers. "You'll like this part of it even more. The ink isn't even dry on the deal yet when Bartel suddenly gets awarded a DOD development contract to see what he can do with the stuff."

Ellery Tweet did not have to tell me more than he already had. Bartel's sudden acquisition was beginning to smell like the mess coming in from the slough.

"Tell me about this CFUS-POLCON-PRIE-MON."

This was the part that Ellery loved; it gave him the opportunity to demonstrate his thoroughness. "Well, first of all, the lab boys call it CpP. There has always been a demand for a power source—single component, multisystem feasible—that could be encapsulated and operate a system five to ten thousand times its weight and mass."

"You lost me, Tweet."

"Think of it this way, E. G., my boy. Picture something the size of a refrigerator with an unlimited power source no bigger than a pinhead. In theory, it could operate the system for up to ten years with no deterioration in performance. My source tells me that no one really knows how long this CpP stuff lasts because they haven't depleted the energy in the first tests—all on computer models of course."

"Back to that DOD contract. Are you telling me Bartel was awarded a contract on a theory?"

"A theory that works," Tweet said.

"But what you're really saying is that no one has ever actually successfully encapsulated and drained the energy source in a controlled, let alone operational fashion, right?"

"If you put it that way, no. But the theory checks out on a computer."

I was being silent because there was one hell of a sick feeling in the pit of my stomach. "Okay," I finally said, "that's a piece of the puzzle, but I need more."

"Have you heard from Placeman yet?" Ellery asked.

"Still waiting."

"Anything else you need from me?"

"Get me some more information on Bartel's DOD award: dates, deliver clauses, authorizations, that sort of thing. Anything that looks interesting to you." For Ellery Tweet, my simple request was tantamount to handing a kid a charge card in a toy store.

"The authorization was signed by a Colonel Patrick G. Lancer, a procurement officer in the AP section at the Pentagon, but I'll dig up whatever I can," Ellery said and he was gone. The phone went dead in my ear but I continued to sit there, still too astonished to hang up. When I finally did, Cyn was staring at me.

"You look like you've seen a ghost," she said.

I made sure the anger didn't come through. "I think it's time to put your cards on the table."

"What do you mean?"

"How long did your father and George Lancer know each other?"

Cyn was a poor liar; she knew it and she knew I knew it. She folded her arms and her face got a little pouty. "They grew up together, why?"

"Because Foster Wallace and George Lancer

pulled an even bigger land swindle than the one you have been accusing Felix Chesterton of trying to pull off."

"My father was a fine and honorable man. I won't have you talking about him like that." She had picked up her purse and was starting for the door.

"I think you better sit down, Cyn."

To my surprise, she did.

"Start at the beginning."

I had to contend with a few tears. She used her handkerchief to dab at her nose and faltered through a couple of false starts before she could get the first words out.

"I only learned about it after it was a done deal, Elliott, honest. Daddy told me about it when he came to Boston shortly before he died in that automobile wreck."

She paused, probably to see if the tears were having any effect on me and to determine whether or not I was going to insist that she go on with her story. I wanted to tell her that tears were effective only when they were legitimate.

"Patrick Lancer is George's son. He told my father about the Bartel contract, and Daddy saw it as a way to kill several birds with one stone. Lancer had a couple of acres over on the slough, but my father knew that most of the land around him near the slough was on the tax rolls. Most of it had tax liens on it going back to the twenties. Daddy bought the land, financed it through the Fort Janes Bank and waited."

"I think I can figure out the rest. Young Lancer suggested that Bartel put the development facility in Jericho as part of the deal."

"Most contracts have certain stipulations," Cynthia snapped.

I waved her off. "But greedy Felix found out, maybe during a little pillow talk even. And all of a sudden he saw a way out of his own financial dilemma—a chance to line his own pockets and keep his slate clean enough to someday run for the governor's chair. So, he and his buddies came up with their own land scheme. That complicated things, didn't it? Young Lancer had already played his trump card and it was too risky for him to do anything more than suggest Jericho as a site. So your father and George Lancer ended up having to low ball the Chesterton price to keep the bank's records clean."

Cyn did a little hard swallowing. "You're forgetting that my father died during all of this."

"But you were there to pick up the pieces, right?"

"He was driving home to Jericho one night after a board meeting at his bank. He must have fallen asleep at the wheel. He just drove off the road. It was a twenty-foot drop. The car caught on fire. . . ."

At that point the lady really did come apart at the seams. She cried hard and I felt like a first-class bastard. But I was consoled by the fact that I knew I was finally beginning to get to the truth about the Bartel plant. I stood there, not quite sure what my next move should be, while Cyn gathered up her girl things and left.

I've thought about that particular moment 100 or more times since that day, and it always

The Lake

comes down to what would have happened if the phone had not started ringing. But it did, and I answered it. It was Benny Placeman.

"That you, E. G.?" Benny Placeman had the prototypical whisky voice.

We spent less than 30 seconds on pleasantries before I hit him with my first question. "What do you know about something called the Jericho Project?"

"The DOD shelled out four hundred big ones to see if Bartel can deliver," he said.

Benny spends 12 to 15 hours a day on the telephone; he brokers information. A person soon learns that Benny doesn't waste time on nonrevenue producing small talk.

"Second question: how valuable is this CpP breakthrough?"

"Put it this way, the biggies—Dow, Borden— they'd like to have it in their own arsenal. Unless I miss my guess, one of the bigger houses will suck up Bartel one of these days just to get their hands on it. Wall Street is already hedging their bets. Word is hard to come by. Bartel is privately held."

Third question: rumor has it that Bartel has never actually encapsulated any CpP, that all they've got so far is a computer model. Is there any truth to that?"

"That's what they bought, but you'll have to ask their Jericho people."

"I'm in Jericho now."

Benny Placeman was quiet for a moment. "I'll cut my fee in half, Elliott, if you can verify a

143

rumor that I picked up a couple of days ago."

"Deal. Try me."

"Word has it that one of their damn test units failed."

"What kind of test unit?"

"The DOD is looking to your friends at Bartel to develop a clandestine device powered by this CpP substance."

"Tell me more."

"Size and configuration unknown, powered by a CpP energy source, go anywhere, hide anywhere, operate on that damn source for years. Rumor is it can monitor everything."

"Another satellite, huh?"

"Shit no, Elliott, this ain't no satellite. This unit operates underwater. In theory our government could seed the floors of the seven seas with these little suckers and Uncle Sam could hear everything in every bedroom from Murmansk to Ho Chi Minh City."

"And you say one of their test units failed?"

"My information is a little sketchy, but from what I'm hearing they built a couple of supposedly operational prototypes and they either lost one or it got away from them."

After that, Benny hung up.

Between Ellery Tweet and Benny Placeman, I felt as though someone had just dropped a bomb in my lap—and it was ticking.

TWO

Saturday P.M., September 4

Ferdinand Porsche would have beamed with pride if he had witnessed his nimble rear-engined creation snaking through the hordes of tourists and snarled traffic on the way to the launch area for the replacement barge. I was packing when Cletus Mackey phoned to tell me it had arrived. Ira Leonard was wasting no time getting the gleaming 40-foot high-tech piece of equipment in the water. The carrier, an oversize, black-and-silver 18-wheeler with an extended flatbed trailer, had been pulled off the road and tucked in a vacant lot a couple of hundred yards from Herd's place. The escort unit, with two additional personnel to assist Leonard, was parked beside it. His entourage was already on the barge setting up equipment.

A throng had gathered around the end of the pier, and when I got there, I discovered why. The two divers Peters had brought in from the

Jericho Volunteer Fire Department had completed their grisly mission. They were standing on Herd's pier next to Peters and Mackey while they supervised the removal of the remains of the two Carmi graduate assistants. When Peters saw me he shook his head. "Just like Graham Hatcher," he said, "maybe worse." Then he trudged up the hill behind the men carrying the body bags. I heard doors slam and saw the ambulance pull away. There were no flashing red lights and no sirens. I could tell from the way the crowd continued to mill around they had no idea what had happened. It was a good thing they didn't.

I gave myself a couple of minutes to get over the feeling of nausea and started looking around for a way to get out to the barge. I found a young entrepreneur with an aluminum rowboat, offered him a couple of bucks to take me out and crawled aboard. Even though the young Carmi scientist was still shaken with the discovery of the bodies, he had decided to press on with the investigation and I gave him an abbreviated version of my phone conversations with both Ellery Tweet and Benny Placeman.

"CFUS-POLCON-PRIEMON," he said. "I've read about it, but I don't see how it ties in with what we're finding here." Leonard was still disoriented, but he gave the name of the Bartel material to a young man sitting at the computer in the wheelhouse and instructed him to run it back through the mainframe on the Carmi campus.

"Maybe you should go some place," I said, "and get your bearings. This damn lake can wait."

Leonard shook his head. "I'll be better off if I keep working." When he looked at me, I could see that he had been crying.

"You get pretty close to some of these kids," he said. "Bake and Simpson were two of my favorites. When they heard what I was coming down here for, they gave up their weekend to work with me."

He slumped down on one of the gear lockers, stared out at the lake for several minutes, buried his head between his hands and started to cry again. Several more minutes passed before he regained control. When he did, he said, "I guess we did get something accomplished." He handed me his clipboard. It contained eight columns of meticulously recorded figures. "We used your friend Freeman's deckboat most of the day and came up with these." The sheets had been torn from a loose-leaf notebook. "Not that it's all that scientific, but it does indicate that the closer we get to the trench, the more the readings appear to be reversed."

"Reversed?"

Leonard nodded. "Actually, they are inverse, just the reverse of what we would expect to find." He pointed to the stone bridge over the channel. "Straight out from the bridge is where it gets weird. Now that we've got more accurate equipment, we're going back out there to verify our readings. According to the DNR charts, we were directly over the channel when we took those readings. There appears to be a bizarre correlation: the deeper the channel, the higher the temperature."

I looked at Leonard the way anyone would have looked at the young Carmi scientist if he had just informed them the readings were 180 degrees out of sync with what he had learned in Physiography-105. It did not seem to bother him. I had the feeling that Leonard, because of his youthful appearance, had been fighting that battle all his life.

He turned his attention to the data displays on the bank of monitors and began explaining what we were looking at. We had both noticed that the vapor cloud had diminished steadily during the course of the day—and now was virtually nonexistent. I asked Leonard why.

"I don't know. The truth of the matter is I've been so intrigued with these temperature readings that I've ignored the vapor cloud. We can check it out now that we've got the right equipment on board. I'll have one of my guys take some air samples if we get close enough to it."

My thoughts turned back to the two young men who had just been carted away in body bags. Their loss was significant. Still I couldn't help but think that Jericho had, in a way, lucked out. So far there had been no reports of anyone else being hurt, and the Jubilee participants were confining their activities to the other end of the lake.

The early evening sky was dotted with a splotchy patchwork of warm weather cumulus clouds that gave us a temporary respite from the sun, and the tourists appeared to be losing interest in the seemingly dull repetition of scientific endeavor. It couldn't be that much fun watching someone drop a weighted line into the water, wait two minutes, draw it out, take a reading and repeat the cycle. Stacked off against the thrill-a-minute midway of the Jubilee, Leonard's colorless crew of data gatherers paled by comparison.

While Leonard and his boys made ready to take more readings, I was going back over my conversation with Benny Placeman and trying to picture what one of Bartel's prototype designs might look like. I had a relatively clear concept of computer-controlled airborne sensing devices, if for no other reason than I had used the information in my last book. I wasn't so sure what the design of a clandestine monitoring device that crawled around on the floor of the world's oceans might look like. Did it have legs? Did it slither along the bottom? Or did it use a propeller powered by what Benny Placeman described as an energy source the size of a pinhead?

The barge got underway, moving due west. The skipper, a young man with a crew cut wearing a Notre Dame T-shirt and cutoff jeans, was keeping us several hundred feet from shore. The two divers from the Jericho Volunteer Fire Department had been left onshore. They had spent the better part of the last eight hours in the water and they were exhausted. If there was any diving to be done from this point on, Leonard and his crew had resigned themselves to doing it.

Thirty minutes later, the skipper brought the barge around so that the bow was facing the stone bridge. The vaguely noticeable vapor cloud was no more than 18 inches off the water, covering an area no more than a couple of hundred feet in diameter and a good 60 to 70 yards off our starboard. Even before the engine came to full stop, Leonard and one of his crew had already begun dropping a series of thick nylon lines overboard. Affixed to each was a small orange temperature-sensing device. The devices transmitted a low-frequency thermal signal back to two onboard display monitors that were vaguely reminiscent of fish finders.

A second set of lines was similarly dispatched. They were sonarlike transmitting devices that broadcast a density absorption signal. Leonard explained that he was profiling the lake bottom and verifying the trench depth as well as validating his temperature data.

When he was convinced everything was operational and functioning properly, he returned to the stern and stood with his thin arms folded, studying the bank of monitors. I was engrossed in what was left of the vapor cloud. For the first time I noticed that there was a vague, almost imperceptible red-orange cast to it.

It was the barge's skipper who saw it first. "Dr. Leonard," he shouted. "Unit 7. Look at the size of that son of a bitch."

Leonard took one look at the monitor, threw open a gear locker and quickly began slipping into a tangle of belts and dive gear. Just before he hit the water I heard him say, "How about it, Wages, coming with me?"

For reasons I can't explain, perhaps some catholic desire to be part of the solution and not the problem, I quickly pulled on a tank, buckled myself in and went in after him.

The somber austerity of the freshwater world of Jericho Lake hit me like a slap in the face. It was a universe largely devoid of the color and other enchantments of saltwater diving. I surfaced just long enough to clear my mask and grab the halogen lamp one of Leonard's crew was holding out to me. I checked my gauges, slipped under the barge to let my eyes adjust and started down. Leonard was several feet below me, his head darting first one way and then another as he looked for whatever had triggered the image on the monitor.

I took hold of one of the nylon probe lines and followed it down. In less than 30 feet of water it had become hopelessly tangled in a mossy, yellow-green, undulating universe. I released it, surfaced and tried a second one. The water was incredibly clear, a green-blue-gray world that looked as though it had no intention of trying to conceal anything from us.

The probe on the second line was lying in a sandy clearing. I swam close enough to read the depth indicator and get a temperature reading. It was hovering right at the 80-degree mark and I was cavorting in 32 feet of water. I did a full three-sixty looking for Leonard, but he was nowhere in sight. My wrist compass indicated I was facing due south or in the general direction of the trench and I decided to head that way. I kicked off, swam 20 or 30 yards and noticed that the water seemed to be getting warmer. I stopped, took another reading, logged

84.7 degrees and checked the DDI gauge on my
monitor. I had been swimming downslope, and
the water was several feet deeper than the point
where I had taken my previous reading. I knew
that approximations wouldn't do Leonard any
good, and since I had lost him, I decided to head
back for the surface.

When I got there, Leonard was bobbing on the
surface. "Did you see it?"

I shook my head while I cleared my mask
and pulled it back into place. He was giving
me hand signals. He went down again and I
followed. On the second pass, the DDI indicated
a reading of slightly over 36 feet when we bot-
tomed out and started working our way toward
the trench again. We swam another 30 yards
or so, the bottom abruptly gave way yawning
into blackness and there was a dramatic elevation in the water temperature. It went from
summer warm to downright uncomfortable in
a matter of just a few yards. I could feel myself
beginning to sweat inside the mask. I pulled
up and waited until I could get my regulator
adjusted. The warmer water was causing my
body temperature to elevate too rapidly and I
was gulping too much oxygen in an effort to
compensate.

Leonard was just ahead of me and pointing to
the expanse of emptiness below him. He gave
me another signal, indicating that he was going
down, and I watched him until the only thing I
could see was the faint illuminating glow from
his probing halogen. Soon the marker balloon
drifted up past me, tethered to a yellow nylon

line, and I knew he had marked the spot and was coming up.

I followed him to the surface again, we boarded and he began barking out signals to his crew. The iridescent orange marker was bobbing, half submerged, about 50 yards off of the stern. "There's our damned trench," he said. "I had one hundred and twenty feet of line on that sucker and I couldn't go any deeper so I wedged it into a recess in the wall of the trench."

"How much deeper do you figure that trench goes?"

"No way of telling." He held out his hands to show me the pinkish tinge to them. "I had a hell of a time just wedging the line anchor into the wall of the trench. Those rocks are actually hot."

Leonard supervised the relocation of the barge directly over the marker, and when he did, we were less than 20 yards from the residue of the vapor cloud. It was hard to believe that earlier that morning it had encompassed a large portion of the lake over the eastern basin.

"What now?" I asked.

"More sensors. As soon as we get these deployed, I'm going back down to have another look. That's where you come in. The longest lines we've got on board are only a hundred and twenty feet. I need you to go down as far as the rim of the trench and feed me line."

"Just exactly what do you expect to find down there, Doc?"

Leonard looked perplexed. "Good question. The truth is I don't know what the hell I expect to find. All I really know is we've got a real anomaly down there. Something has to be causing those temperatures to soar like that. I've got a theory that, when we find what is causing those elevated temperatures, we'll find the source of your vapor cloud as well. When whatever is causing that is remedied, the odor everyone is complaining about goes away too. One gets you two, two gets you three, that sort of thing."

"They teach you that at Carmi?"

Leonard was still smiling when he dropped over the side and pulled his mask into place.

The last thing I remember as my field of vision went from light to dark was the zenith of that azure September sky. From there on, the water evolved through a spectrum of yellow into green and finally a silver grayness. Leonard was little more than a shadowy image below me, leaving a trail of telltale bubbles and a luminous glow from his halogen.

I checked my gauges, counted to ten, waited for the sound of my pulse to subside, turned top over bottom and started down, descending hand over hand along the lifeline. At a depth of 45 feet, the lake bed was clean sand with only the occasional atrocity of an empty beer can or some other misguided tourist's contribution to pollution.

By the time I got to the first level, Leonard was anchoring a dual-knotted lifeline along the edge of the trench. He gave me hand signals indicating that I should work east toward the basin at a depth not more than 30 feet down from the rim, while he went in the opposite direction and deeper. I snapped my tracer line to the cable, checked my air reserve and went over. There was a lot of emptiness below me and I wasn't able to see the other side of the trench wall.

The wall itself was solid rock with a slimy, clinging moss. I aimed the beam of the halogen up and down, saw that there was a natural line of demarcation where the rock had been stratified and started my sweep. Leonard propelled himself past me, knifing his way through the water, descending down into the trench's deeper recesses. The blackness swallowed him up almost immediately. The elevated temperature of the water was already starting to get to me and I checked my elapsed time. I had only been in the water 11 minutes on the second descent and already I was becoming uncomfortably warm.

My foot came in contact with something smooth and solid and I worked the light back and forth until I realized that I had come to a ledge. It jutted out a good five or six feet to another drop off. I dropped to my knees, ran my hand back and forth, determined that it was a striation in the rock formation no more than a foot and a half in thickness. A plate had probably shifted hundreds of thousands of years ago, and if the formation held true to form, there was likely to be a compensating shift in the opposite direction underneath, creating a recessed area of some kind.

I lay down, poked my head over the rim, swung the beam of my light in a 180-degree arc and started to work my way down to the level where Leonard had tied the depth knot. A hot, salt-rich sweat was causing my mask to cloud and burn my eyes. I pulled one of the thermal sensors out of my ballast belt, held it up, counted to 60, added ten more counts for good measure and read it. I couldn't believe it; I had just recorded a temperature of 127 degrees Fahrenheit at a depth of 67 feet. Still suspended over the ledge and facing back into the recess in the rock formation, I was attaching the thermal sensor to a D-ring on my utility and ballast belt when I got the first unnerving sensation that there was something hiding back in the deep shadows.

I adjusted the drop line, locked the swivel and stabbed the beam of my halogen into the darkness, but it had already started toward me.

There was one terrifying split second when my mind recorded what was happening. Even in the surge of water that gushed out in front of it, my mind was rejecting it, telling me that I couldn't possibly be seeing what I thought I was seeing. Bolting straight toward me was a bloated, lesion-covered creature with a grotesquely deformed head twisted to one side. It was a giant gar, easily twice the size of the one that Graham Hatcher had caught.

I rammed the lamp out in front of me, using it as a shield, and tried to deflect its charge. It hit me head on, in what had to be the same ramming motion it or one just like it had used to spear the hull of Cyn's boat. I spun around on the swivel, quickly becoming disoriented but holding on to the halogen with a death grip.

I was still spinning when it made its second pass. It caught me broadside, and the impact sent me gyrating through the water still tethered to the lifeline. I slammed against the ceiling on the underside of the striated ledge and the mouthpiece to my air supply was dislodged. While I struggled to get it back in place I knew I was dangling in the creature's lair like a piece of live bait.

As it circled, I jerked the pinion hammer out of my auxiliary belt. I had the light in one hand and the hammer in the other. My eyes were clouded with sweat, and I was having one hell of a time determining just how far away the gar actually was from me. It didn't attack, instead it cruised by me, taunting, appraising, deciding, I imagined, how it was going to finish me off. It was during that passing that I was finally able to get a good look at the huge body networked with deep fissures and crusted with scar tissue. It blinked indolently in the light of the halogen and I wondered if I had enough time to work my way back up and over the ledge. Anything was better than just dangling there, presenting myself as an entree for the big bastard's late afternoon dining pleasure.

When it made its next pass I jabbed out with the handle end of the hammer, gouging out a huge chunk of rotting flesh in the monster's underbelly. It rolled to one side, righted itself and came around at me again. That time it was even more sluggish. I jabbed again and felt the hammer sink deep into the beast's body.

Finally I realized that the creature was sick, maybe even in the throes of dying. It peeled back again and charged, its long ugly snout open to display its gatorlike mouth full of decaying teeth. It crashed into me with a spearing action and the mouthpiece exploded out of my mouth again. My head started spinning and I dropped the hammer, but still somehow managed to hold on to the light. I tried to curl my legs up under me, the idea being to make myself less of a target.

I felt like a spinning ball on the end of a string. The giant gar came up and circled. At that point I was convinced he was moving in for the kill.

As it charged, I coiled my legs, kicked off my fins and prepared to kick out. Some kind of brain stem survival instinct had taken over. The gar made its pass. I kicked and one foot sunk into the improbable brute's corrupted flesh. I brought the halogen down hard and felt it crush and fragment the beast's rotting snout-like mouth. It peeled away again and I began groping for the mouthpiece to my air supply. My mask was fogged completely over, and for the moment, I was blind to his next charge.

The gar came up from beneath me and I felt him pass within inches. Its sandpaperlike skin rubbed away the top layer of flesh on my right thigh. The water was instantly clouded with the sickening pinkish tinge of blood, and I coiled again, trying to regulate my breathing. The gar circled up, overhead, and started down again. My mask had cleared enough that I could see it—and I remember vowing to myself that, if he was going to get me, he was going to pay one hell of a price for the privilege.

It started down and I had the beam of the halogen aimed right in its empty black eyes.

When it was close enough, I jabbed the torpedo-shaped lamp out to create one final barrier. I braced myself, knowing there would be one hell of a jolt when the impact came.

The collision pitched me into a confused world of pure terror, and for one split second, I thought I had bought the farm. Maybe, looking back, I was even more afraid that the end would not be swift enough to spare me that agonizing kind of realization that I was certain a man had to endure when he knew he was taking his final breath.

My arms went numb and the death grip on the halogen wasn't enough. It ripped out of my hands and undulated down to the floor of the cave under the ledge, the purposeless beam still probing the murky darkness.

The great beast looped around under me, started up and swerved to my left. The last desperate thrust with the light had been more devastating than I realized. The entire left side of the creature's head was gone, and the skin was gradually shredding away to reveal some kind of primitive skeletal structure devoid of all those things that distinguish the living from the dead.

After that last impact, its courtship with death was brief. It careened down to the floor of the cave, registered a final protest and then lay motionless.

In the darkness, my fingers worked with the anchored D-ring as I tried to loosen it. It was tangled and knotted. It took several more minutes to work out of it and lower myself a good eight to ten feet to the floor of the cave, less than ten feet from the wall that plunged on down into the blackness of the trench.

The giant gar was dead. I moved around it, recovered the battered halogen, then examined the carcass a little more closely. It was at least 11 feet long and had obviously been in its final moments when I discovered it. My unexpected intrusion had only hastened the inevitable.

I waited for several minutes, tried to get my equilibrium, regulated my breathing and finally began to look around the recesses of the creature's lair. The rocks were hollowed back so far the beam of the halogen was unable to violate its secrets.

I inched farther back into the tunnel, stabbing the light ahead of me, and then I stopped. The reality of what I was looking at finally registered. The beast had been protecting its treasure: the mutilated upper half of a human torso, shredded and ravaged almost beyond any recognition.

I sagged to the floor of the cave, my brain refusing to accept the reality of the ghastly image being etched into it. I had never met the young man, but somehow I knew it was all that remained of Abner Barker's young friend with the sailboat.

It took every last ounce of energy I could muster to get to the surface.

Saturday P.M., September 4

Peters and I were driving to Marlboro and Leonard's meeting with Felix Chesterton. I was attending only because Leonard insisted that I be there. "You're the one who had the encounter with that damn giant gar, and you're the one who discovered the Kinder boy's body," he had said. "Chesterton doesn't have any choice but to listen to us now." That was his opinion; I was not so certain.

Leonard was still operating on the assumption that Chesterton would back down and allow Marlboro to close the lake when he was presented with the right kind of evidence, which was another assumption I did not share. From what I had observed so far, the Jericho mayor was motivated by something other than the principle of the most good for the most people.

Cyn had given me a good dose of tender loving care on my injured leg, and it was feeling better under a liberal application of salve and gauze. I had donned a pair of long pants to conceal the results of my encounter with the sandpaper-skinned, oversize gar.

"How are you feeling?" Peters asked.

A grunt seemed adequate. Key West was starting to look appealing again, even with the tourists, but I didn't tell him that. Instead, I said, "Tell me how Foster Wallace died."

Peters looked surprised at the question. "Traffic accident, why?"

"Were you the one who investigated it?"

"If you want to call it that. It wasn't much of an investigation though—it didn't have to be. It was pretty obvious what had happened."

"How so?"

The sheriff had the dismayed look of someone rummaging back through old files trying to recall half-forgotten details. "Hell, Elliott, that happened almost four years ago now. Old Foster had been to a meeting at his bank. The meeting must have run late. On his way home, he ran off the road up on highway 120. There's a stretch of road between here and Fort Janes where the road runs through an old bog. There's a twenty foot drop off on each side of the road. No curves though. In fact, the road is straight as a die. Doc Hoppkins was the coroner. He figured Foster went to sleep at the wheel."

"What do you mean, he figured? Didn't he do an autopsy?"

Peters appeared to be slightly befuddled by my line of questioning. He shook his balding head. "What for? It was obvious what happened.

Besides, there wasn't a hell of a lot left to perform an autopsy on. When his car went over that embankment, it dropped twenty feet, rolled over a couple of times and burst into flame. I wouldn't want Cynthia Wallace to hear me say this, but by the time we got to him, there wasn't much more to work with than a pile of ashes. Casket was closed, of course. Biggest damn funeral I ever attended."

"Who reported the accident?"

Peters had to think awhile. "Not sure I recollect. It may have been someone who saw the fire. Most everyone around these parts figured that old bog was pretty well played out, but it burned for days. We had a hell of a time just getting to Foster's car. The truth is we didn't recover the body until the next day, if you want to call it a body."

"How do you know it was Foster Wallace's body?"

The sheriff took his eyes off the road just long enough to give me one of those what-the-hell-is-this-all-about looks. "Hell yes, it was Foster. We had dental records, it was his car, and Hoppkins confirmed it on the death certificate."

"You said it was late at night. Was it common for Foster Wallace to have his bank board meetings late at night?"

With that question, Peters took his eyes off the road completely. He slowed and pulled over to the berm. "What the hell is this all about, Elliott? Why are you suddenly so interested in something that took place four years ago? Is Cyn Wallace saying I didn't do a thorough job of investigating her daddy's death?"

"On the contrary, I'm curious."

The big man turned off the ignition. "Bullshit, Elliott, that ain't your style. You've been digging around in this damn Bartel affair and you've come up with something. What is it?"

At that point I had said nothing to Harrison Peters about my second conversation with Ellery Tweet, and he had no way of knowing Benny Placeman even existed. I had my reasons. First of all I had not had an opportunity to double-check any of the information. Second, the CpP substance both Tweet and Placeman talked about was fairly exotic stuff and pretty much of an unknown and I still had some digging to do. Third, there was no way of knowing just yet if anything I had learned had any bearing on what was happening in Jericho. Relaying the fragmented bits and pieces I had come up with so far would have accomplished little more than adding even more confusion to the situation.

"Did you ever talk to anyone about why they held that particular bank board meeting?" I asked.

Harrison gave me his lopsided smile. "So you've heard that old story about how Foster and George Lancer bought that old tax land to sell to Bartel, huh?"

"Then that part of it is true?"

Peters had both hands on the steering wheel. "When you're sheriff in a small place like Jericho, you hear a lot of things you're not supposed to hear. But the thing that surprised everyone about George Lancer and Foster Wallace buying that

166

slough land was that it was worthless—just plain worthless. That land had been on the tax rolls for years. They bought it for a song. All they had to do was pay the back taxes. Half the town was snickering, saying old Foster had finally flipped his lid. The other half was laughing at George Lancer. What the hell were he and Millie going to do with it? There was no way he could use the land to expand his dairy operation. Most folks was calling George and Foster our version of the odd couple."

"A couple of more questions," I said, hoping Peters did not decide to clam up on me. I had been able to get more information out of him in the last 20 minutes than I had in all of our summer-long beer talks put together.

Harrison looked at his watch. "Fire away. We're already late to that damn meeting."

"Can you find out what the board meeting was about the night Foster Wallace died? Even more important, who was there that night? Then I want to know who was involved with Chesterton on the purchase of that parcel of land they couldn't sell Bartel."

Peters thought for a while. "There might be a way. I know a man who owes me a favor. The last part, about who was involved with Chesterton, that should be easy. Ask your girlfriend. It was her bank that loaned them the money. Seems to me she would know as well as anybody."

"Are you telling me Wallace's bank loaned Chesterton the money to buy the land they intended to sell Bartel? Then Foster Wallace and George Lancer undercut Chesterton's deal

R. Karl Largent

with Bartel by offering them the old tax land?"

"The big city ain't the only place they play hardball," Harrison said.

When the sheriff started up the engine again, I was once again reminded just how much there was about the town of Jericho that I did not know.

Ira Leonard and Felix Chesterton were locked in a heated debate when Peters and I walked into the room. The look on the mayor's face told me he was not all that thrilled to see that the two of us had joined the proceedings. I took a seat, but Peters was content to stand by the door with his arms folded across his sweat-stained shirt. Marlboro had positioned himself at the far end of the table. He wore the expression of a man standing by, waiting for the time to play his role in the unfolding melodrama. Leonard was sitting across from me, slouched in his chair with several pages of scribbled notes in front of him.

The battle lines had been drawn. Chesterton, Becker Herd and Bert Freeman—the Jericho village council—were the opposition.

Chesterton leaned forward with his arms on the conference table and a belligerent expression on his face. "Well, Dr. Leonard, we're all waiting for this so-called evidence of yours."

Leonard straightened in his chair and began sorting through his papers.

"Yes, Doctor, I'm curious," Herd said, "just when is this so-called disaster supposed to take place? I'd like a little warning so I could stock up on beer. My beer sales skyrocket every time

168

we have a disaster." Becker looked around the table to see if anyone appreciated his humor.

"You're going to have a disaster all right, Mr. Herd. The only problem is there isn't any way to guarantee you when it's going to occur." Before Becker could work up another of his multijowled smiles, Leonard said, "But it could happen as early as tonight."

"You know how this strikes me, young man. It seems to me this is a whole lot like the nonsense those people living in California have to put up with. Every day they hear another doom spreader telling them that their world is going to split open right beneath their feet and swallow them up. Only problem is it never seems to happen. Is that what we're dealing with?" Herd didn't smile this time; he sneered.

"What we're dealing with," Leonard said patiently, "is a physiological time bomb that could go off at any minute."

Chesterton leaned back in his chair with a tired smile. "No, let me rephrase that. What we have here, gentlemen, is a vivid illustration of just how many different approaches there are to this life. I submit that I am an optimist. Dr. Leonard here is a pessimist. How do I know that? Quite simply because all academics are pessimistic. They take the perspective that, if something could happen, it will happen. Our young scientist friend here is warning us about a very long shot. Isn't that correct, Dr. Leonard?"

Marlboro cleared his throat. "On the contrary, we're dealing with what Dr. Leonard feels is a certainty. The only thing at issue here is the

R. Karl Largent

timing involved. Dr. Leonard has accumulated a great deal of data in the last several hours. We now know more than we did this morning and what we have learned in the past few hours is very disturbing."

Chesterton continued to smile. "The problem remains, Commander, no one, not even our learned Dr. Leonard here, can tell us with any degree of certainty when this so-called cataclysmic event is going to happen. Now I'm certain that what Dr. Leonard has to say is very interesting, Commander, but I for one am very tired. It has been a long day. If Dr. Leonard is in possession of such data that will prove, without the shadow of a doubt, that we are jeopardizing life and limb of the people attending the Jericho Jubilee, I suggest that he present it. Otherwise, let us adjourn until such a time that you have the conclusive proof I have insisted upon since the outset."

Leonard was undaunted. "Mayor Chesterton, I don't think you realize just how dangerous this situation is becoming."

"Do you have proof?" Chesterton demanded. "Do you know precisely when this so-called physiological disaster is going to occur?"

Leonard ignored the question. "Let's start with the water temperatures first. According to our records we've taken over four hundred readings in the last thirty-six hours. The water temperatures in the east basin of Jericho Lake are abnormal. They are not only abnormal, they are dangerously elevated."

"What are you talking about, Doctor, a couple

170

of degrees? Hell yes, the water temperatures are higher than normal; this has been one of the hottest summers on record."

"No, Mr. Mayor, I am not talking about a couple of degrees. There is a near catastrophic elevation in some places. We have found temperatures a full ten degrees above normal in swimming areas along the shoreline near the east basin. And it appears that those areas are spreading."

"All right," Chesterton said with a sigh, "you've made your point. The water temperatures are higher than normal. Now just exactly what does that tell us?"

"Earlier today, Mr. Wages and I explored the Jericho trench that connects the lake to the Montana Mills slough. There we encountered temperatures of extraordinary proportions, some in excess of one hundred and twenty degrees. Even allowing for depth, source contribution, time of year and thermal layering, these are freshwater temperatures of cataclysmic dimension."

Becker Herd started to laugh. "Come on, Dr. Leonard, Felix and I have lived around this lake all of our life. The only way you could possibly get the water in this lake to those temperatures is to cook it."

"Precisely." He looked around the table. "That is exactly what is happening, your lake is cooking. Something in that trench or the east basin is superheating the water."

"And you call *something* hard evidence?" Herd said.

"Do you know what is causing these elevated temperatures, Doctor?" Chesterton was no longer smiling. If anything, he had become even more impatient. "Are you telling us that the foul odor or that vapor cloud is somehow tied in with all of this?"

"We believe they are," Leonard said. "We also believe that this condition somehow relates to the mutated life forms that have been found in the lake in the last forty-eight hours and that it contributed to the deaths of at least four people."

"Why do you insist on attaching some dark and ominous dimension to an unfortunate string of circumstances, Dr. Leonard? Very likely, the same careless boater who ran down the Barker boy hit the Kinder youth as well. Unfortunate, yes, but hardly an omen of an impending disaster."

"And you would explain away the deaths of the two young men on the Carmi barge just as easily?" Leonard asked.

"Let me ask you questions about those young men, Dr. Leonard. They were college students, correct? They were alone at night on the barge, correct? Were they working, Doctor, or were they fooling around? Did you know that shortly after you left that evening these same two young men came in, docked their barge, bought a case of beer from Becker Herd's store and then went back out on the water? Did they drink too much, Doctor, and then maybe decide to take a little swim? Sounds rather risky and undisciplined, don't you think?"

172

The Lake

The steam went out of Ira Leonard. He sat down.

That's where I jumped in. "I was with Dr. Leonard down there today. I saw those mutations. The one Graham Hatcher caught was sick—just as sick as the one I saw today. Not only that, but that creature's nest is where we found the remains of the Kinder boy." Actually I was surprised at how controlled my voice sounded.

"Tell me, Mr. Wages, don't you think it's rather curious that there were, at different times, three, perhaps even four hundred boats out there on that lake today and you and Dr. Leonard are the only ones who encountered these beasts?"

Chesterton got up from the table and walked to the window. "How many people would you estimate attend this Jubilee every year, Dr. Leonard? Five thousand? Ten thousand? Twenty thousand?" He turned around. "I'll tell you how many. Last year on Saturday alone, forty-two thousand people attended the Jubilee. Do you have any idea how much money forty-two thousand people spend when they are having fun, Dr. Leonard? Some of the merchants here in Jericho tell me they make twenty-five percent of their annual income during the Jubilee alone. That's rather important, wouldn't you say? Twenty-five percent. Then let me ask you the second half of my question. Do you honestly think these people would come to this hick town if we didn't have the Jubilee as a drawing card? Bottom line is this town cannot survive without the Fisherman's Jubilee, and I will be damned if I will let

173

a couple of freak fish, a rash of untimely acci-
dents and your half-assed theories about some
as yet unidentified impending disaster screw up
the lifeblood of this town."

Leonard's jaw tensed.

Herd pushed himself away from the table,
got up, walked around and put his hand on
Leonard's shoulder. "I know this ain't what you
wanted to hear, sonny boy. But I gotta go along
with the mayor. So far you ain't proved there's
anything bad enough in that lake out there that
we oughta be closing it down for."

Marlboro began gathering up his papers.
"Well, Dr. Leonard, it appears that we have
no choice. I will call the governor's office and
tell him what we decided."

"And what exactly did we decide, Commander?" Felix demanded.

"That we don't have enough hard evidence to
take any definitive action."

Chesterton appeared to be satisfied. He looked
at Peters. "Better get a good night's sleep,
Harrison. Looks to me like we can expect a
big crowd tomorrow."

Ira Leonard was the only one in the room
when I started to leave. He was still shoveling
papers into his briefcase.

"You tried," I said.

"Four deaths don't mean a thing to those
clowns."

"Think we can get through two more days?"

Leonard shrugged his shoulders. "Who the
hell knows, Mr. Wages? Maybe it's guys like

you and me who don't understand. Maybe the Chestertons and the Herds of the world are right."

"Where to now?"

"Back to the barge. I want to check to see if the mainframe dug anything up on that CpP you were telling me about. Can I give you a lift?"

I shook my head. "It looks like a nice night for a walk. Thanks anyway."

Leonard left and I stayed there for several minutes before stepping out into the muggy night air. It was a Saturday night and the Jubilee revelers were out in full force. The streets were glutted. The midway was worse: three balls for a dollar, get your cotton candy here, win a little prize for the lady by tossing the wooden ring over the bottle. Lights. Noise. Crowds. Voices. Music. Street vendors everywhere. A kaleidoscope of color. A cacophony of sound. Yessirre bub, America was sure having fun.

I stuffed my hands down in my pockets, thought of the patch of abraded skin on my leg and started toward the Lake Road, regretting for the moment my decision to walk.

"Where you headed, big fella?"

It was a sweet voice, all honey with a tinge of street smarts about it. I looked around and for the moment, at least, was dragged out of my muddled thoughts. Cyn was walking toward me. She looked ravishing. She slipped her arm through mine and graced me with one of those paradise-found smiles of hers.

"The word on the street is that you and the boys couldn't come to an agreement."

"You heard right. Your old boyfriend is a hard sell. He isn't convinced we were able to come up with anything even remotely close to conclusive proof that there is any real danger."

I steered the lady up the long cement stairs leading to the seawall adjacent to the street. The wall served as a breakwater for the village's winter storms. There was a patch of grass between the sidewalk and the water. We threaded our way through legions of lovers who had decided cuddling was more fun than the merry-go-round. We found an empty park bench with a glorious view of the moon-baked lake and sat down. Cyn kicked off her shoes and wiggled her toes in the grass.

If Cyn was willing to forgive and forget, why the hell shouldn't I? I slipped my arm around her shoulder and we sat staring at the lake.

"Do you think there is something bad out there?" she asked.

"Depends on your definition of bad. I know what I saw, and in my frame of reference, it didn't look good."

"Felix gets his way again, right?"

I nodded.

"So what's going to happen?"

"I don't think anybody knows. Ira is plenty concerned though."

"I wasn't talking about the lake; I was talking about us. We never did get a chance to spend that weekend in the city."

"Maybe next year."

"Or you could invite me down to Key West."

I wondered how that would work out.

The Lake

"I'm going to miss you, Elliott Grant Wages. This has been quite a summer."

I held her a little closer and we sat there, watching a Saturday slip into the past tense. The crowds were starting to thin out and the carnival rides were shutting down. The lights dimmed and soon the music stopped altogether.

We ended up at Cyn's place. Mrs. Fern had already retired for the evening and Basketcase seemed reluctant to make much of a fuss about my being there. The lady fixed each of us a tall scotch on ice, and we sat on her deck listening to Linda Ronstadt sing love songs.

From time to time we reflected back on the events of the last three months, laughing and sometimes regretting. It was as if we both understood that we were playing out the roles of lovers who were running out of time.

Then I dozed off.

Later she tugged on my arm. "Come on, let's go to bed, little man. You've had a busy day."

I managed to get out of my clothes, sprawl across the bed and watch Cyn undress. Somewhere in the twilight before sleep took over and shut out my conscious mind, I saw her walk to the window and stare wistfully out at the lake. Her voice was distant and muted by the thin veil of first sleep.

"Elliott," she said, her voice coming at me from a distance, "it looks like that thing you called a vapor cloud is getting bigger again."

"That's nice," I muttered. "Now, come to bed."

Sunday A.M., September 5

Someone was shouting my name and someone else was trying to tell him to be quiet. I heard a door open and close and more muffled conversation.

"Shhhh," the second voice said, "it's Sunday morning. Everyone is still asleep."

A contrite silence followed, punctuated by the distant sound of a barking dog and more conversation in loud whispers.

All of this was coming at me through a gossamer fog. I had one eye open, waiting to see what happened. The dog kept barking and I heard the second voice say, "I don't even know if he's here. Is his car out there?"

The first voice continued to mumble.

"I'll ask Miss Cyn," the second voice said. "You wait right here."

When I heard the heavy footsteps assaulting the stairs, I knew it was Mrs. Fern. It was her

178

semidiscreet way of letting us know she was in the area. The inevitable timid knock followed.

I groaned. It was the only response I could muster. One of the real drawbacks of being a rational, freethinking human is that, the first thing when you wake up in the morning, you're confronted with a major issue like whether or not to get out of bed.

"Miss Cynthia?" Mrs. Fern asked.

"She is still asleep," I said.

"Is that you, Mr. Wages?"

"Who the hell do you think it is?" I bellowed. Responses such as that contributed to my constantly eroding relationship with Mrs. Fern, yet for some unexplained reason I continued to make them. Maybe it was because Mrs. Fern, whom I suspect of secretly burning candles at the foot of the statue of Saint Chastity each night, disapproved of the way her employer and I carried on.

"There's a Mr. Freeman here to see you, Mr. Wages."

"Tell him to go away. Better yet, tell him I went back to Key West."

"Mr. Freeman says it is very important," Mrs. Fern said.

"You tell Mr. Freeman that my mother said I couldn't come out and play today and he'll go away. Mr. Freeman gets discouraged easily."

There was another impatient pause. "Mr. Freeman says Sheriff Peters wants to talk to you."

I cocked the other eye open and heard Cyn giggle. "They probably need a fourth for their Sunday morning gin game," she said.

"I better see what he wants," I said, getting out of bed. Cyn promptly covered her face with a pillow, curled into the fetal position and pulled the sheet over her as I put on my trousers. "Tell Mr. Freeman that I'm coming right down."

All 160 or so pounds of Mrs. Fern waddled away from the door and I went into the bathroom and took care of the chores I tend to in order to make myself presentable. Then I went downstairs.

In the kitchen, Mrs. Fern gave me the cold eye that she reserved for the occasions when I didn't go home like a good boy, then she informed me that Bert Freeman was waiting in the foyer. I ignored her, headed for the Mr. Coffee, poured a cup and started a series of slurping sips only because I have never figured out a way to mainline that first jolt.

"Mr. Wages will be right with you," Mrs. Fern told Freeman. From my perspective, the time it took me to join Bert Freeman depended entirely on how fast the caffeine jump started my brain.

All the while, Cyn's mangy cur was appraising me with a low, throaty, somewhat-intimidating growl. "What's wrong with the mongrel?" I asked Mrs. Fern when she came back in the kitchen.

"He doesn't like you," she said. She added, "Either," when she got to the other side of the room. With that warmer than normal assurance to fortify me, I walked into Cyn's foyer and asked Freeman what he wanted.

Belligerent since youth, I refused to look contrite for having been discovered in my playpen.

180

The Lake

Bert Freeman wasn't smiling. "Peters needs you," he said. He was altogether too grim for a Sunday morning. "I think he wants you to hurry."

I didn't ask why. I trudged my way back up the stairs, ferreted out my shoes and a golf shirt Cyn had given me and told Freeman I was ready.

Freeman drove. We made good time until we came to the roadblock. There, a sober-faced deputy checked us out and let us through, admonishing us not to attempt to cross the bridge. And even though Bert got us close, there was no way we could have crossed the bridge if we had wanted to. There were two police cruisers at one end, both carrying the insignia of the state police, and one of the Jericho County Sheriff's units at the other. All three of them had their bubble machines working.

I rolled the window down and realized that the air was cool—or at least cooler than it had been any time during the past two weeks. I also noticed that the Sunday of Jubilee weekend had dawned with a slight gray cast, or was it the misty pall of colorless air that was being referred to as the vapor cloud? I double-checked its size and location, and I was disconcerted to find it had grown both bigger and grayer and covered a larger area of the lake than before. The entire east basin of Jericho Lake appeared to be under its spell.

Fifty yards from the bridge, we were as close to the scene as we were going to get. Bert pulled

off to the side of the road, turned off the ignition
and we walked the rest of the way.

There were at least seven people clustered
around the two state police cruisers blocking
the southern end of the bridge: Marlboro, Ira
Leonard, Harrison Peters, Cletus Mackey, two
state troopers and a man I had never met before.
Peters broke away from the group and met me
halfway.

"Freeman said it was urgent."

The sheriff motioned for me to follow him.
When he turned back toward the bridge, I realized there was another car, one I hadn't seen
until just that moment. It was sitting in the middle of the bridge and the door was open.

"Mackey found this on his first patrol around
the lake this morning."

At first glance the car appeared to be a '74
or '75 model Chevrolet four-door sedan. As it
turned out, it was newer than that. After what
had happened, the exterior was badly in need
of paint. I walked around the front of the car,
noted that all four tires were flat and looked in.
The results wouldn't have been any different if
someone had butted me with the handle of a
shovel. My stomach started looking for a place
to hide, clawing its way into recesses normally
reserved for other purposes. There were four
bodies: two boys and two girls, all severely disfigured, and all very, very dead. If someone had
asked me how I thought they had died, I would
have said that I didn't know, but it was obvious
that the killer had dumped some kind of acid on
the bodies to conceal his handiwork.

The Lake

Each of the babes in joyland was covered with large, open sores and hideous blisters, where there was any flesh left to be violated. In each instance, an assortment of anatomical parts was missing.

The boy in the back seat was completely naked; the residue of his trousers had melted in a chemical flash fire as they lay draped around his ankles. He had a charred and partially melted beer can in one hand and a flame-blackened upper body skeletal appendage locked around what remained of the girl's body lying underneath him. Her legs were wrapped around him. Most of his face was gone and most of hers was still there. Her head was back, her mouth was open but the features had become something revolting and unrecognizable. She had no lips and no eyes, and the parts of her face that remained were both bloated and distorted. I reeled backward, sucking in hard to find enough air to keep from losing it altogether.

Peters closed the right rear door and opened the front. The girl had died while she was removing her clothing. What was left of her did not look all that appealing. The boy sitting beside her would not have been much of a lover. Both his arms were missing, blunted. They had become blood-gorged stumps that protruded ludicrously into the air. On the floor, near what was left of his right foot, was an unopened, foil-sealed rubber. The bizarre thought occurred to me that they had at least intended to practice safe sex. It had not quite turned out that way.

My stomach continued to do a slow, undulating pirouette as it tried to screw itself into a new hiding place. The wave of nausea had already set in. But this time it was the horrifying sight of the four young people and not the odor that sickened me.

Either way, I knew I had to get out of there or become one very, very sick writer. I backed away and looked at Harrison Peters. I realized that he probably did not know the answer, but the question came out anyway. "What the hell happened to them?"

Peters was numb. He shook his head and fumbled through his pockets for one of his ever-present cigars. When he lit it, his hands trembled. "They're from out of state," he said in a monotone. "They probably came to town for the Jubilee."

"Any identification?"

"Don't know. Haven't had the balls to get in there and dig around to see if I could find any."

I heard the scraping sound of footsteps on the tarmac behind me. Ira Leonard was coming toward us, looking like a man who already had put in a very long day. "What do you make of it, Ira?" I asked.

He shoved his hands down deep in his pockets and looked out at the vapor cloud hanging over the water. "I don't think there is any doubt about it, Elliott. That cloud out there is your culprit."

"That's what I wanted you to hear," Peters said. "Ira here has a damned interesting theory."

Leonard's voice was hollow and his eyes even more so. "When I left the meeting last night, I

184

came back to the barge, reworked some of my calculations and then curled up in the cab of my truck to try to get a little sleep. About three o'clock this morning, the two students working the barge came ashore to advise me that the vapor cloud was expanding again. They said they could see traces of it stretching all the way back past the bridge up and into the slough."

"It had almost completely dissipated late yesterday afternoon," I said.

"I know, but I'm starting to develop a theory. The pattern we have noticed so far is that the vapor cloud seems to expand during the course of the darkness hours when the air cools. Then it appears to diminish as the day warms up."

"But you said there were traces of gas in it; gas expands as it heats up. If that's the case, wouldn't the cloud be more obvious in the daylight hours?"

"Under most circumstances," he said, "but we're not dealing with most circumstances. That kind of thinking is based on our expectations to the normal reaction of a gaseous vapor to ambient temperature. When the sun goes down and the free-air temperature cools, most vapors tend to condense. When the vapors condense, the unique properties of that particular mass become evident; examples, in this case, obviously being an acidlike toxicity and volatility."

"Then what is causing that vapor cloud?"

Instead of answering me, he motioned for the man I hadn't recognized when I arrived. He walked toward us, purposely avoiding looking at the blistered carcass of the Chevrolet. He was tall, soft bodied, bearded and mostly bald. He was wearing a windbreaker with the words *Carmi Institute* on his chest.

"This is Dr. Arnold Manion, Chairman of the Carmi chemistry department," Leonard said. "He's the one who got us the information on the CpP yesterday. When he heard that we had a situation where the substance might be involved, he came down and brought something interesting to show us."

Manion walked back to Leonard's truck, opened the tailgate and removed a large metal container. Inside of it was another container. And inside of it was a third that appeared to be made of lead with a blanket of heating coils. There was a vacuum-sealing device in the middle of the stainless-steel lid. Manion put on a pair of rubber gloves, broke the seal and extracted a small object that looked like a fountain pen.

"This, gentlemen, is stabilized CpP, diluted to one part per million. We are told that the maximum stabilization quantity, under the most stringent of laboratory conditions, is no more than five grams."

Even at one part per million, Manion treated it like something exotic and deadly. He selected a golf ball-sized stone, placed it in the middle of the tarmac and took out his handkerchief. Placing it over the lower half of his face, he advised us to step back at least 20 feet and prepare to hold our breath for at least 45 seconds. He removed the top of the penlike cylinder and ever so carefully touched the tip of the instrument to the stone. His touch was so deft it was tantamount to a hummingbird's wing momentarily grazing a mountaintop.

Nothing happened for several seconds. Then the small stone began to disintegrate. The CpP quickly ate a hole clear through it. The molten stone puddled and gave off a gaseous vapor with an odor identical to the one we had been living with for the last several days.

Manion waited for several minutes, then took the handkerchief away. He did not have the look of a man who had just successfully completed a controlled experiment. He was wearing the expression of a man who had just played God. "I had no idea what would happen," he said. "I have never handled CpP before, I have only read about it." I was glad he hadn't told me that beforehand.

Like Leonard, I approached Manion's little demonstration with a whole lot of trepidation. Leonard plucked a blade of grass and held it in the proximity of the stone. It turned brown and burst into flame. He looked at his watch and then at me. "Elapsed time, two-point-three seconds."

"Holy shit," Peters muttered in the background.

I was trying to remember just exactly what Benny Placeman had told me about the Bartel development contract. He had said that Bartel had purchased the British technology that enabled them to stabilize and control the CpP. But both Ellery and Benny were referring to an encapsulation process. What control did Bartel have over the device that the substance powered? And assuming it was in one of those clandestine monitoring devices, what happened to the CpP power source if it was exposed to a hostile environment for any prolonged period of time?

Leonard's face was even more sober. "Gentlemen, assume for a moment that everything Mr. Wages heard from his associates yesterday is true. Assume also that Bartel really does have a contract to build a prototype subsurface, self-powered monitoring device for the DOD. Let us also suppose that it is being built over there at the back of the Montana Mills slough and that it is in fact powered by some form of encapsulated CpP. Where do you test such a unit?"

"You test it a hell of a long way away from people," Peters growled.

"If you are acting responsibly and are environmentally aware, that's what you do. Has Bartel acted responsibly? Or have they been testing one of their units in Jericho Lake?"

"Placeman indicated they were having test problems," I said.

"If that substance is somehow escaping into the lake, that could explain the mutated life forms, the elevated water temperatures, many things." He looked at me. "You're a logical man, Mr. Wages. If I were to ask you where the derelict Bartel prototype was likely to end up in that lake, if in fact it exists and has been lost, what would you guess?"

I didn't hesitate. "The east basin. It's the deeper of the two basins, and according to the DNR

188

charts, there is a deep trench that runs from somewhere in the slough all the way to the basin."

"I still don't get it," Peters said. "If this damn device you're talking about is lying in the basin and spewing out crap that causes the vapor cloud, how come we're seeing that vapor cloud move back up into the slough each night?"

"Perhaps the device was leaking. Perhaps it trailed this substance the entire length of the trench before losing power and mobility."

"How do we prove all of this?" Peters demanded.

"We start by obtaining an admission by the Bartel people that this device actually exists, Sheriff. If they have lost one, they need to confirm that fact. Then we will need their cooperation. They will have to tell us when they last verified its location, where it was programmed to go, how volatile the situation is. There are many, many questions we need to ask the Bartel people. And even if we had those answers right this minute, I would be willing to wager that we don't have enough time to rectify the situation. We need to impress upon them that we are sitting on an almost certain disaster if we don't have their prompt cooperation."

"Yes," Manion said, "Ira is right. For the moment, all you have is a theory and, from what I've heard so far, a reluctance on the part of Bartel people to even admit that they have a problem."

"I'm supposed to meet their man Blackmonn at nine o'clock this morning," I said. "He's supposed to have some answers for me."

"Let's hope we get his cooperation," Leonard said. "When I went to the airport to pick up Dr. Manion, I heard the weather forecast. We've got a cold front moving through. The last thing we need is some kind of thermal instability. If my theory is right and that vapor cloud starts expanding in periods of cooler weather, there is no telling what kind of disaster we could have on our hands."

Peters drove me back to Ginny's place. Then I picked up the silver Carrera and headed for my meeting with Roger Blackmonn. At three minutes before nine o'clock I pulled into the parking lot next to a late-model Oldsmobile with New York plates and started looking around. Blackmonn had been painfully explicit about both the time and place of our meeting.

I parked so that I had a view of the front and west side of the Bartel facility as well as a limited view of the slough behind it. Low-hanging gray tentacles of the vapor cloud had searched their way clear to the far end of the slough.

When the pedestrian door of the Bartel facility opened, Blackmonn stepped out. Stripped of his corporate trappings, he looked even less imposing. He was wearing a pair of wash pants, a blue knit shirt and deck shoes. Attired as he was, he would easily have blended in with the Jubilee throngs and no one would have known the difference.

"Good morning, Mr. Wages," he said. His demeanor was confident, and he had the body carriage of a man going forward to meet a challenge.

Blackmonn was not quite big enough for me to look him square in the eye. He stood with his hands in front of him, clasping a bulging manila file folder. If anything, he gave me the distinct impression he wanted to get on to more important matters. He looked at me with casual indifference and finally asked how I fit in the picture.

"You might say I'm amicus armiger, Blackmonn. All the official titles were taken."

Roger Blackmonn was quick with his small smile. "The sheriff's friend, huh? That wouldn't make you a deputy, would it?"

"He's operating shorthanded. Forty thousand people," I said, using Chesterton's numbers, "can keep one sheriff and two deputies busy."

The way Blackmonn just stood there, I figured he needed to be prodded into action. "Since your home office encourages good community relations, Blackmonn, I assume you made it a point to look into some of those matters we discussed yesterday."

The aura of confidence was evident. "As a matter of fact, I did, Mr. Wages. And I'm prepared to assure the authorities in Jericho that I was unable to uncover anything that could be even mildly construed as an operational irregularity." It was easy to believe that Blackmonn was used to having enough clout that he expected everyone to take his word as the immutable truth.

"When I said we weren't looking for assurances, that we were looking for proof, Blackmonn, I meant it."

The challenge hit him right between the eyes. He stiffened and I had the feeling it had been a long time since anyone had displayed the audacity to question his integrity. He recovered nicely, though, and continued to assess me with the level, practiced, controlled appraisal he had probably been told he was good at. I had the distinct impression Roger Blackmonn was a politician, and because of that, I was going to get only the answers he wanted me to have.

"Mr. Wages," he said and sighed, "this is a high-security facility. We have built what industry analysts and psychologists like to call the typical toy company paranoia compensators into this operation. Unfortunately, it is the nature of our business. The mission of toy companies is often a better kept secret than what goes on in some of our nation's most sophisticated top-secret defense installations." It was beginning to sound as though Blackmonn's appeal was based on some supposed inner propensity by the average man to let an American corporation go blissfully on its way because it was the nature of the industry.

I did not tell Roger Blackmonn that, while my suspicious little mind accepted the tenet that individuals might be innocent until proven guilty, it was the other way around with corporations. Anyone who made it a practice to walk all over the guy making the bread to appease the folks who had invested in the bakery did not

The Lake

deserve my respect. In Blackmonn's case, it was guilt by association.

"Proof," I said again.

The Bartel superintendent was starting to get a little tense. The lines around his thin mouth tightened, his jawline hardened and his eyes narrowed. He wasn't quite ready to tell me to get the hell out of there, but he wasn't all that far from it either. "I caution you, Mr. Wages. . . ."

I wasn't certain how Blackmonn would handle a display of old Elliott Wages's aggressive behavior, but I decided it was worth the effort. The worst that could happen was that he would take a swing at me, but because of his size, I figured I could handle that too. I took a step toward him and saw him blink. I was banking on the belief that in the boardrooms people usually didn't go around hitting other people in the mouth. Blackmonn had a lot of money invested in dentalwork and he took a step backward. He looked slightly befuddled.

"Let me clear the air, Blackmonn. This is not a damn toy factory, and that lake over there is not some pretend pond in a fairy tale. That lake is spring fed, but it also backs up to the slough behind your plant. And after what I've seen over there this morning, there are a whole lot of people in Jericho that are convinced your toy plant is dumping something very, very nasty into their lake. Do you understand?"

Blackmonn nodded.

"Now, four and possibly eight people have died because of some very, very strange things that have been going on over there. And the only

R. Karl Largent

variable in this dirty little scenario is the fact that Bartel has fired up its operation in recent months. Can you say lawsuit, Blackmonn? Think about it: big, ugly, nasty, expensive and time consuming lawsuits. Because that is exactly where you and the Bartel Toy Company are headed if we don't get some cooperation and some answers, pronto." There was a bit of theater in what I was saying, and I was being careful to make my speech sound just strident enough to make Blackmonn think the crazy man he was talking to was on the verge of losing it.

Blackmonn did not blanch. If anything, he was surprised I had not trundled off with my tail between my legs. His voice had lost that edge of authority though. "I assure you, Mr. Wages, this facility is in full compliance with—"

I hit him with a second volley just to keep him off balance. "This facility is not a toy factory, Blackmonn, and you know it. The sole purpose of this operation is to develop an oceangoing, clandestine monitoring device powered by a highly unstable material known as CFUS-POLCON-PRIEMON. The word on the street is that you have had a test failure and that you are trying to conceal it."

"That is nonsense!" Whatever cool-quotient standard Bartel had established for its executives, Blackmonn had just failed it. The denial was too quick, too vehement and too awkward. Even the sardonic little laugh was missing. Blackmonn had the kind of eyes that betray what a man is thinking. They were darting nervously first in one direction and then another.

The Lake

"I want you to see something," I said, still pushing. I started for the nearest pedestrian gate in the security fence with Bartel's man dutifully following. "Open it."

He fumbled through his keys, unlocked the gate and we stepped out into Lancer's field. I bent over, snatched a handful of grass and showed him the greasy green residue on my hand. From there I walked him toward the rear of the property and pointed out the defoliated trees. If I had not been so preoccupied with making my point, I might have noticed that Blackmonn was rapidly regaining his composure. When I looked at him, he was actually smiling again.

"The shoe is on the other foot now, Mr. Wages. If you had done your homework, you would have known."

"Known what?"

He opened the manila folder and handed me several photographs. "I took these photographs myself, the morning after we concluded negotiations with Ms. Wallace on the purchase of the property. That was exactly four years ago, in July, and you will notice that those trees were defoliated at that time as well. As for the grass, perhaps we were a little careless in the way we applied the coloring, but the fact remains that it is a harmless coloring, developed by Bartel chemists to make this and the adjacent property look a little more attractive." Blackmonn, to prove his point, plucked up a blade of the grass and stuck it in his mouth. "It is quite nontoxic, Mr. Wages."

I stammered before I was able to say, "Okay, I'll buy the trees and grass part of your story, but you still haven't satisfied me about what Bartel is dumping into that slough."

"As for our RANASUR unit, it is true, Mr. Wages, that we have had some problems. The preliminary design did have some operational problems, but those are being corrected."

"RANASUR?" I asked.

"An acronym, it stands for Random Area Surveillance Unit. And I can assure you, it is quite safe and poses no threat to the ecological balance of your lake. Would you like to see one?"

Blackmonn's offer caught me flatfooted. It isn't often that nonunit, nonauthorized personnel are permitted past the gate of a DOD facility and even more bizarre for him to invite me into a restricted one.

"Little out of the ordinary, isn't it?"

"Under the circumstances, I think it is justifiable. You appear to be the kind of man who will exercise discretion about what you have seen."

We entered a door at the rear of the building and Blackmonn led me through a labyrinth of dimly lit corridors, up a flight of steps, through a door marked *Authorized Personnel Only* and finally out on a viewing platform that overlooked the same large, open bay I had seen the day before. The tiny red blinking lights had been turned off, and the area was illuminated by banks of fluorescent lighting.

"That, Mr. Wages, is a working prototype of the Bartel RANASUR."

The Lake

I couldn't tell much about it, which is probably why Blackmonn felt comfortable letting me catch a glimpse of the unit in the first place. It was made of metal, titanium, I guessed, or some exotic kissing cousin and appeared to have a seamless outer skin. On balance, it appeared to be little more than a miniaturized torpedo—vented, shrouded and apparently controlled by what looked to be a series of jet exhausts spaced at intervals around the hull. There were a small vertical stabilizer and two tiny horizontal fins at each end of the device, which made me think it could probably be programmed to travel forward or backward. A tiny nodule like pod protruded from the nose.

"For four hundred million, I expected something a little more exotic," I said dryly. I did not tell Blackmonn that I was also using the opportunity to get a good look at the facility itself. The bottom of the bay where the RANASUR unit was contained was covered with water, but there was no way to determine how deep it was. The water was being agitated, and I suspect, because of the temperature in the bay, heated by a series of submerged, rotating fans. The room was an uncomfortable combination of both heat and high humidity. I was certain it was not the comfort-zone dryness of conventional air-conditioning.

Blackmonn kept me moving, at the same time keeping up a barrage of distracting statistics. He knew I couldn't be mentally recording what I was seeing if he confused the input with more than I could assimilate. We left the RANASUR's

197

R. Karl Largent

chamber, went up another flight of steps and into his office. He offered me a chair and sat down at his desk. "Now, Mr. Wages, I must ask you if this appears to you to be the kind of facility that would be willfully dumping some sort of undesirable element in the slough?" The corporate charm was back. He had managed to regain control and he knew it.

"At the risk of appearing ungrateful, Blackmonn, I'm still not convinced. Something is decidedly different out there and your plant is the obvious variable."

Blackmonn tented his hands and ran the tips of his index fingers along the underside of his lower lip. "What you saw in the bay chamber was the only working prototype of the RANASUR. A second unit, with certain design modifications is being fabricated and assembled in New Jersey, but it will not be delivered to this plant until next spring."

He turned in his chair, touched a small switch on a panel next to his desk and activated a bank of television monitors. A tape cartridge engaged and Blackmonn began to narrate over the video. "This is a copy of the tape prepared for a board review in New York as recently as last Monday, Mr. Wages. What you are seeing is the RANASUR being launched in the slough behind this facility. As you can see, it is in a surface configuration, and then it is submerged in response to computer-generated positioning and maneuvering commands. The test you are watching took place on the morning of July seventh and lasted fifty-seven minutes. The tests were repeated the next day and test data compared and verified."

The screen went blank, there was a pause and a new image appeared.

"In early August, the second and third phases of the preliminary round of testing were completed. On the first occasion, the RANASUR traversed the full length of the Montana Mills slough and for a brief period actually entered Jericho Lake. Six days later we repeated those tests. During the entire testing cycle, there was only one minor glitch. A small programming error resulted in our having to activate the backup retrieval system to bring the unit in. Dr. Mueller made the corrections in the software and a simulation test conducted the following day indicated that the problem was indeed corrected."

"And these tests used the CFUS - POLCON - PRIEMON as the energy source?"

"It performed admirably," Blackmonn said. The video played out and he turned off the bank of monitors. He was smiling.

I did not tell Blackmonn that something bothered me about his little presentation because I wasn't quite sure what it was. But I seldom ignore that old feeling that something isn't quite right.

"Any more questions, Mr. Wages?"

I shook my head. "Not for the moment."

Blackmonn had the look of a man who had just defused a nasty situation. "Then I can assume that your writer's curiosity is assuaged?"

"Writer?"

"Please, Mr. Wages. You may indeed be here on behalf of the good people of Jericho, but I would never have extended these courtesies if I had not first checked you out, as they say. That is the reason I originally suggested a meeting next week. I wanted to give our security people time to run a profile on you."

At that point I allowed a small degree of civility to return to my own demeanor. "I have to admit at this point it looks like Bartel's skirts are clean."

Still, I was disappointed that Blackmonn had not made at least a small expression of dismay over the loss of life of so many people. He simply sat there, obviously relieved that I was finally getting out of his hair.

"One small favor," I said as I started to get up.

"Of course."

"Get in touch with us if you come across anything that might shed some light on this matter."

"Rest assured, Mr. Wages, you will have our full cooperation."

The man pressed a button on his intercom and there was an annoying little buzzing sound. The door opened and a colossus entered the room wearing the top half of a security uniform. A pair of bib overalls constituted the lower half. He was big enough to bale hay and eat it too. "Please show Mr. Wages to the front gate," he said.

We shook hands and King Kong escorted me through the maze of corridors and out to my car. He locked the gate on his return.

The Lake

By the time I had situated myself behind the wheel and started the engine, I had put two and two together. Kong was the security guard standing with Blackmonn that day on the balcony overlooking the slough when I was watching them watch me. Another thing was certain. Kong, no first name, looked big enough to go in the water and manually retrieve something called a RANASUR if it did malfunction.

Sunday A.M., September 5

It was strictly an impulse. After leaving the
Bartel plant, I saw George Lancer's name on
a mailbox and turned onto a long, potholed
gravel lane that led up to a two-story, dilapi-
dated farmhouse. If there had been windfall
profits for George and Mildred Lancer in sell-
ing the slough tax lands, they had not marched
right out and spent it on renovating the family
farm.

It was all there: whitewashed rural Americana
with wooden screen doors, flowerpots, a porch
swing, two cane-back rockers and an old mongrel dog sleeping on the porch. Mildred Lancer
came bustling on the first knock, wiping her
hands on her apron.

Pleasant was the only word to describe
Mildred Lancer. She had a pleasant smile,
a pleasant voice and a pleasant manner. She
asked what she could do for me and I inquired

202

if George was around. She told me he was in the living room and invited me to go right on in.

George was looking out the window, sitting with his back to me. I put on a friendly face and walked around to introduce myself. I stopped just in time.

George Lancer was 75 going on 200. His sickly, weathered face was the repository of vacant, empty eyes. He had a slack mouth and the heartbreaking look of a severe stroke victim. I swallowed the words I had intended to say and started inventorying the things that I had overlooked, beginning with the old wooden wheelchair.

Millie Lancer was watching me. She could tell by the look on my face that I was not prepared for the sight of the human wreckage called George Lancer. "One is bad enough. Three would kill most men, but not my George," she said. There was a peasant's pride in her voice, an exultation in life, the kind that says, "Dish it out, big boy. Whatever you've got in store for me, I can handle it."

"I'm sorry, Mrs. Lancer, I didn't know." The moment I spoke, I knew I sounded stupid and inadequate.

"Call me, Millie," she said. "Would you like some iced tea?"

I nodded. Millie left the room, made some kitchen noises and returned with two tall glasses. The ice rattled around when she handed one of them to me. I started to introduce myself, but she waved me off.

R. Karl Largent

"Shoot, Mr. Wages, I know who you are. A friend pointed you out the other day. You're the fellow who's dating Foster's daughter." Millie Lancer did not need to know my credentials. The stamp of approval and acceptance came from the fact that Cynthia Wallace saw fit to go out with me. I had the feeling that in Millie Lancer's version of the world boys and girls still sat on front porch swings and held hands until they were old enough to get married and have babies.

"You didn't know about George?" she asked.

"No, I'm sorry."

"Oh my, don't be sorry. I still got him, ain't I? Lots of women my age have already had to put their menfolk into the ground."

Fresh from my heady victory over Roger Blackmonn, I had stopped at the Lancers' place with every intention of extending my streak of one by nailing George Lancer to the wall on his land scam. There would be no holding the feet to the fire this time, no blasting a man about his sense of ethics, no playing judge and jury, because I don't hit a man when he is down— and George Lancer was clearly down.

"If you wanted to talk to George about something, maybe I can help you," Millie said.

"Perhaps you can," I said. I tucked away all the indignation and hostility and put together the best story I could on the spur of the moment. I told her I was a writer, which was true, and that there might be a story in the Bartel Company, which was also true, but not very likely to be marketable. I ended up by saying, "I wanted to

The Lake

talk to George about the sale of the slough lands to the Bartel Company."

"Oh my, I'm afraid George doesn't know anything about that. He has no idea that Foster has been taking care of us all these years."

Slam dunk two. "Perhaps you better explain, Millie. I guess I don't understand."

Millie was only too happy to have a chance to talk about it. "Right after our son was born, George had his first stroke. But Patrick and me, we held it together. We made a go of it. When Patrick's reserve unit got called up to go to Vietnam, I had to have some help and Foster found me a hired man. He worked out real well. Only hired man we ever had who wouldn't take no money. He said all he wanted was his room and board."

Millie rattled on, but I was beginning to get a whole new picture of the relationship between Foster Wallace and George Lancer. "Mr. Wallace and your husband were good friends for a long time I take it?"

"Oh my, yes, thick as thieves from grade school on." There was a tiny twinkle in her eye. "I had a hard time making up my mind between the two of them. They were both very handsome." She caught me stealing a glance at the wreckage of George Lancer and I halfway expected to get a lecture on judging books by their cover.

"So it was either George or Foster. Why one and not the other?"

For Millie it was simple. "George needed me, Foster didn't. When Foster went back east to school and George stayed here to start farming, the choice was easy. Haven't you heard that old saying, while the cat's away the mice will play?" She winked.

Foster Wallace was redeeming himself fast.

There was a long sigh. "I guess if it hadn't been for Foster there would have been some hard times. Oh, we would have made it all right, but it would have been hard. It was even Foster's idea to buy that old tax land. He said he would loan us the money to buy it, and then we could sell it to the Bartel people. He said if we did, I'd have enough money to take care of George for a long, long time. And that's exactly what I'm doing. Foster put that money Bartel paid us into some annuities for George and me, and the checks come every month just like he said they would. I have to admit that I was worried though after signing all those papers. When Foster was killed in that accident, I was really frightened, but Cynthia stepped right in and took care of things."

Two different portraits of the same man—and woman.

"Oh my," Millie said, giggling, "by now you are probably saying to yourself, 'How that woman does go on.' I just don't get many chances to talk about my blessings and how good a man my husband is." She looked a little embarrassed and wiped her fingers on her apron again.

I wanted to hug Millie Lancer and tell her I thought she just might be the most beautiful woman in all of Jericho County, but I didn't. Instead I asked her about the old slough tax lands.

The Lake

"'Course I don't remember it myself, but my father used to tell me about it. It was an old proving grounds for the military during World War I. I guess near everybody in Montana Mills and Jericho used to work there during the war. When the war was over, the government closed it down and deeded the land to Montana Mills. Then during the depression, this part I remember," she said and smiled, "Montana Mills just sorta became a nothing. George used to call it a wide spot in the road. And when that happened, most of the land went on the tax rolls. There was always talk about turning it into some kind of park, but the county never seemed to have the money. Before George had his first stroke, we used to talk about how we could expand our dairy herd if we had that land, but I always knew we couldn't after George got down. When Foster came up with his idea, I talked to George about it. Then I prayed real hard and it all worked out."

After that, Millie was finished. She had talked. She refilled my glass of iced tea, fussed over George a couple of times, showed me her late summer tea roses and walked me to my car. I think she was surprised when I bent down and kissed her on the cheek.

On the way back into town, I did my old weather bureau routine, appraised the skies and tried to remember if or when I had seen anything quite like it. To the east the sky was clear. But a pallid yellowish-gray cloud hovered over the eastern half of the lake. I came to the

207

T in the road, drove around the roadblock and headed for Ginny's cottage to check my answering machine.

When I pulled into the Western Shores cul-de-sac, I found the Carmi contingent waiting for me. I was glad to see them. Leonard was certain to be interested in a complete rundown on what I had learned from Roger Blackmonn. The two men followed me into the house, and I supplied Manion with a phone so that he could call the Institute; then I started to brief Leonard.

"Blackmonn cooperated. He admitted that they had conducted tests of a prototype unit in both the slough and the east basin. He showed me videos of the actual tests. The tests were conducted on three different dates between the end of July and early August. The tapes clearly show the unit submerging and surfacing."

"Then you're satisfied it isn't Bartel?"

"On the contrary, I'm only telling you what Blackmonn said and what I saw."

"Then Bartel actually does have a way of harnessing the CpP?"

"Look, Ira, your guess is as good as mine. I'm a writer, not a scientist. Maybe the tapes were phonies, but if they were, don't ask me why. Things get a little weird when you're talking four hundred big ones. I'll tell you this much. You can't tell much from the design; it looks like a bloated torpedo with stabilizers at each end. At one end there is a projection, like some kind of sonar device." I took a piece of paper out of Ginny's desk drawer and attempted to sketch what I had seen. Leonard was still studying my crude effort when Manion walked in the room.

"I feel like a man with a three-piece puzzle and only one of the pieces." Leonard sighed. He slumped down in a chair, looked at the drawing and frowned.

At that point I realized that Leonard was stalled until either Manion or I could get him more and better information.

"What did Groves have to say?" Ira asked.

Manion tended to mumble when he wasn't certain what he wanted to say, and Leonard hadn't given him enough time to mull over his conversation with Groves.

Manion cleared his throat. "He says there are three possibilities. But until we can confirm the fact that we're dealing with some form of stabilized CpP, we would only be shooting in the dark."

"Let's hear them," Leonard said.

"Possibility number one is based on the assumption that we are dealing with some isolated form of CpP. Groves believes that in such a case the CpP's molecular weight would cause it to sink and the water would dilute it. Bottom line: extensive damage to aquatic life forms."

"Just as I thought," Leonard said. "He's saying it would act like an acid agent in the immediate area of the discharge, just like our little demonstration this morning. Does he know we've checked the soil samples from the bottom of the lake? Rock and marl, the ideal lake bottom to exacerbate the problem.

"Ira is right from the standpoint that it provides recesses for the CpP to seep into," Manion said.

They were losing me. "I don't get it. Neither of you seem overly alarmed. I was told the stuff was both volatile and toxic."

"Correct," Manion said, "but the lake is acting as a natural diluting agent. The rationale goes like this: if some of Bartel's CpP did escape it shouldn't do much more than kill a few fish and fry some underwater vegetation. The natural cleansing action of the lake will eventually disperse and break down the CpP, rendering it harmless."

"Lay the second scenario on me," I said.

Manion hesitated. "Groves says all bets are off if the CpP escaped into the deeper recesses of the trench. It becomes trapped, isn't diluted, and in its concentrated form, it does extensive damage to the ecobalance of the lake."

"And the worst-case scenario?" I asked.

"Suppose there was something down there," Manion said.

"Like what?"

"Like gas."

Manion was several jumps ahead of me. "How could there be gas down there?" I asked.

Leonard walked to the window and looked out. "Makes sense, Elliott. If the bottom of the lake is made up of rock and marl, it means we have limestone and stratified rock. That would mean that there is a high probability that we have pockets of gas down there. The two conditions go hand in hand."

The Lake

Manion leaned forward in the chair with his elbows on his knees. "It works like this, Mr. Wages. The CpP violates the lake bottom and eventually eats its way through the composition into one of those pockets of gas. The gas begins to escape. If too much of it builds up too fast, you can get one hell of an explosion."

"A very frequent and natural phenomenon," Leonard said. "It's happening all the time. It becomes dangerous only when too much escapes too fast."

"But that still doesn't explain the odor or the vapor cloud."

"Obviously, we don't have all the pieces of the puzzle," Manion said, then grunted. "We're still operating in the dark. There are far too many ifs. The theory that Dr. Leonard advances does not explain the elevated temperatures, the deformed fish, the—"

That's when an idea hit me. I picked up the crude sketch of the RANASUR, dropped it, grabbed the telephone with one hand and thumbed through the phonebook for the Bartel number with the other. I was in luck. Someone answered.

"Bartel security. Hammond."

"Is Roger Blackmonn still there?"

There wasn't much formality. "I'll check," Hammond said. Seconds later, Blackmonn was on the line. Neither Harrison nor Cyn would have believed it.

"Roger, this is Elliott Wages. I think I've come up with something. Put that tape of the RANASUR tests on and fast forward to

R. Karl Largent

the third sequence. Run a frame by frame on the submerging procedure, and then do the same thing with the surfacing maneuver."

Blackmonn did as I requested. I could hear him fumble with the tape cartridge and the whirring sound as he advanced it. There was a stop, a click and then a rewind. Then he repeated the sequence. "Do you mind telling me what the hell I'm supposed to be looking for, Wages?"

"That small pod on the nose of the RAN-ASUR—"

"What about it?"

"What is that, the sonar?"

"Hell no, it's the power pod. The pod contains the heating coils for the CpP. The coils have to be there to keep the CpP from cooling too rapidly." With that Blackmonn fell silent. He knew he had just let a very important cat out of a very secret bag. CpP was stabilized with heat, another way of saying that Bartel's big advance in the use of CpP was the ability to maintain a constant operating temperature in the colder water.

My heart did a slow roll. "Check your tape again. This time just watch the power pod. Does it look any different to you?"

I heard the tape wind, rewind and wind again. He must have had the receiver lying next to the control panel while he punched the buttons.

"You're right, Wages. It looks a little odd, but it could be nothing more than the angle of the camera. Let me check it on the computer." I could hear the hollow-flat click-click-click of his fingers searching out the keys. There was another delay before he said, "Ah, here it comes."

212

"Read it to me."

"Which one: elapsed time-depth or depth-temp?"

"It doesn't matter. What we're looking for is any kind of variation or interruption, some anomaly in the data transmission."

"What kind of interruption?"

"Damn it, Roger, I don't know. I'm playing a long shot. Start reading. If you see an anomaly, shout it out."

Blackmonn began reciting elapsed time-depth readings. "Dive interval checks, thirty seconds: 0701:00 -4, 0701:30 -8, 0702:00 -11, 0702:30 -15. From the looks of these figures, Mueller had it in the accelerated descent mode, four to five meters every thirty seconds."

"Mueller? I thought you were running that damn show?"

"Mueller runs the projector, Wages. I manage the damn theater."

"How deep did the RANASUR go on this test?" I could hear Blackmonn scanning ahead. "Forty-nine meters."

"Jesus, that's one hundred and sixty feet. What was the temperature?"

There was a silence, then he said, "Wait a minute. I'm getting a data void—now a malfunction code."

"I think we're on to something. Now, go back to the video."

Blackmonn was punching up a new set of commands. "Now what?"

"Magnify and isolate on the power pod."

The machine was rewinding. It stopped, started and indexed again. "I see it," he said. "The pod position appears to be altered."

"How much?"

"What the hell do you mean? How much? Even the slightest alteration could be critical. When the encapsulated CpP is mounted to the RANASUR, the fuel-feed membrane allows a controlled flow to the cooling unit so that it can expand and power the unit. If that membrane is ruptured, we've got big problems."

"You told me you brought the RANASUR to the surface on the backup recovery system because of a software problem."

"Damn it, Wages, I know what I told you. That's the information I was given. Mueller was running the tests."

I was in no mood to listen to buck passing. I slammed the phone down and looked at the two professors. "Forget scenario number one. We're already in number two."

We turned left out of Ginny's drive, heading in the direction of the stone bridge over the slough because we could still see Marlboro's men working there. Manion continued to sort through the variables now that we had verified that it was likely that the RANASUR unit's CpP pod had been compromised.

"As CpP cools, it gains energy, becomes more volatile and decidedly more toxic," Manion said.

"And therefore, more active," Leonard added.

"Temperature variation is the real culprit," Manion said. "Too much, too little, but we're getting close. We now have to assume that our escaped **CFUS-POLCON-PRIEMON** is interacting with something down there. The question is what?"

When we got to the bridge, the entire area was shrouded in a thin, misty hangover from the vapor cloud. Following the same pattern it had for the last several days, Jericho Lake's patch of unpleasantness had started to drift away from shore and subside again, seeming to grow smaller as the day grew warmer. I looked up and down the shoreline. The cloud did not appear to be overland at any place along the beach.

The bridge had been cleared, the car removed and the area cordoned off. I couldn't help but wonder where the bodies of the young people had been taken and who had been assigned the unfortunate task of handling them.

Marlboro saw us coming and broke away from the throng of people clustered around his officers. The people started to follow him, but two of the troopers held them back.

"Damn press," he muttered. He looked straight at me. "Peters was hoping that you might be able to get some information out of the Bartel people that would tell us something."

I paraded Commander Marlboro through what I had learned from Blackmonn and then turned it over to Leonard and Manion. They took him through the same drill they had used on me, explaining in detail what could happen in each of the scenarios. Manion concluded by saying, "It's important to remember that several pieces of key information are still missing, Commander. We can't tell you what killed those young people. Unstable CFUS-POLCON-PRIEMON can result in an explosion and it is toxic. But there is no data to indicate that it would do what was done to the young people we found on the bridge this morning. Secondly, we don't know how long the situation will remain unstable. At this point, I think what we don't know is likely to give us even bigger problems than what we do know."

Marlboro frowned and straightened his shoulders. "It's becoming too big a risk. I will inform the governor that I'm ordering the mayor to close it down and that we intend to conduct a full-scale evacuation of Jericho."

Sunday P.M., September 5

As we headed back to the car, I tried to decide what to do with the bits and pieces of information I had accumulated during the past few hours. I was strongly tempted to say the hell with it, head back to Ginny's place and start the packing and tidying-up process. But that old good-neighbor ethic was telling me that, plans or not, I'd better hang around as long as there was something I could do to help. Or was it simply a good old-fashioned case of morbid curiosity about where the situation in Jericho was headed? Obligations to publisher and agent notwithstanding, there was one hell of a story unfolding in that upstate village by the lake.

Marlboro headed out to give Chesterton the bad news, leaving Leonard, Manion and me standing alongside the road. At that point, I could not see where I could contribute anything further to what had to be accomplished. I had told Leonard everything I knew about the Bartel situation, and with the exception of a few questions for Harrison Peters, who was far too busy to answer them, I was done. "So where do you go from here?" I asked.

"Back down in that trench," Leonard said. "Until we know what's causing that vapor cloud our work isn't done. If your friend Blackmonn is right and the filter membrane between the RANASUR and the CpP power pod ruptured and started leaking out down there, we know we've got a problem. But CFUS-POLCON-PRIEMON by itself, Manion assures me, wouldn't be causing that vapor cloud. The CpP is probably mixing with something, attacking it and causing a reaction."

Manion nodded agreement. "Ira is right. Based on what we know now, it's only going to get worse. Given the right set of climatic conditions, that vapor cloud could well invade most of the homes along the shoreline here on the east basin."

"If we can get to the deepest part of the basin, get some soil samples of the lake bottom and run some tests, we might be able to figure out a way of neutralizing the situation," Leonard said.

"How are you going to do that?" I asked.

Leonard gave me a wry smile. "There is a way, Elliott, but I need some help," he said, looking straight at me.

"No way. I went down there once. Once is enough. Take Manion with you."

Dr. Arnold Manion unbuttoned his shirt pocket and took out a small bottle. "There

218

was a time when I wouldn't have let you get in my way, Mr. Wages." The bottle contained nitro tablets. "I have a very uncooperative ticker."

"You're talking at least one hundred and forty foot of water and one hundred and twenty degree temperatures," I said.

"There is a two-man, open-cockpit seasled aboard this barge. It's better equipped than the *Harrington*. We use it for underwater exploratory work. It's not sophisticated, doesn't even have special equipment, but it could get us down there. I could take soil samples and we could be back on the surface in less than sixty minutes." Leonard took out his notebook and sketched the configuration of the trench, indicating the place where he thought it would be most advantageous to take the core samples. "Since the trench slopes down to where it culminates in the deepest part of the basin, we know where the flow of sediment would carry any foreign substance and, consequently, where the most significant accumulation would be. That's the point where we should get our data."

"How do you know it's there?"

"The current from the slough would carry it there. In effect it traps it there," Manion said.

I studied Leonard's sketch. "It looks to me like you're overlooking a couple of things. First of all, the water is already superheated. We had trouble breathing down there yesterday and we were only halfway down. Second, we've already seen what that stuff does to the marine life even in its diluted form."

"The temperature of the water is a problem," Leonard said. "But since we'll be working from the survey sled, we can carry a spare tank. It won't matter if we use our air supply at an accelerated rate—within reason, of course. My guess is that we can get in and out of there in plenty of time."

"I don't like when you have to guess," I grumbled.

"It will take two of us," Leonard said. A quirky crooked grin was playing with the corners of his mouth again. "Look at it this way, Elliott. If we can get down there, find out what's causing the cloud and figure out a way to put a stop to it, you'll have yourself one whale of a plot for your next book."

"If you don't," Manion said with an ominous air about his voice. "Jericho Lake could end up being uninhabitable for years to come, a veritable modern day version of a ghost town. Until we know what's down there, we have no way of predicting what happens when the weather cools and the sun doesn't generate enough heat to dissipate that vapor cloud."

Two thoughts played tag with my addled brain while Leonard and Manion made their appeal. One was telling me that going back down in that trench was a mild form of lunacy. The other was telling me I would never be able to live with myself if I didn't.

Leonard knew he had me when I asked, "Do we have everything we need?"

"It's all there," he said. I couldn't tell whether Leonard really believed we could get in and out of there with a minimum of risk, or if he didn't feel like he had a choice in the matter.

The old Elliott Grant Wages penchant for getting himself in over his head inundated me with waves of doubt and recriminations while we drove to the barge. We took Becker Herd's launch out to the Carmi barge, and while Manion and Leonard readied the seasled, I checked over the diving gear.

The sled was primitive, not the kind I had seen used in deep-water exploration in the Caribbean. It was a 12-foot-long, two-seated affair with an open cockpit, saddle seats and a small cluster of controls on a metal panel in front of each diver. The frame was made of titanium, and the sled was powered by four rapid-charge, extended-performance 12-volt marine batteries with, Leonard assured me, enough energy capacity to keep us going for an hour. Since there was another bank of batteries sucking up juice from the barge's generator, I knew that the battery pack could be replaced and the seasled made ready for a second dive in a matter of minutes.

Propulsion came from a single variable pitch prop and the ballast, if any, was probably in the bottom of the two tool lockers. Plain and simple, the bare minimum. It was designed to get us there and back and do a minimum of sight-seeing along the way.

Leonard gave me a quick course in hand signals and informed me that it would be my job to baby-sit the sled while he took the core samples. As the three of us hefted the sled over the side, Manion was droning out his own set of instructions.

"You have exactly forty-five minutes of operation time. Your safety factor is fifteen. When the chronometer indicates you are at positive fifteen, start for the surface. The tether line to the barge will be at the forty foot level. I have attached a strobe so that if the water is murky you'll have something to shoot for. You each have seventy-five minutes in your tanks. That's the main plus auxiliary. The spare tank on the sled has fifteen. Don't use it unless you absolutely have to—that tank is your last refuge. There is no way to predict how those elevated temperatures will impact your usage. Allow yourself enough time to come up. You need at least ten minutes at the eighty-foot level. And try to get a fix on the location of the vapor cloud. Even though it's backing off, you don't want to surface right in the middle of it."

I remember checking the mission time/ elapsed time chrono on the safety bar curved over the abbreviated console in front of me. The indicator read 0107 and 44:31:30 when Leonard plowed the bow of the sled beneath the surface. The plan was to head, underwater, for the vapor cloud and then to descend. The water instantly began an ugly metamorphosis from blue-clear to gray-cloudy, and I could already detect a decided elevation in temperature. At the 40-foot level, I pulled the D-ring, disconnected the tether and activated the homing strobe. I watched it drift back. The rush of air filled the bladder, stabilized and began flashing.

The Lake

Leonard leveled the sled, reconfigured our descent pattern and put us into a slow, circular, downward glide. At that point we were eight mission minutes into our energy supply. Ira corrected to a forward 090 and motioned for me to turn on the port halogen with a sweep of 180 degrees. The light knifed through the wall of opaque gray in front of us. We skimmed through a thinly populated school of small fish and glided out over the edge of the trench. The gray went to black and a chasm of nothingness yawned out beneath us. The moment we were out over the trench I felt the temperature spike. We began the circular descent pattern again and the sweeping halogen began picking up the gray-green algae-coated walls of the trench. I remember thinking we were trying our little maneuver between two walls of solid rock, actually nothing more than a tiny crack in the earth, and I hoped that the gods did not decide to choose that time to repair the crack.

Sweat began to trickle under my mask and search its way into my eyes. I squeezed them shut, blinked and checked the single-needle depthometer—35 meters. At that depth the light from the halogen was being sucked up by the darkness no more than 30 feet in front of us. Leonard gave me the signal to turn on the starboard lamp and aim it down. I did. Sweat was cascading down my back inside the wetsuit. When I checked the temperature gauge, I realized the lens was loose. It had filled with water and the indicator lay to one side. It was rapidly becoming a sensory world in reverse.

The deeper the sled plowed the warmer the water was getting. My breathing had accelerated and a tenseness gripped my entire body, causing my arms and hands to ache and my legs to tremble.

The seasled swirled abruptly to one side and Leonard momentarily lost control in a thermal upcurrent. I righted myself in the saddle and watched Leonard veer first left and then right as he corrected our course. I spotted a bloated and lesion-covered fish. It was unusually large— and it was dead, its cancerous head flaking off skin as it undulated in the agitated water. There was a stream of bubbles directly beneath the fish and I brought the halogen around until I spotted the source, a spring. In what should have been a nutrient-rich stream of cold water, I saw a tangle of brown seaweed, even more brown algae and the skeletal remains of thousands of fish. The bottom of the trench was covered with the debris of death.

Leonard leveled us, then headed forward again, and I aimed the halogen directly in front of us. I watched him get off the sled, unfasten his safety tether and make a circular motion with his hand. He lifted a two-foot-long section of pipe out of the stow locker and selected one of two short-handled sledges. With one end of the pipe against the sediment, he began to hammer on the other end. When he finished, he clamped his hand over the end, extracted it and sealed both ends. He put the pipe in the box, then he motioned for me to move the sled forward and took a second sample. The dive-time indicator read 29:06:14, which meant we had less than 16 minutes before we would have to do some serious thinking about how we intended to get out of there.

Just as Leonard finished, I saw him look up from what he was doing. He straightened and started moving away, shoving the beam of light along like a broom in front of him. I maneuvered the sled in as close as I could and started playing the sled's forward halogen ahead of us.

A thick, undulating, murky gray cloud hovered over what appeared to be a moundlike irregularity in the topography of the lake bottom. Leonard began circling around it and motioning as if he was getting ready to move in to examine it. When both beams of light were finally focused on the scene, I realized we were looking at a pile of barrels, dozens of them—old, corroded and coated with heavy red-yellow rust. The corrosive action had actually eaten through the metal on several of them and the contents were bleeding into the water. He gave me a signal that I interpreted to mean that we had found what we were looking for and he started to kneel down to flake away enough rust to see if he could determine what was in the barrels. The moment he touched one of the barrels, there was a small muffled explosion. I saw Leonard's body pitch backward, stirring up clouds of sediment. The halogen spiraled out of his hand and his entire body began to spasm. From that moment on, everything in that underwater nightmare unfolded in a terrifying frame-by-frame slow motion. I managed to get the tether line unbuckled and off of the sled. My

tanks caught on the saddleback and I fell down.
I got up and my feet went off from under me a
second time. With sweat blurring my vision, I
clawed into the tangle of barrels after him. He
was directly in front of me, tearing at his wet suit,
arms flailing. When I reached for him, he spun
away from me. After three attempts, I realized he
did not want me to get a hold on him. I brought
myself around and planted both flippers against
one of the barrels. It collapsed under my feet and
discharged a thick, inky-black substance into the
water, creating a blinding cloud of syrupy confusion. Jagged shards of rusting metal swirled in
the water. One of my flippers caught in one of the
rotting barrels, and I instinctively reached down
to peel it off. When I looked up, Leonard was
coming straight at me. He stabbed at me with a
piece of crenulated steel in his hand, slashing the
deadly object back and forth in the water like a
rapier.

The sweat forced me to close my eyes. Blindly,
I went to one side, stumbled and plowed into the
sandy bottom. My fingers closed around the snap
end of the webbed nylon tether line. I jerked it
up, laced it tightly between my hands and got to
my feet just in time to fend off Leonard's second
charge. Using the snap end as a barrier, I held
it out in front of me. The jagged piece of steel
sliced through the water, but missed me. Within
inches of me again, Leonard faltered and went
to his knees. While he struggled, I moved around
behind him, slipped my arm around his neck
and felt something spongy under the fabric of
his wet suit. I pulled his head back, dislodged

the shard of metal from his hand and pulled him around to face me. Through the lens of his mask I could see his face disintegrating. There was no mouth, just a crimson-black tear in the flesh revealing the horrible violation that was taking place throughout his body. A torrent of thick pink mucus pumped from his body through the acid-etched holes in his wet suit. It was as if his circulatory system was boiling his body juices and what was left was escaping the prison of his body by erupting through the flesh that imprisoned it.

Ira Leonard's body slowly evolved into something hideous and unrecognizable.

There was a moment of panic, a rapid wave of sense-numbing nausea and then the sensation of total hopelessness. A voice inside told me that I was holding on to a dead man. When I loosened my grip, he fell away and his body began undulating in the subtle yet deadly current from the slough.

I have no idea how long it took me to marshal my senses. I know I stayed there for some time, trying to get a grip on reality, trying to plug myself back into the urgency of the moment. Slowly, a reorientation to the situation at hand, of things living and my own vulnerability began to creep over me. I checked my air supply and went back to the seasled. Elapsed time was 41:09:41—not enough time. Manion's words were etched in my brain. "If you see you can't make it, forget the sled and save your own hide."

I began to devise a fevered plan. I would take the sled up as far as it would go, thinking that if

227

it could get me to the 80-foot level, I could take the ten minutes and still make it to the surface. I unhooked the spare air tank, cradled it in my lap and made sure the tether line was loose.

For some unexplained reason, I played the beam of the bow halogen back over the scene one final time. Perhaps I was thinking that maybe, just maybe, there was hope, hope that at the last minute I might learn something that would in some way help to justify the death of Ira Leonard. It is more likely, though, that the one long last look was nothing more than an attempt at reassuring that I was not deserting him, that there was no hope.

Leonard's body had come to rest near one of the barrels. In the combination of the eerie, muted light of the halogen and the murky yellow-grayness of the water, it seemed as though he had found a way to give me a clue to what had happened.

I bent over and began to brush away the rust and debris, careful not to puncture the corroded side wall of the drum. There were letters painted on the side of the barrel. I was able to uncover the letters COC, but the rest was obliterated. Beneath it were more letters—an O, an S and a G. I knew I could end up the same way as Leonard if I pushed my investigation any further. I stopped and checked my air supply. I was out of time.

The sled was history. It was obvious I would have to leave it behind. The needle on the battery reserve indicator had collapsed to the far left side of the danger zone. The lone issue I cared about was saving Elliott Wages.

When I started up, I was all too aware that I was heading up without the answers that Ira Leonard had sacrificed his life to obtain.

Only after I had negotiated the rim of the trench and saw the pulsing beacon of the strobe did I think I really had a chance to survive.

When I came to, I saw the craggy face of Arnold Manion staring down at me. Looking up into that hawkish, homely face, I told myself he was the most beautiful sight I had ever seen. Then thoughts began to ricochet around my head like a pinball in play: Manion was on the surface, and if I could see him, so was I. If I was on the surface, I was safe.

The expression on his face was a different matter. It told me he realized what had happened. He didn't have the details of course, but the bottom line was the same. As the blurriness began to fade, I could see the pain in his angular face, which mirrored the questions he wanted to ask.

He gave me a few minutes to regain my equilibrium. I pushed myself up on my elbows. As I felt the pain in my chest and the throb in my head, I told myself that being in the world never felt so good. When he saw that I was starting to come around, he sagged back until he was sitting on the deck, then wrapped his long arms around his knees.

"How long have I been out?" I sounded mushy mouthed.

"Five minutes—no more. You never actually

lost consciousness. Your pulse was accelerated and you had an irregular heartbeat, but you settled right down. If I was guessing, I'd say you came across something that scared the hell out of you."

I reflected back on tank gauges that were reading empty at the 40-foot marker. It felt as though someone had a stranglehold on my lungs and was still squeezing.

"Can you talk?" he asked.

I nodded. "Try me."

He had a one-word question: "Ira?"

I shook my head, full well knowing that the time would come when I would have to spell out the details.

"Did you find anything?"

The words came out slowly, as if I was piecing them together letter by letter. "We found barrels, rusted and corroded. I'm no scientist, but it looks to me like the combination of CpP and the escaping contents of those barrels is the culprit. The floor of the trench is littered with dead fish, damn near all of them mutilated. The water is hot, real hot. I can't tell you how elevated because the temperature gauge malfunctioned."

"The sled has a min and max temp gauge on it. Any chance we can recover the sled?"

"It's still intact, but I don't think we should risk going back down to get it."

"We'll retrieve it," Manion said. I did not hear a lot of conviction in his voice. "Any idea what was in those barrels?"

I tried to remember the few letters I had been

The Lake

able to make out and their sequence. "Some of the barrels had lettering on them, but the words were obliterated, all I could see was an O and an S and maybe an H, but not necessarily in that order."

Manion wrinkled his primitive brow and contorted his mouth into a series of funny shapes. "Nothing else?"

I shook my head. I had forgotten all about the COC on the line above. "Makes you wonder what the hell those barrels were doing there in the first place. This isn't the kind of place where folks go around dumping garbage and trash in the water."

Manion took out his pipe, loaded it and lit it. He did not have to tell me that his mind was rummaging over and over the few sketchy facts I had given him. "What color were those barrels?"

"Couldn't tell."

"Were they a bright orange like the ones used to transport toxic waste?"

I shook my head. "Not bright. Drab looking, but hard to tell with all that rust."

"Drab," Manion said. "Drab-colorless, drab-dull, drab-no appeal." He was trying to get a hold of something. "Drab—drab—drab—olive drab." His eyes brightened. "Military green?"

"Could have been, but it's hard to say, they blended in with whatever the hell was happening down there."

"Olive drab," he said again, rolling his eyes up until he looked like he was trying to peek under his own eyelids. "How? Why?"

"The only way they could have gotten there is for someone to dump them."

"Or could they have washed down the slough?"

I looked at Manion and my brain began to click. At the same time my heart began to sink. "That's it." I reasoned my way through the sequence a second time looking for the holes in my logic. "That Bartel plant is built on the site of an old proving ground."

Manion slapped his forehead with the palm of his hand. "Damn! The old Montana Mills Proving Ground." He laid down his pipe, whipped out a pencil and began writing the letters on the deck itself. Then he laid the pencil down and closed his eyes. "That damn power pod of Bartel's is attacking and releasing seventy-five-year-old barrels of carbonic dichloride, otherwise known as Phosgene. They were producing it at Montana Mills when the end of the war came."

"Phosgene?" I asked.

"Causes edema, an abnormal accumulation of fluid in the cells, rapid swelling in the tissue and cavities of the body. Coupled with the barrier penetration properties of the CpP, it would cause something to keep swelling until it exploded."

I closed my eyes, remembering Ira Leonard. "Is that what that damn vapor cloud is?"

"That's exactly what it is. Now it's all beginning to make some sense. COC-2 and CpP would create a near-perfect inversion process, the exact opposite of the behavior we would expect. Heat, not cold, controls it; it expands, intensifies and then liquefies when it cools. In other words, the damn heat wave this town has been enduring has been saving this town's bacon. In effect, the stagnant air has had the effect of containing it. Rain, wind, a cold air mass, a weather front moving through—any or all of the above would allow the gas to concentrate. The vapor would then become thicker and invade any organism that inhales it or allows the mixture to penetrate the skin."

Manion had thrown a lot at me, and I was trying to digest it. His face somehow managed to drain of color even further as he grappled with the enormity of the discovery.

"It's worse than I feared." He sighed and started shaking.

"Potential catastrophe?"

"Certain catastrophe, Mr. Wages. Certain catastrophe."

Sunday P.M., September 5

We took Becker Herd's launch back to the pier and found Cletus Mackey waiting for us. His expression was harried. "Peters sent me to find Dr. Leonard," he said. He was out of breath.

I gave the deputy an abbreviated version of what had happened just moments before in the trench and started looking around for some indication that the evacuation had started. If it had started, it wasn't all that evident. The shoreline was still clogged with onlookers. "I thought Marlboro said he was going to inform Chesterton he was shutting the Jubilee down."

"They haven't been able to locate him. Marlboro is looking for him. But now something else has come up. Maybe you and Dr. Manion better come with me."

We crawled in the cruiser with the deputy took a hard right out of Herd's lot and headed south on the lake road. Where the pavemen

The Lake

forked off to the east into Fort Janes, the state police had set up a roadblock. One trooper had his hands full trying to turn back the stream of traffic still headed into Jericho for the big Sunday night fireworks display. If that duty wasn't bad enough, he also had to keep the road cleared for the trickle of Jubilee goers who had had enough of the festivities and were on their way out of town.

"Shit," Mackey muttered, "the way this traffic is jammed up it'll take us another hour to get to Peters."

Manion and I got out of the cruiser and started walking. Mackey pulled the unit off to the side of the road and caught up with us.

Manion walked at the brisk pace of a man who had a lot of practice. "Good for the heart," he said as he looked up to assess the cloud cover. "I don't like the looks of that sky, Elliott. Those clouds are beginning to thicken and the temperature feels like it's dropped a good five degrees since earlier in the day."

By the time we had located Peters a couple of hundred yards north of the bridge, Manion had reiterated his concern that any appreciable drop in the temperature could allow the cloud to stabilize and perhaps even cause it to spread again. "As long as that son of a bitch stays out over the water, we have a fighting chance. If it comes ashore again, all bets are off."

Peters saw us coming, broke away from a small cluster of reporters and started toward us. Several of them followed. "Where the hell is Dr. Leonard?" he demanded. "He can answer

235

those reporters' damn fool questions a hell of a lot better than I can."

I gave Peters a full account of what had happened in the trench, but decided to let Manion interpret the part about Bartel losing the integrity on the CpP power pod. Peters listened, scowled and then motioned for us to follow. He led the way out onto the nearest pier to get away from the reporters.

Then he said in a low voice, "After we got the mess cleaned up on the bridge, I instructed Mackey and Hargrove to make a sweep through the area and advise the cottage owners along the shore through here that they were going to have to evacuate. This is what they found."

Like a big, agile cat, Peters stepped down into a small aluminum fishing boat. Carefully pulling back a piece of tarpaulin so that no one on shore could see what he was showing us, he sucked in his breath. "I must have had my head up my ass this morning. By the time we got around to warning folks, it was too late."

The body in the boat was that of an old man, rigid and grotesquely twisted into a telltale configuration that indicated he might have been trying to get out of his boat when the mist hit him. I didn't know the man, but from what was left of him, I probably wouldn't have recognized him even if I had. The body was split right down the middle like an overcooked sausage. A tangle of inner parts only seen in anatomy textbooks had been exposed; they were gray, bloated and nauseating. The small amount of skin that still managed to cling to the muscle structure was badly burned, and the hands protruding from the long-sleeved fishing jacket looked like clumps of spoiled meat.

"His name is Calet Phillips," Peters choked out. "He worked for the power company in Fort Janes. Went fishin' every night after the skiers quit for the evening." He avoided looking at the body when he dropped the sheet of canvas back in place to conceal the remains. Then he stepped back up on the pier. "Hell, this is only the tip of the iceberg. It wasn't until we finally got the bodies of those kids out of here and the car off the bridge that I realized I hadn't seen any of the cottage owners out and stirring around along this stretch of the lake."

He handed Mackey his clipboard, and we followed Peters to the cottage adjacent to the one where Calet Phillips lived. There he showed us the bodies of Sam and Joann Larkspur. The elderly couple were sprawled across the bed. The bedroom faced the lake and the large sliding glass doors were open. The same slimy residue I had seen on the *Harrington* when it emerged from the vapor cloud was evident throughout the room.

"I've known old Sam here since school days," Peters said stiffly. "He used to tell me how he and Joann used to sleep with their doors open to catch the breeze coming in off the lake at night."

I took one last look at the Larkspurs and went back outside to get some fresh air.

I didn't tell Harrison Peters, but the three bodies he had shown us all had a great deal in common with the disfigured creature Graham

Hatcher had pulled out of the lake four days earlier and the dying gar I had encountered in the trench.

After seeing the Larkspurs, Manion had turned white and his hands began trembling. He looked like a man who knew he was going to be very, very sick. "It's a goddamn shame about Ira Leonard," Peters said. "I figured maybe he was going to be the one who was able to tell us what happened here." His eyes darted back into the Larkspur cottage and then he turned to Manion. "I'm in over my head, Doc. Got any ideas?"

"Better tell Harrison your theory," I said, prodding Manion.

"I don't think we need to call it a theory anymore, Mr. Wages." He was still visibly unnerved. "When Dr. Leonard and Mr. Wages here went down in the trench today, they discovered a number of discarded barrels containing what we believe to be carbonic dichloride, otherwise known as Phosgene—a poison gas manufactured during the First World War."

Peters's eyes narrowed. "Phosgene?" he said. "I've heard of it."

"A gas," Manion said, "three to four times heavier than air. Boils right around fifty degrees Fahrenheit. The Bartel people have confirmed that the fuel cell membrane in the RANASUR power pod was ruptured, and sometime during the course of one of their tests they lost a portion of the contents of the power pod's CpP in the vicinity of the trench leading to the east basin. From what Mr. Wages tells me he saw down there, I now believe it's reasonable to assume that the spilled CpP is acting as a broad-based releasing agent by eating through the metal surface of the containers. Then it is mixing with and elevating the temperature of large amounts of escaping concentrated carbonic dichloride. The elevated temperature of the water resulting from this mixture is carrying the gas to the surface. Bottom line: our little lake out there is becoming more and more unstable by the hour. And the more unstable it becomes, the faster it cools when it reaches the surface. The way I see it, Sheriff, it's beginning to look more and more like we have the potential for a major disaster."

Peters listened in resigned silence. Shoulders hunched, he looked out at the lake and then at what was left of the deadly cloud of vapor gas. The situation had changed drastically. He wasn't dealing with a kid in a hot car or one of the local drunks or a domestic squabble. He had trouble with a capital T—the kind of thing Harrison Peters had never dealt with before. He went through the ritual of lighting one of his cigars, then looked at Manion. "Okay, you tell me where the hell we go from here, Doc?"

Manion shook his head. As he did, I wondered if either of them had noticed that the wind had shifted around to the west with a slight increase in velocity.

Peters took a crumpled piece of paper out of his shirt pocket. "All tolled, counting Dr. Leonard now, we've got a total of seventeen victims."

Mackey moved into the conversation. He was looking at the clipboard and nodding. "Near as we can determine, that fog didn't work its way any farther north than Bert Freeman's place."

I grabbed the piece of paper out of Peters's hand and scanned the list of names. When I came to the last two, an icy realization hit me. At the bottom of the page were the names of Candy and Bert Freeman. The half-scrawled entry indicated one of the men had found their bodies on the patio. I swallowed hard. Somehow, there wasn't any doubt in my mind what Bert's last words were: He died telling Candy it was the worst damn smelling vapor cloud he had ever seen.

"Are you saying that all you have to do is breathe this damn stuff?" Peters asked, trying to comprehend the approaching disaster.

"Unfortunately, Sheriff, that appears to be the case," Manion said.

"Which means we can't take any chance on routing the exiting traffic anywhere near the vapor cloud."

"What it means, Sheriff, is that we will have to be especially alert to make certain that we keep a close eye on the track that vapor cloud takes throughout the day and the night. You'll have to appoint someone to monitor its movement full-time. The observers will have to be equipped with gas masks and communication gear. They will have to be alert. The position of the vapor cloud will be critical to the evacuation process. We have two enemies: cooler temperatures and darkness. The cooler temperatures will enable the cloud to expand and the darkness will hide its movements."

The Lake

"Shit!" Peters said. "When the hell are we going to get a break. The gaseous son of a bitch has us by the balls. How the hell are we supposed to track it when it's dark?"

"We have one very small advantage, Sheriff. We can smell it coming."

Peters grunted, started toward his cruiser and stopped. When he turned around, he had squared his shoulders and set his jaw. "Cletus! tell those troopers we need to round up as many gas masks as we can lay our hands on. Then go over to Sam Patton's place and deputize anyone sober enough to keep their eyes open and carry a flashlight. Keep appointing deputies until you run out of badges and masks. Then see that they are stationed all around the perimeter of the lake. Tell them we have to establish some kind of communications network to keep track of that damn vapor cloud. If Harley Sanders has already closed his Radio Shack up for the day, don't waste time trying to find him. Break the damn door down and grab every walkie-talkie and piece of communication gear you think you can use." Then he looked at Manion and me. "You two, come with me. I need you to explain what's happening to Marlboro so he'll know what to tell the governor."

Thirty minutes later we had fought our way through the traffic and throngs of people to the Jericho council building. For whatever reason, I remember making note of the precise time when Marlboro finally got through to the governor's office to advise him what we were doing.

Maybe I was curious about how long it would take them to get the village evacuated. On the other hand, maybe I was simply wondering if the evacuation order was a case of too little too late. Whatever the reason, it was exactly five minutes after five o'clock when Marlboro instructed his men to notify the vendors along the midway that they were to assemble at 5:30 in the hospitality tent outside the council building.

What I did not know at the time was that Felix Chesterton had not yet been located or told of the impending shutdown. Under the circumstances it seemed as if informing Chesterton would have been a mere formality. The governor's order had taken the matter out of his hands, and Marlboro, by virtue of a state-of-emergency order, was in control. Chesterton, if he stayed true to form, might do a little political posturing, but the die was cast.

As it turned out, Chesterton heard about the closing order before Marlboro was able to inform him, and the moment he stormed through the door, I knew he was ready to do more than just posture. "What the hell is this all about, Marlboro?"

"It's out of your hands, Chesterton. The governor's office declared a state of emergency less than fifteen minutes ago. I'm shutting the Jubilee down. It's too risky."

"By whose goddamned authority?"

"The governor himself. We're shutting the midway down and I'm ordering a complete evacuation of the village."

The Lake

"Evacuate the village?" Chesterton said. "What the hell for?"

"Because Manion informs me we've got the potential for one hell of a disaster here. And the faster the weather deteriorates, the more critical the situation becomes."

At that point something snapped in Felix Chesterton. He lunged at Marlboro, but Peters was quick enough to step between the two men and push him back. "Cool it, Felix, it's his show now. I was here when he talked to the governor. He's been ordered to shut it down."

"If you do, you'll bankrupt this goddamned town." Chesterton yelled.

Marlboro was showing restraint. "Dr. Manion believes that a sudden change in the weather could trigger a movement in that vapor cloud, possibly bringing it ashore. A worst-case scenario says that, if that cloud moves in over the village with all those people out there, Jericho could be another Nagasaki by tomorrow morning."

Chesterton turned as though he intended to leave, spun back again and threw a punch at Marlboro. The trooper sidestepped him, and Harrison Peters, moving quicker than I had seen him move at any time in the three months I had known him, leveled Chesterton with a chest-high block, burying his shoulder in the big man's midsection and knocking him to the floor.

Chesterton got to his knees, uttering a string of profanities. "Put your mayor under arrest, Sheriff!" Marlboro said. "Keep him there until he decides to cool off and cooperate."

Mackey led the dazed Chesterton into an adjacent room just as Marlboro was informed that the majority of the vendors, ride owners and officials of the Jubilee had assembled in the Council's hospitality tent on the front lawn. Peters and I followed. Marlboro didn't mince words: all booths, rides,. food stands, displays and stores were to be closed immediately. "You will move no equipment. Just shut down, lock up and make provisions to get your people out of the area. At ten o'clock, I will order the troopers to conduct a sweep of the village. If you're not out of here by then you will be forcibly removed."

There were howls of protest, demands to know what was going on. Several people said they wanted their fees back and some insisted on talking to Chesterton. Through it all, Marlboro held his ground. "It's five forty-five, gentlemen. It appears to me you've got a hell of a lot to do in the next four hours. At ten o'clock, when I look out there, I want to see nothing but deserted streets."

As the crowd dispersed, Marlboro went back into the council building and began parceling out more assignments. Some of Mackey's recruits from Patton's Pier were instructed to inform the people in the campgrounds. Others were sent to the municipal beach, where the crowd had already started to select the choice spots for the fireworks display. "Every cottage owner has to be notified. Use bullhorns, sirens, anything it takes to get their attention."

Someone in the back of the room mentioned the fact that the people at the Bartel facility

244

had to be warned. I wondered if Blackmonn and Mueller had any idea how much damage the ruptured fuel membrane on the CpP power pod was causing.

In the confusion, I heard someone else say that one of Peters's men had been trying to get in touch with the Bartel people for the last two hours with no success. When Peters pulled me aside, he wanted to know if I had any idea how many people would have to be evacuated from the plant. "You've been over there twice, Elliott. What are we talking? Two, twenty or two hundred?"

"No way of knowing, Harrison. It's a Sunday night, so there's probably no one there. Maybe a couple of security guards at the most. Actually, I'm more concerned about George and Millie Lancer. Millie will need help getting the old boy out of there."

Peters ordered a nervous little man wearing thick glasses and a deputy's badge to drive over to Montana Mills to tell the town marshal what was happening. "On the way back, see if you can roust anyone out at the Bartel plant. Tell them the state police are ordering an evacuation of the entire Jericho area." Then he added, "After that, help Millie get George into the car and tell her to go stay with her sister in Helgo until we get a handle on this situation."

The deputy hustled out wearing the expression of a man on a mission, and I went back outside to check on the weather. It had taken a decided turn for the worse. There was a heavy cloud deck building up over the western part of the lake and blocking out the sunset. The wind had picked up to a steady eight to ten knots. I had seen too many storms roll in off the Gulf in the last few years to be mistaken. With the freshening breeze, I thought about Manion's theory of what could happen if the air cooled and wondered if there had been any discernable change in the composition and location of the vapor cloud.

Out on the midway, the Kentucky Fried Chicken and Taco Bell booths had shut down. Cars were already lined up bumper to bumper getting out of the parking lot. Kids were crying, mothers were complaining and fathers were leaning on horns.

Manion sidled up to me, hands in his pockets and a semipleased look on his face. "Looks like it's finally happening," he said. "They tell me the parking lot down at the marina is starting to empty out." He put his finger in his mouth, wet it and held it up in the wind. "So far the evacuation appears to be running smooth. But if these folks get wind of what happened down at the other end of the lake today, Jericho could have a first-class panic on its hands."

"That's one of the things that's bothering me, Doc. There were two or three mobile news units down there earlier this afternoon. At this point it's likely the only thing that's keeping the truth off the air is the fact that neither Peters or Marlboro have confirmed anything. If people suddenly learn that they'll be in danger when that vapor cloud comes ashore, we could have one hell of a mess on our hands."

The Lake

Peters came out of the building, fumbling through his pockets until he found his lighter. He lit what was left of his cigar and exhaled. "I hope to hell we can get the biggest part of the crowds out of town before the storm moves in."

"Storm?" Manion said. "Is it confirmed?"

"Yeah, Mackey just informed me that one of the radio stations in Fort Janes is reporting that a line of thunderstorms is expected to move through Fort Janes any minute now." I studied the western sky and finally saw the brief, muted, yellow flash of distant cloud-to-cloud lightning. Then I heard the faint low, telltale growl of far-away thunder.

Harrison Peters shook his head as he looked at me. "I've got a feeling, Elliott, that this is going to turn out to be a very long night."

"Or a very short one," Manion muttered.

An hour later, I still hadn't figured out a way to leave. Every street in Jericho was congested with honking cars and short tempered motorists. Marlboro had called in 11 more troopers, and they had been dispatched to various locations throughout the Jericho area in an effort to get the town evacuated by the deadline. A complete command post had been set up in the council's hospitality tent, and one of the troopers was valiantly fending off a barrage of questions from the handful of reporters still on the scene. The first wave of thunderstorms had passed. There had been lots of thunder, but not much wind and very little rain. The state police had a direct line to the Fort Janes Weather Bureau, which was updating its storm bulletins every ten minutes. Manion was even more alarmed when he learned that the Early Storm Warning Center at Kansas City Weather Central had isolated a developing series of squall lines preceding an approaching cold front in the western portion of the state. Those same radar reports indicated that the cold front was less than 75 miles west of Jericho.

Through it all, I had been formulating my own plan. I had called Cyn twice during the last hour, giving her traffic updates. On my signal, she was to get Mrs. Fern and Basketcase loaded in her car. When she saw the lights of the Carrera in her driveway, she was to lock up and follow me. "Don't worry," I said. "I figure we've got another hour at least. I'll be there in plenty of time."

After that second call, I went back into the council building to check out three gas masks and discovered that they had all been issued. "We only had a dozen or so," the trooper on duty said, "and we issued them to the folks monitoring the vapor cloud. Marlboro has sent for more but they'll have to be brought in from the Clarridge post. That's seventy miles north of here." When I left to rejoin Manion, I ran into Harrison Peters. He had been out checking the progress of the evacuation and was just pulling back into the parking lot. By the time he got out of his car, I knew we had a new concern.

"Has Marlboro talked to you yet?"

I shook my head.

"We just got a call from the Bartel people in New York. They've been trying to get through to their Montana Mills facility for the past several hours. They haven't been able to get any response; so they called the state police post in Fort Janes. They say they have a potential problem and their security people aren't responding. They want us to check it out."

"What do you mean by a potential problem?"

Peters went through his cigar routine. Finally he found his lighter, bit off the end of the cigar and lit it. "From what the dispatcher over at Fort Janes got out of it, this CpP stuff is stable only if it is stored and maintained in a very narrow temperature range."

"How narrow?"

"One hundred and thirty-three to one hundred and thirty-seven degrees Fahrenheit. Apparently the chamber where they keep it is controlled by computers that monitor infrared ovens with alarm gauges. For the last three hours they report they have been getting an insecure code."

"Insecure? What's that supposed to mean?"

"Insecure, unstable. Mary Lou wasn't sure. They want us to see if we can roust out somebody from the local Bartel plant and have them check it out."

"Just how critical is this potential problem?"

"They don't know for sure. From where they are, they can't tell whether they've got a systems malfunction or a computer problem. Marlboro and I figured since you've been in that plant twice in the last couple of days you'd be the logical one to ask."

"What about that deputy you sent over there earlier?"

"Haven't been able to get through to him," Peters said.

"Hell, Harrison, he's had time to go over to Montana Mills, check out the Bartel plant and stop to check on the Lancers a couple of times."

The way Peters looked at me I knew I wasn't telling him something he didn't already know. "I realize that, and that's why I think we better check it out." His voice was flat.

At this point there were two things I was certain of: it wasn't the time to back out on Harrison Peters, and I had to let Cyn know that the plans were being changed. I called her, told her that I was still tied up and that she would be smart to load up and head out. "I'll meet you at the Holiday Inn East in Fort Janes as soon as I can get there," I said.

There was a whole lot of uneasy silence on the other end of the line. When her voice came through, it was small and frightened. "Elliott, what is going on? You're not making a whole lot of sense."

If you've ever tried to condense a long, convoluted story with lots of loose ends into something coherent, you know what I was up against. Worse yet, the more I tried to explain, the more it sounded like pure babble.

"Damn it, Cyn, I know that," 'I said, trying to keep my voice calm. "Nothing in this whole fiasco makes any sense."

"What if you can't find anyone over at Bartel? Then what?" It was the same question I had asked Peters. He didn't have an answer either.

"Look, it's probably something like a broken security seal or something. If we can't find anyone over there, we'll have to call the Bartel people in New York and ask them what the next step is." I wondered if she was even less convinced there was merit in the plan than I was.

"Can't I wait for you?" she asked.

"It's risky. If you do, you'll have to keep your eye on that vapor cloud over the east end of the lake. The moment you even think it might be getting closer to the shoreline, bail out of there. Don't wait for me. Understand?"

"It's already raining hard enough that I can't tell exactly where the vapor cloud is," she said.

"You can smell that damn thing," I said. "If you even think you smell it, hit the bricks."

"Elliott," she said. "I'm frightened." She paused, then added, "I love you."

"Keep your eye on that vapor cloud," I said in answer. I wondered if the bravado sounded as hollow and plastic to her as it did me. "Holiday Inn, okay?"

When I heard her confirming okay, I hung up. Just as I did, there was a cracking noise, like a bullwhip. I saw Peters bolt for the door and disappear down the hall. There was a distant peal of thunder and then something that sounded like a moan. Peters was crouched down by the men's room at the end of the hall. He was bent over the figure of Cletus Mackey.

"Chesterton's loose!" he said. "He shot Mackey."

I raced to the front door of the council building and looked up and down the street. I couldn't

see anything, but it was raining hard enough
that I was convinced that I couldn't have seen
him if he had been directly across the street.

By the time I got back to Peters and Mackey,
the sheriff had his deputy sitting up. There was
a spreading black-crimson stain covering most
of his left side. At first I thought the bullet had
hit him in the lower left quadrant of the chest,
and then I realized it had caught the deputy in
the meaty underside of his left arm just above
the elbow. The blood came from a flesh wound
that probably looked a whole lot worse than it
actually was.

Mackey was already blubbering out excuses.
"He said he had to take a—but he said he couldn't
do it with his hands cuffed behind his back. So I
let him. . . ."

Peters was nodding. "He's got your .38, right?"

Mackey looked down, realizing for the first
time where Chesterton got the gun. He knew he
had been played for a fool.

"Has he been talking to you?" Peters asked.

Mackey shook his head. He was still rattled.

"Are you sure he didn't say anything that
might indicate what he might have been thinking
about? About getting out of here? About where
he might be going?"

Cletus Mackey was too confused to think
straight. For the moment, all he could do was
shake his head. Peters pulled the angular man to
his feet, took his handkerchief out of his pocket
and made a tourniquet.

"Come on, Elliott. Let's get him out to the
state police command post and see if they've

The Lake

got any first-aid gear. Then we're going after Chesterton."

I looked out the window at the downpour and darkness. I didn't like the idea of looking for a screwball with a police special, but my real concern was what the latest squall line was doing to the vapor cloud. When I shivered, I realized how much the temperature had dropped.

Sunday P.M., September 5

Peters headed out behind the council building to get his cruiser. I grabbed a phone, tried to call Cyn and let the phone ring ten times. While I waited, I watched the crew in the command post wrap something bulky and white around Mackey's arm.

By the time Harrison screeched around to the front of the building, he had received word from his dispatcher that one of Mackey's temporary deputies had spotted Chesterton running toward the marina. "At least we know where to start," Peters said.

The old man knew how to make time. We covered the five blocks to the public pier and the Jericho Marina in nothing flat. He jerked the Mercury into a broadside slide and blocked off the entrance to the pier. As I started to get out, he slapped open the door to the glove compartment, reached in and came out with a .32-

caliber Ladysmith. When I raised my eyebrows, he said, "No smart-ass remarks, Wages, I won it in a poker game. Know how to use one?"

I knew it wasn't the time to start telling Harrison Peters clever little stories about the nifty little survival kit I usually carried. I nodded, checked the safety and chamber, hefted it and hoped for the best.

The pier leading out to the marina complex was a good 50 yards wide with a montage of small souvenir shops and fast-food stands lining both sides to the boathouse. There was a ponderous ancient vintage Buick parked in front of the entrance to the marina. "Cover the other side," Peters said. He threw his door open, crawled out and darted into the shadows. I did the same thing on the other side of the pier. The brief but heavy rainstorm had slackened into an annoying drizzle, and I could feel water running down the back of my neck. For a moment or two, all I could hear was a pregnant silence. Then I began to be aware of other sounds: cars on the lake roads, horns honking, an occasional shout, a door slamming somewhere off in the distance. Then I heard running footsteps, a metallic clatter and a car door shut—sounds with an urgency about them. A car came around the corner, sliding on the wet pavement, from Baker Street and stopped next to Peters's Mercury.

The headlights turned off and Cletus Mackey, arm in a sling, got out. He had cozied the nose of his cruiser up tight against Peters's car so that the entrance to the pier was completely blocked off.

Across the pier, Peters was doing an older man's version of the police crouch, weapon drawn, moving toward the marina, keeping close to the storefronts. He was moving from shadow to shadow, disappearing then reappearing again.

"How's the arm?" I whispered back at Mackey.

"Hurts like a son of a bitch. I'll stay here and make sure Chesterton doesn't get past the two of you." His voice had the ring of a man who had a score to settle. I watched him lean across the hood of his car with a double-barreled shotgun, and I remembered that Chesterton still had Mackey's police special. I knew the shotgun wasn't sheriff's department issue, but I had a hunch Cletus Mackey was just as comfortable with it as he was with the .38 Chesterton was packing.

I curled back around, worked my way past a Tastee Freeze stand and slipped into the shadows of a place that had been offering Jubilee goers foot-long hotdogs with Jericho sauce.

"You movin' up?" Peters hissed from his side of the pier. He sounded as if he was out of breath. I couldn't see him. All of the lights had been turned off except two mercury-vapor security lights at the end of the pier. One was focused out over the flotilla of rental boats, while the other bathed the entrance to the marina shop in a bleached yellow. The rain gave the rest of the world a muted gray-black wash that made it almost impossible to see.

"Spotted him yet?"

"Not yet," Peters said, "but he's down there. I heard him."

I managed to get all six foot two inches of me hunkered down into what I figured would be the hardest target for Chesterton to hit and started inching my way toward the marina again. When I got to Sandy's Fish Shack, I straightened up again, glanced back and saw Mackey still sprawled over the hood of his car. If Chesterton decided to make a run for it, he had to get past the man with the double-barreled shotgun stationed in front of the giant billboard that read, *"Welcome To The 45th Annual Jericho Fisherman's Jubilee."*

From Sandy's, I moved ahead again, saw Peters work his way around the turnstiles, through the gate to the transit pier and position himself behind a trio of empty trash barrels.

"Stop right there, Harrison!" Chesterton shouted.

Peters didn't respond. From where I was positioned, I couldn't see either of them.

"I'm warning you, Harrison. Don't try anything stupid. I've got Rudy Perrymore in here with me."

I didn't have the slightest idea who Rudy Perrymore was, but when the small figure of a boy was momentarily thrust out into the light of the mercury vapors and jerked back into the shadows again, I got the message. Chesterton was holding the boy hostage.

"Let the kid go," Peters said. This time his voice was measured. "You're only making matters worse."

At that point I had no way of knowing whether Chesterton knew I was there or not. I crept up another ten or so feet, making certain he didn't see me.

"I'm getting out of here, Harrison," Chesterton said, "and I'm taking the Perrymore kid with me." That time around I heard a stress in Chesterton's voice I hadn't heard before. "Be smart. Stay where you are, Harrison, and no one will get hurt. I know you got a gun, so drop it. Drop it so I hear it hit the planking. Then I want you to move out into the light so I can see you better."

There was another silence.

"Damn it, Harrison, I said I wanted you out in the light where I can see you. Now move."

The rain had started coming down again, harder than before. I saw a brief flash of lightning over the boathouse and heard a low, continuous roll of thunder.

"You're acting like a goddamn fool, Felix," Peters shouted. "Let the kid go. It isn't worth it. Taking that boy hostage will only make matters worse."

"Worse?" Chesterton said. "How the hell can it get any worse? You still don't get the picture do you, Peters? You and the goddamn hick-town mentality of the people in Jericho make me sick. The way everyone around here sees it, there is always a tomorrow. Well I got news for you, Harrison. There ain't going to be any more waiting for tomorrow for Felix Chesterton. I'm out of time. I've played out my string. I'm through waiting."

The Lake

I was surprised when I saw Peters stand up and step out from behind the barrels. He dropped his revolver. It made the kind of sound Felix Chesterton wanted to hear. "Look, Felix. Whatever is wrong, we can fix it."

"This was my way of fixing it, Harrison. This was my trump card. My hand is played out. I lost everything I had on that Bartel deal. Foster Wallace was trying to break me. He loaned my syndicate the money to buy those damned farms outside of town, and then he undercut me with that damn tax land. You know why, Harrison? Because he wanted to ruin me. He wanted to ruin me so his damn daughter wouldn't have anything to do with me. He wanted me to get out of her life, and then he wanted me to crawl out of town with my tail between my legs."

Peters stood in the rain listening.

"But I got even. I ran the old bastard off the road and then I set the bog on fire. Without Foster Wallace, there was no way Bartel could have pulled off that deal on the old tax land from the proving ground. If it hadn't been for Cynthia coming back and pushing her daddy's deal through, I would have come out of that Bartel deal set for life."

"You got your wires crossed, Felix. Shutting down the Jubilee has nothing to do with all of that," Peters said calmly.

"You still don't understand, Harrison. Cynthia Wallace, Jericho's bitch banker, is behind all of this. She's putting the heat on me; she knows I can't come up with the money. I was desperate. I mortgaged everything I had. I bankrolled this whole damn festival for a cut of the action. Every cent I could scrape together is behind those guarantees. When Marlboro closed us down, he cut off my last hope. I could have held Cynthia Wallace off with my slice of the action."

Peters was silent for a moment. Then he said, "You better let the Perrymore kid loose and get out of this before you get in any deeper." The rain was dripping down off the rim of his hat.

"Not this time, Harrison. I got a better idea. I heard about what's going on over at that Bartel factory, and I got an idea that can make you and me a lot of money."

I knew Harrison was stalling when he said, "Let's hear it."

Chesterton's voice cracked on the verge of hysteria. "The people at Bartel in New York are nervous, right? Nervous about the stability of that stuff they're storing over there. I overheard you talking to Wages about it."

"What about it?" Peters asked.

"We go over to that Bartel plant. Then we call them and we tell them that we can fix what's wrong." There was a pause before he began again. "But we want bucks—big bucks." His voice was stretched to the limit. "They can't afford not to, Harrison. They've got millions invested; they'll gladly pay it. They can't afford to let this whole thing blow up in their face."

Chesterton's voice trailed off into a childlike whimper; they were the sounds of a desperate man makes while he watches his dreams go down the proverbial tube.

"Won't work," Peters said. His voice had become dry and unemotional. With the slightest tilt of his head he was giving me a subtle signal to move in. I slipped around a couple of trash barrels, and all of a sudden I spotted Chesterton. He had the muzzle of Mackey's revolver tucked up under the boy's chin.

"He's got the kid right in front of him," I whispered back to Peters. "I don't think I can get a clean shot."

I saw Harrison change his stance; obvious body language—the old boy was clever. He looked as though he was actually thinking about Chesterton's proposal. "Know somethin', Felix? That little scheme of yours, it just might work. You're right. Those Bartel people do have a ton of money tied up over there. They just might be willing to pay."

Chesterton straightened up. "Hell yes, they'll buy it. They've got more to lose than we do." If Chesterton believed that, I thought to myself, he wasn't just irrational, he had completely lost touch.

"If we're gonna pull this off, Felix, we'll have to get with it," Peters said. "They're makin' noises like we're runnin' out of time."

Chesterton was gaining confidence. "It'll work, Harrison, it'll work. I know it will. You and me— we're their only hope. What's a few bucks to a firm as big as Bartel?"

It occurred to me that, if I ever sat down and talked to a rational Felix Chesterton again, I'd tell him exactly what money was to someone like Bartel. I crouched deeper in the shadows, waiting and getting wetter by the minute. Peters was playing the string out little by little, inch by inch. I was using the darkness and the shadows of a big Bomark double-deck party barge for cover; the name *Good Times* was lettered across the stern.

Then the break we were waiting for came. There was a sudden shift in the wind blowing across the pier and a single-masted Bird Song anchored to Chesterton's left swung around and banged noisily against the pilings. Chesterton momentarily lost his concentration, and I bolted out of the shadows straight for him.

My plan was sound. My timing was atrocious. Chesterton was just as big as I was and, as it turned out, a whole lot quicker. He shoved the Perrymore kid at me, and the youngster's hurtling body hit me knee high, taking both legs out from under me. Our bodies tangled, the kid hit the planking butt first and old Elliott landed right on top of him.

Chesterton, rattled, didn't wait; he opened fire. I heard one slug rip into the oil-stained oak boards next to my head and splinters peppered my face and neck. A second bullet gouged out a piece of wood the size of a baseball next to the Perrymore kid's head. I rolled over, grabbed the boy, shoved him toward the *Good Times* and kept rolling myself. Two more shots chunked into the floor of the pier and I heard the metallic click of a firing pin striking an empty chamber. Chesterton reacted the same way I would have—he threw the .38 at me. It ricocheted off the pier a good three feet from me and splashed when it hit the water.

The Lake

By then Peters had recovered his own weapon and I saw him out of the corner of my eye. Chesterton made his move—a dive straight for the Perrymore boy. I came up on my knees and catapulted everything I had right into His Honor's midsection. The air went out of him, he groaned, rolled over and came up with one of those Bruce Lee moves that only true athletes can make. His leg took both of mine off from under me and I hit the deck again— on my back, hard. He got two quick blows in before I could roll over, scramble to my feet and jerk my knee up into his crotch like a sledgehammer. He reeled backwards, yelling profanities and protests, rolled right on over and came up again. He lunged and buried his big muscular shoulder right in my face. Something went ping in my brain and the world of E. G. Wages went all haywire. I dropped to my knees and Chesterton's foot caught me in the side of the head. My head wobbled sideways and a big black hole opened up and pulled me in. There was a strange vibrating high-pitched noise.

From somewhere in my fuzzy little world came the sound of a shotgun, a scream and metal shredding, but someone was thoughtful enough to close the manhole cover and I didn't have time to think about it.

Reentry was like walking through a mental mine field. Mushy-mouthed hobgoblins tried to claw me back into the hole with them. I couldn't understand a thing they were saying. They sounded like munchkins, with irritating little voices. I peeled one eye open in the hopes I could catch a glimpse of Dorothy and Toto, but the kid staring down at me didn't look like either of them. Finally the words that were all out of sync with the way his mouth moved began to get through to me.

I pushed myself up on my elbows and looked around. Peters was flat on his back, thrashing around like a speared fish. The monster Buick was gone, and there was one hell of a space between where Mackey and Peter's patrol cars had been guarding the entrance to the pier.

"He took your gun, and he shot Sheriff Peters," the kid blubbered. "Then he jumped in my car and rammed his way in between the two patrol cars. He got away."

Your car?" I said. What the hell was this world coming to? The kid didn't look old enough to pay adult fare on the rollercoaster and he owned a car? I struggled to my feet and hobbled over to where Peters was. The big man didn't even wait for me to ask him what had happened. It came spewing out of him peppered with every four-letter word in his limited vocabulary. "I couldn't get a shot at the son of a bitch because you and the Perrymore kid were in my line of fire. If I ever get my hands on him, I'll castrate that asshole."

It occurred to me that Peters had a few wrinkles in his anatomical plans for Chesterton, but I didn't point them out. Instead I started poking around to see where he had been hit. The Ladysmith had made a tidy little hole in the fleshy part of his left thigh, and a second

shot had creased his left shoulder. The two-inch
barrel on a .32 in the hands of an amateur can
leave a bit to be desired. I told Peters I had to
check on Mackey and went up the Pier to check
on the deputy's condition. He was a lot worse off
than his boss. The shotgun was still clutched in
his hand and he was breathing, but barely.

"How fast can you run?" I asked the kid.

"I was on the Jericho track team," he said.

"Then get your skinny little butt in gear and
see how fast you can get to the state police command post up at the council tent. Tell them what
happened and tell them we need help."

He sprinted off, leaving me to tend to Peters
and Mackey. There was an electric crackling
sound directly overhead, like the belch of fire
from a giant howitzer, and the instantaneous
crescendo of a thousand kettledrums followed
on its heels. The deck of low-hanging clouds
shredded into a soaking downpour and everything was again obscured. "Go ahead," I said to
the sky, "everyone else has."

The nerve center of the state police command
post turned out to be a good place to take inventory. One of the troopers peeked, probed and
picked at Peters's bullet holes until he could make
an assessment. "The one in his leg is superficial.
The one in his shoulder is about the size of a
golf ball." The same lady who had been pouring funseekers watered-down lemonade earlier
in the day inspected Peters too. Satisfied, she
went to a first-aid kit, extracted a handful of
supplies and put an end to Peters's bleeding.

She had me rinse my mouth out with distilled alcohol, counted my teeth, then made sure my nose was in one piece and still situated in the middle of my face before pronouncing me fit to return to battle. "Keep your eye on him though," she said, pointing to Peters. "He's lost a lot of blood." I felt better when Peters informed me that the lemonade lady used to be a nurse before she married for money.

I was still half afraid to ask Peters what our next step was when Marlboro and Manion arrived. The man from Carmi was white as a sheet and the commander didn't look much better.

"Damn glad we found you," Marlboro said. "We've got more trouble."

Manion, visibly shaken, confirmed it. "The vapor cloud came ashore less than thirty minutes ago when the wind shifted. The whole eastern basin of the lake is socked in. We've got cars backed up, bumper to bumper, all the way from Herd's grocery to the edge of town."

Marlboro went to the map of Jericho Lake where the traffic-control points had been established. He was pointing to the fork in the road marked *CP-A*. "The trooper at this checkpoint says that when the wind shifted in that last squall line, the vapor cloud changed direction and started moving toward shore. He's estimating that there may be anywhere from forty to fifty cars trapped in there."

"These squall lines have erratic wind patterns," Manion said. "We can't be certain which way the stronger gusts of wind will push the vapor cloud

266

or, for that matter, how fast. The movement of that damn thing is solely dependent upon the wind shifts."

Fighting with Chesterton had given me a splitting headache, but I still tried to comprehend the significance of what Manion was saying. "Then you're telling us the east fork of the Fort Janes road is sealed off?"

Marlboro studied the map. "For the moment. Even if it recedes we don't know what that does for us. The road could be clogged with cars just like that one we found with those kids on the bridge this morning." He looked at Peters. "Tell me about these other roads."

A wobbly Harrison Peters traced his finger along the routes of the various roads in the Jericho Lake vicinity. "This one takes you through Montana Mills, but if the vapor cloud is over the shoreline at that end of the lake, that means you would have to pass all of the Fort Janes traffic over the stone bridge. You've seen that bridge, it's narrow, one vehicle at a time. If the cloud should happen to shift back in that direction it becomes a choke point. Anyone caught in that vicinity wouldn't have any way out—except to get out of his car and run." His finger jumped to another place on the map. "This road circles back and goes up on a ridge overlooking the lake; it's gravel, narrow, has a good thirty foot drop off on either side. What really makes it bad is the old iron bridge over Mackmore Creek; it's been condemned for years. It might hold up for a while, but it wouldn't take anything heavier than a passenger car."

R. Karl Largent

"What about this one?" Marlboro asked, pointing to a blue line leading directly west away from the lake.

"That's a firebreak line through the state forest. Four-wheelers could get through there, but not much else."

Manion perched himself on the edge of the desk and studied the map as Peters stoked new life into what was left of his cigar. "According to the weather bureau, these squall lines will be sweeping through for another three or four hours. Every time one comes through we'll have to be on guard for a shift in the vapor cloud."

Peters's jowly face was a complete grimace. "Suppose we didn't try to outrun it?"

"You've seen what happens when someone inhales that stuff, Sheriff," Manion said. "Anyone caught in its path is going to suffer the same fate as those kids on the bridge."

"Look, I know it sounds farfetched, but what if we routed the folks that are left down to the old high school and then started sealing the building off from the inside."

"How the hell are you going to do that?" Marlboro asked.

"Plastic sheeting, furnace tape, anything we can lay our hands on. Seal every window, every entrance and exit, the vents on the roof, everything."

Manion looked around the tent. The rain had subsided again. "It sounds farfetched, but it could work. It's one hell of a long shot though. If it didn't work, the people trapped in that building would face certain death."

The Lake

Peters grabbed a felt-tipped marker and began sketching the layout of the old high school on the map. "The school was closed down two years ago when Jericho County consolidated its school system. The school complex consists of three buildings. The big building is where the classrooms are located. It could hold up to two thousand, the gymnasium might hold another twelve hundred or so and the maintenance building another hundred—maybe a few more."

"Hell, Sheriff, there are at least seven to eight thousand people still trapped out there. You're talking about trying to save no more than a third of them."

"What if we keep routing them out of Jericho on some of these narrow back roads until we get clogged up and then use the old school complex as our last resort?"

Marlboro looked at Manion. "What do you think? Think we can seal off that building well enough to keep the cloud out?"

"It's risky," Manion said. "If we have two or three thousand people holed up in that school and the vapor-cloud gases start seeping in through some vent or window that we've overlooked, we could have another Dachau on our hands."

Peters went back to the map again. "The first step is to get your men to start routing traffic on the two alternate routes. Tell them they'll have to pull the big RVs off the road. Have the people in anything bigger than a passenger car or a van ride out with strangers. I don't know how long that old bridge will hold up but at least we can

269

stack the cards in our favor. Tell them to pass the word along to the four-wheelers that they can try the old firebreak up through the state park—but only the four-wheelers."

Manion looked apprehensive. "We need Lady Luck on our side for a while, and we need to be able to keep people out of the path of that damn vapor cloud until these squall lines quit marching through. If we can do that, we just might be able to help some of these people survive what may turn out to be the worst night of their lives. It's a good thing you and Wages were able to get through to the Bartel plant and get that situation stabilized. The last thing we need is to start pumping highly toxic and unstable CpP into this environment."

Peters shook his head. "We never made it to the Bartel plant. We were called back when Chesterton escaped."

Manion made a noise like someone had let the air out of him. "You mean we don't know what the situation is over at Bartel?"

"That's exactly what I mean," Peters said.

A few minutes later Charley Marlboro had everyone gathered in the council tent. The state police had established a direct line to the governor's office and we were no longer working through aides. Governor Vernon Matthews himself was doing the talking. The schedule called for Marlboro to update the governor every 30 minutes.

Two of Marlboro's troopers had been pulled in from the roadblocks and brought back to the nerve center. One of them was assigned to coordinate the effort to get the traffic rerouted off the lake road, back through the village and north on the gravel road over the ridge. Some cars were being allowed to filter out an access road used by the power company, and their drivers were instructed to stay south of the Montana Mills road and avoid the stone bridge. A few four-wheelers were starting to be dispatched up the firebreak, but progress was slow on all of the roads. The storms were coming in sudden but brief, drenching torrents, and the access road and firebreak lanes were quickly becoming quagmires.

Peters instructed his dispatcher to get through to the Fort Janes Telephone Company. He wanted them involved in trying to make contact with the Bartel people in New York, because we had to know what the latest was on their security situation.

After finishing his conversation with the governor, Marlboro hung up the phone and turned toward Peters. "Governor Matthews is ready to activate the Air National Guard if we can figure out a way to use their help."

"Hell of a lot of good that will do us," Peters grumbled. "There's no way to get them in and no way to get them out once they get here."

"Unit Two just reported in," the trooper monitoring the field communications said. "They report they've got a situation developing over at the grocery store near the roadblock. They've got two carloads of drunk kids who're getting belligerent. They're insisting on going through the roadblock. Unit Two is requesting assistance."

"Send two men out there," Marlboro said, "and tell Parker if anyone else gets out of line, he has the authority to cave in some damned heads. That'll get their attention. While you've got him, have Parker give us a check on that vapor cloud."

The trooper made the request and waited. I could hear static on the other end of the line. Finally he said, "Parker says it has spread all the way across the road back up into the woods. Says it's about five hundred yards down the road from him and definitely moving."

"Ask him how many gas masks he has and how far out over the lake it's reaching," Manion said.

The young man repeated Manion's question and waited. "Can't tell," he finally said. "Parker has two masks and he claims it's raining too hard to tell where one begins and the other ends."

Peters chewed on his cigar, lit it, took one drag and let it go out again. He continued to stare at the map. "What about the unit on the ridge road. If CP-A is close to that damn vapor cloud, that means it's getting close to the junction in the road leading up to the ridge as well."

"CP-C, this is base. Give us a status report."

Static.

"Repeat, CP-C, this is base. How about an update?"

More static.

The operator turned to Marlboro. "Could be the damn rain or it could be something else, sir."

Marlboro snapped up the phone and hit the button on the hot line. There was a momentary lull. "Matthews here," a man said.

Marlboro cleared his throat. "It's getting worse, Governor. We just received a report that indicates the vapor cloud has moved across the only main road for getting the traffic out of town. For all practical purposes, the people still here are trapped."

The dispatcher leaned over and whispered in Peters's ear. "I just got through to CP-C. A Winnebago tried to get through the old bridge and it collapsed. They've got a family of six trapped in the wreckage down in the ravine. CP-C is requesting the assistance of a medical team."

"Put a call out for any EMTs that might be willing to help," Peters ordered. He tapped Marlboro on the shoulder and relayed the news.

"We've just been informed that one of our alternate routes has been closed off as well," Marlboro said.

There was a prolonged silence at the governor's end of the line. Finally he said, "How many people do you estimate are still in the Jericho area?"

Marlboro was guessing. He shrugged his shoulders. "Seventy-five hundred, maybe more. The Fort Janes weather bureau says that the string of squall lines seems to be building in intensity. In Montgomery, west of here, they are reporting winds up to thirty-five miles an hour and gusts to forty-five with golf-ball-size hail, lots of damage."

I was beginning to think Peters's idea about
herding people into the old high school building
had some merit.

"What about helicopters, Commander? Could
we evacuate some of these people with helicopters? The guard unit at Culver City has those big
T-77-A personnel carriers."

"It's worth a try, Governor. How soon can you
get them here?"

Matthews's end of the line fell silent again. It
was obvious he was working two phones. His
voice began to crackle through again. "I've got
Gen. Kaplan on the other line. Most of his units
are in Wisconsin on maneuvers. He has three
standby units he can mobilize. But it will take
them a couple of hours to get there and then it
will depend on the weather."

"We need 'em, Governor. Pray for a break in
the weather." He hung up and looked at Peters.
"What's our power situation?"

"Most of the village doesn't have any. We are
operating on generators but I think I know where
I can get my hands on a few more."

"Find them and get them down to the football
field at the old high school. That'll be where
the choppers put down if we get a break in the
weather. Without those lights, we're dead in the
water."

Peters limped out the door followed by one of
the troopers.

Marlboro turned to the dispatcher. "Anything
new from CP-A?"

The young trooper's voice was shaky. "Yes,
sir," he nodded, "I just logged a transmission

from CP-D, Barkdull. He said he lost sight of the roadblock at CP-A ten minutes ago."

Manion looked at the map and mentally calculated the distance between the two checkpoints. "That can't be more than two hundred yards. It must be raining very hard down there."

"No, sir," the young man said hollowly. "He said they were swallowed up by that vapor cloud."

It was Marlboro's turn to fall silent. He sat looking at the bank of communication gear until he realized that they were waiting on him to give the order. He cleared his throat as though the announcement would have to carry out to all the checkpoints by itself. "Put me through to CP-D," he said.

"CP-D, Barkdull."

"Larry, turn 'em around if you can. Head 'em back into town. If it's going to take too long to get them turned around, tell them to abandon their cars and start walking. Tell them they'll be able to see the lights from the high school football field in a few minutes. That's where they should be headed."

"Commander?"

"Go ahead, Larry."

"I saw that damn vapor cloud swallow up Masters and Hamilton. After I get these folks headed back into town, I'd like to go up there and check on those two to see if there is anything I can do."

"Better not chance it," Marlboro said. "If they inhaled that stuff there isn't a damn thing you can do for them."

THREE

Sunday P.M., September 5

Marlboro parceled out assignments to his dwindling cadre of human resources, and when he finished he turned to me. "Look, I know this isn't your problem, Wages, but we need all the help we can get. Are you still with us?"

I looked at the beleaguered hulk of Harrison Peters sitting on a bench across the room and thought about what other real options I had. What else was there to do with a rainy Sunday night?

"Where the hell would I go?" I said, forcing a smile. Deep down inside a little voice was asking me whether Clive Cussler or John D. MacDonald ever managed to get himself in situations like this.

"Good, because I need someone to start around the far side of the lake and make certain that everyone along the south shore has gotten the word on the evacuation. You'll have to hustle

though. The problem is getting stickier by the
minute, because with the power outage there is
no way to tell who has been informed and who
hasn't. You'll have to check every cottage, Elliott.
If you find people, tell them to grab a couple of
blankets and hightail it to the high school. I've
got a crew working on hooking up a couple of
generators so that we'll have enough lights for
those choppers to get in."

"What about Bartel?"

"As soon as we get something definitive from
the Bartel people, I'll get word to you."

I left Peters in the care of the overworked
lemonade lady and headed for the parking lot,
wondering if the Air Guard pilots would be
able to thread their way in and out between
the squall lines. Behind the driver's seat of
Ginny's Carrera, I dug out my old E. G. Wages
survival kit and fished around until I found a
couple of essentials: the Broomhandle Mauser,
a couple of spare ammo clips and a heavy duty
flashlight. I tucked the Broomhandle in my belt,
crawled behind the wheel and headed out of the
parking lot.

Most of the homes along the south shore of
Jericho Lake fell into the slightly ostentatious
category; all were good-sized estates. The upside
of that was there would be fewer places to check.
The downside was that they were also the folks
least likely to be involved in Jubilee activities
and, therefore, the least likely to be aware of
what was going on over on the other side of
the lake—unless of course they were fortunate
enough to have their radios on.

The Lake

To get to the south shore from the state police command center in the council tent, I had to drive through the darkened village. The absence of any light gave the streets an uneven, almost spectral dimension. Compounding the darkness was a cloak of swirling mist interspersed with frequent lightning and thunder and an occasional downpour; it was the stuff of surrealistic paintings. By the time I had threaded my way through the side streets to the southern edge of Jericho, the whole scene was playing weird games with my imagination.

The beams of the Carrera's headlights had difficulty piercing the wall of opaqueness. There was a temptation to move up a notch from a straining second gear, but it would have been folly. Most of the time I couldn't see more than 70 to 80 feet in front of me, and I was developing a disturbing sense of aloneness.

Fullmer Street was blocked. So I turned down the alley behind the darkened Jericho Music Store, passed to the rear of Cartwright's Plumbing Supplies and emerged on Seventh Street. Seventh, if it was clear, would take me through a tree-shrouded residential area that ran parallel with Front and eventually to the lake. The headlights picked up images of things I knew didn't exist in the real world, and I kept slowing for specters born out of nothing more than sheer apprehension. The narrow street ran north-south and melded into a long sweeping curve that followed the contour of the lakefront. At the intersection of Seventh and Lilac, I came to a small park with a pedestrian overlook. There

281

was a sign in front of the park that read, *"The Jericho Chamber of Commerce Invites You to Sit a Spell."*

I had no intention of sitting a spell, but I did intend to stop just long enough to see if I could get a fix on the vapor cloud. I remembered Cyn telling me the overlook was a place where the kids usually parked. From the lack of cars, I judged that the kids had apparently decided some things even had a higher priority than necking.

There was a six-foot-tall wooden observation platform and I climbed the steps. It gave me a vantage point from which I could see most of the downtown section of Jericho and the entire sweep of the southern shoreline. Everything was dark except for the marina's security lights and bunched clusters of headlights along the road where the state police were attempting to reroute the north shore traffic back into town toward the high school football field. The telltale muted, pinkish glow of the revolving lights on top of the police cars indicated where Marlboro had repositioned his men in hopes of averting further disasters. It was easy to conclude that there were far too many sets of headlights trying to thread their way back into the village and far too few officers to control them.

Looking out over the lake during one of the storms, I found it was no longer possible to determine where the spreading, shifting vapor cloud ended and the swirling obscurity created by the rain and mist began. It was gray on gray, black on black, accompanied by one continuous discordant symphony of distant thunder. As far as I was concerned there could have been a wall across the lake and I wouldn't have known the difference. I sniffed at the damp air to see if I could detect the odor and decided it was safe to proceed.

Back at the Carrera, I got in and rolled the window down as a precaution. Hoping to catch the smell of the vapor cloud before I drove right into it, I resolved to keep my speed under 20 miles an hour.

As I started to pull away, I caught sight of something out of the corner of my eye. Whatever it was, it was totally out of concert with the surroundings. I stopped, put the Carrera in reverse and brought the front end around so that the headlights would shoot out over the water.

What I saw was a small aluminum-hulled boat, beached on a sandbar about 20 yards offshore. On the shore lay a sandcastle, some toys, a portable radio, a beach chair and three bodies. I crawled out of the car, grabbed the flashlight, went down to the edge of the water and played the pale wash of light back and forth across the silent scene. The man's body was lying half in, half out of the water. The woman was lying face down on a beach towel and the child, or what was left of it, was lying beside her. It was impossible to tell whether it was a little boy or a girl.

I stood there for several minutes before deciding I could do nothing and headed back to the car. Less than a mile up the road was Sam Patton's place. I rationalized that I could report my macabre discovery from the phone at Sam's.

By the time I pulled back on the road, my imagination had already started playing mind games with me again; it seemed as though everywhere I looked I saw the vapor cloud. I rolled the window up, then down, sniffed at the damp air a couple of times and realized that, after 30 minutes, I was only at the edge of town.

South of the village, the road took a 90-degree bend east and then south again before dropping down to Sam's parking lot. It's situated on a little narrow strip that juts 60 or 70 yards out into the lake. As Cyn liked to point out, it was possible to pull a boat up to Sam's pier, tie up and do some serious drinking without having to worry about the drive home. She had not elaborated on the potential problems for an oversauced boater.

The moment I turned into Sam's parking lot I knew something was wrong. There was a Ford stationwagon stalled in the middle of the entrance to the parking lot. The lights were on and the driver's door was open, but the driver was nowhere in sight.

I pulled around the deserted car, turned the ignition off, took a quick sniff to make sure I wasn't walking into something I couldn't handle and snapped on the flashlight. It hadn't been raining for several minutes.

Sam Patton ran the kind of establishment that stayed open as long as the patrons wanted to drink, but at that moment, Patton's Pier was alarmingly quiet. There were seven cars scattered around the parking lot.

I had driven into Sam's convinced that I would find subdued but serious drinkers, who, having

284

assessed the network of clogged roads, decided there was no place to go and nothing better to do than hoist a few by candlelight. If I knew the crowd at Patton's Pier they were probably betting on the next direction of the vapor cloud. I had been at Sam's during power outages before, and the main man simply kept a running tab on a small slip of paper beside the cash register. Settle-up time came when the cash register was working again. If anything, I expected Sam and the boys to be discussing just how poorly Marlboro and his men were screwing up the evacuation process.

That wasn't the case.

The front door was standing open and it had rained in. Water had puddled just inside the door, and the floor was damp all the way back to the coat-check room. I held my breath and jabbed the pool-cue beam of light around the silent room. The thing that Ira Leonard had called a vapor cloud had come and gone.

Sam Patton was slumped over his beloved bar in front of the television set. I knew it was Sam because of the Cubs hat. If it hadn't been for the hat, I'm not sure I would have recognized him. He looked worse than Graham Hatcher's garpike. On the blackboard behind him, he had listed the specials and the Cubs's score:

Fish, all you can eat, $5.95
Seven Bean Soup, $1.95 a bowl
Giants 5 Cubs 4, 13 innings.

Sam Patton had not died a happy man.

I shoved the beam of light around the room. nsidious and deadly, the vapor cloud had carved its way into every nook and cranny. There was nothing selective about it. A couple had been sitting in one of the booths along the wall. There was a purse sitting on the table, but I wasn't able to tell which one it belonged to.

There were three more bodies at the bar and three cans of Colt 45. Beside them lay a deck of playing cards and a ten dollar bill. The boys' night out hadn't turned out quite like they had planned either. There was a body in front of the cigarette machine and one in the phonebooth. I decided not to try to call in. At this point it didn't seem to matter.

There may have been more, but I didn't want to hang around and take inventory. I had seen enough. The damage had already been done. The warning Marlboro had sent me out to deliver was way, way too late, and I was well aware that the vapor cloud could return at any time. As I left, I realized I might be the only person who had gotten out of Patton's bar alive in the last two or three hours.

Halfway across the parking lot I saw something move near Ginny's Porsche. I stopped, tried to focus and listened. It was one of those choking silences, the kind that convinces you there is a ringing sensation in your ears.

"Who's there?" I shouted.

As I waited, my eyes skimmed from one shadow to the next. There was the sound of gravel being scuffed.

"Who's out there?" I said again.

I dug out the Broomhandle. I wanted it where I could make use of it if I had to. I took three or four steps, aware of the sound of my own breathing, and I saw something emerge from the shadows behind the Porsche. It was upright but staggering and weaving with outstretched hands. Whoever he was, his face was little more than a subhuman mask of open sores and scalded flesh. He had a fat, protruding tongue around which he struggled to force out words.

"Help me, Wages," he pleaded.

I tucked the Mauser back in my belt and threw the beam of light up in his face. Half of the face was gone, but the other half belonged to Becker Herd. His acid-etched clothing was little more than rags.

"Wages," he moaned. He was reaching back into that part of his world where it all began. I was watching a man disintegrate into something that had never existed.

I reached out, but it was too little and too late.

He gasped for air and his bloated body pitched forward into the gravel. I knew there wasn't a damn thing I could do for him, except maybe tell someone, someday, that he tried to die with a modicum of dignity.

There were several seconds, maybe minutes before the thing that he was destined to become began to evolve. I closed my eyes until there were no more sounds.

Homage was brief—little more than a couple of seconds of silence during which I acknowledged that I had known him and that if I didn't get my ass out of there I could very well end up in much the same fashion. I muttered something that I intended to be an appropriate prayer, but which came out sounding more like an expression of fear.

I headed for the Porsche with a clearer understanding of Leonard's vapor cloud. It was spelled killer with a capital K. It had become an entity unto itself, an insidious, merciless, destructive force with a mind of its own, a thing with tentacles that reached out to kill indiscriminately. It was plundering everything in its path.

As I got back in the car, I began to realize that there was a pattern developing. The vapor cloud was sneaking ashore under the cover of the storms. It came ashore and retreated. In and out. There and gone. The unsuspecting were trapped. The heedless paid a terrible price. Even with the odor giving us warning, it had become a consummately efficient killer.

I rolled the window down, but more than ever, I was ready to retreat into my metal cocoon— poised to roll up the windows, turn off the vent fan, close the vents and pray like hell that the weather seals on the Porsche were good enough to keep out the poisonous vapors.

After what I had witnessed in Sam's place, the combination of mist, rain, wind and darkness had somehow managed to take on an even more ominous dimension. I turned on the ignition and began inching my way through the wall of chalky gray, muttering one prayer after another, wondering how much of my anguish resulted from an imagination stretched taut and how much from the reality of Jericho Lake.

The Lake

* * *

Several moments later, I came across the body of a dog lying in the middle of the road. Then I saw the bodies of several birds; they looked as though they had just dropped out of the trees. At each of the first three cottages I checked, there was no one at home. At another, an old man was just getting in his car, preparing to leave. He assured me that he and his neighbors had already heard the evacuation bulletin on the radio and had left for the high school. "Me and Gladys will be fine," he said.

I turned into the drive at Cyn's place and headed down the long lane toward the lake. Cyn's 450 was either gone or in the garage, and since she never took the time to put it away, I was betting on the former. I had already turned around and started back down the drive when something told me to double-check. I tested the air, got out, went up to the door and knocked. When I did, the door creaked open and it occurred to me that the summer-long creature comfortable world of Cyn's big house no longer seemed inviting.

"Cyn!" I shouted from the vestibule.

There was no answer.

"Hey, is anybody home? It's me, Elliott."

More silence.

I started shoving the beam of the flashlight around the foyer and listened. There is a difference in silences; that one made me feel uneasy.

My stomach was staging a minor revolt and I felt that funny little hard-to-describe feeling in my legs. I worked my way through the familiar foyer, down the corridor and into the kitchen.

Mrs. Fern was sitting in a chair next to the radio. The melted and pooled candle gave testimony to the fact that she had tried to cope with the darkness. I knew it was Mrs. Fern because of the beehived mouse-colored hair. I wouldn't have known her otherwise. On impulse, I reached down to see if she had a pulse, and a chunk of flesh fell away from her wrist when I touched her. My stomach did another somersault and began spewing out warnings that it wasn't going to tolerate much more.

From the appearance of things, she had made the transition from one life to another with a minimum of fanfare. Somehow though she had managed to avoid the ravages the others had suffered. Here and there, the cause of death was evidenced by small open sores and a tiny network of tears in the skin. I had no way of knowing it at the time, but in the next few minutes the devastation that was still going on inside her body was destined to ravage her like it had everyone else.

I looked around the kitchen. Behind her, an open window indicated how the killer had entered. What I couldn't explain were the wet footprints on the carpet. I probed the beam of light around the room several times more before I saw the cloud's second victim—Basketcase. The mangy cur that Bert Freeman would have no doubt described as the yappiest damn dog he had ever seen had found a way to look even worse than he had when he was alive. Patches of hair and a few unidentifiable body parts were all that remained.

290

The Lake

I went to the pantry, where Cyn kept what she called her romance package. I took out a couple of candles, lit one, sat it on the kitchen counter and diffused some of the darkness.

On a hunch, I decided to follow the wet tracks on the carpet. They went to the bottom of the stairway, then led to the second floor before they dried out.

On the landing there was a large oriental rug. I reached down, felt it and detected dampness. I heard a noise, raced down the hall and found Cyn in the bathroom, cowering like a terrified animal. Her lovely, symmetrical face was twisted into a mask of bruises, and she was sobbing. When she saw me, she screamed, covered her face with her hands and tried to retreat deeper into her nightmare world.

"What the hell happened?" I asked as I started to bend toward her. She struck out at me and kicked, and then she screamed.

"Don't touch me," she hissed.

"Cyn, it's me, Elliott."

She closed her eyes tight, shutting out the world, and then she covered her face with her hands again.

"It's all right," I said, trying to keep my voice even. "It's me, Elliott. I'm here."

She opened her eyes. They were puffy and bloodshot. She was trembling. There was no trace of recognition.

"Cyn, what happened?"

She was staring through me, as though I was something she didn't want to see. Her swollen lips quivered, and there was a trace of blood at the corner of her mouth. She blinked, started to reach out for me and withdrew again.

I stood, got a washcloth, dampened it with cold water and touched it to the battered areas of her face. "What happened?" I said evenly.

She continued to stare at me, but finally there was a flicker of recognition. Like an uncertain child she began to reach out. After a momentary withdrawal came a desperate grasping, a clutching, then holding and clinging accompanied by racking sobs. She finally managed my name. With a small voice she said, "Elliott, is that you?"

"Hold on, Cyn, just hold on. Everything is going to be alright."

It was neither the time nor the place to tell her what had happened downstairs, but I was worried that Bartel's silent killer would come back again. Unlike whoever had hurt Cyn, it didn't leave bruises. It left a silent and insidious trail of death and destruction.

Cyn was still holding on with all the strength she could muster when I said, "Look, we're in a tight spot. We've got to get out of here. It isn't safe here."

She looked up at me and her eyes were still glazed. "He won't dare come back with you here."

"Who won't come back?"

Her eyes searched my face. "Felix," she said. Her voice was barely audible, as though there might have been an immense risk in revealing who had assaulted her.

"Felix Chesterton was here?"

She nodded. "He said this was his way of getting even with me for carrying through on my father's deal with the Bartel people."

"Did you know about your father's plan to ruin Chesterton?"

Cyn closed her eyes for a moment, then nodded.

"And you threatened to call his loan anyway?"

She nodded again.

There was a hell of a lot more that needed to be explained to get to the bottom of the Bartel land deal; but the vapor cloud clawing its way around and over Jericho Lake had to get first priority.

"We've got to get out of here. Can you walk?"

"I think so," she said and nodded.

I helped her to her feet and started her toward the door. When I did, I noticed just the faintest trace of the telltale odor again. I flashed the beam of light down the stairwell and saw the searching gray tentacles of the vapor cloud creeping up over the first two or three stairs as though it had returned to search out more victims.

I slammed the door, grabbed a handful of towels, and crammed them up against the opening under the bottom of the door. Then I opened the window slightly and tested the air. When I decided it was safe, I opened it the rest of the way. "Kick off your shoes," I said, "and follow me."

When she hesitated, I said, "Hurry, damn it. We don't have much time."

There was a five-foot drop down to the roof of the house's east wing, and from there it was anyone's guess. As I crawled along, I coaxed

Cyn through and we worked our way along the rooftop searching for a place where the ground-hugging vapor cloud didn't have the house surrounded. The beam from my flashlight searched out the Porsche, and I knew I was going to have a whole lot of explaining to do. Ginny's silver pride and joy was cloaked by the clinging gray death cloud. It was too easy to remember what had happened to the car on the bridge.

The vapor cloud had not worked its way all the way to the back of the house, and it looked as if there was a safe area to drop to the ground from the roof of the garage. Cyn didn't have to be told the second time. "Over the edge," I said, grabbed her arm and lowered her as far as I could. She fell the last two or three feet, hit the ground and rolled over. When she stood up, I tossed her the flashlight, then jumped.

By the time I got to my feet, the stench of the vapor cloud was overwhelming. My eyes began to tear and I clamped my hand over her mouth. "Hold your breath. Run as hard and as far as you can. I'll lead the way."

We ran the entire length of that long winding lane before we dared to stop. My chest was pounding. I sniffed cautiously once, then again. Then I opened my mouth and gulped in the untainted air.

Cyn, chest heaving, sagged to her knees. She cried, then giggled, then started to cry again. I crouched down on the blacktop beside her and put my arm around her. Cyn had held on tight before, but never quite as tight as she did then.

"We're not out of the woods yet," I said. "Now we've got to figure out a way to get back to the old high school."

While we knelt there in the darkness, I was aware of the increasing frequency of the lightning and thunder. It had started to pour again.

There is no way of knowing how long we had been walking when I saw the headlights of a car approaching. I felt elation before I remembered it might be Chesterton; he had taken Cyn's 450. I got a grip on the Broomhandle, just in case.

When the vehicle slowed, I recognized the Carmi insignia and the anxious face of Arnold Manion. "Where the hell have you been?" he said, reaching across and opening the car door. "Marlboro has been looking for you. We've managed to get a clarification on the Bartel situation."

I put Cyn in the back seat, wrapped a blanket around her and crawled in beside Manion. As he headed back for the village, I gave him a capsule summary of what had happened, and he brought me up to speed.

"Peters said to tell you they found the body of a guy by the name of Hoppkins. They found him in his car. It had rolled down the bank behind the hospital. It was half submerged in the river. Peters seemed to think the body had been there for a couple of days. There wasn't much left of him."

Hoppkins was a name and a face, and I didn't know him as well as I did Hatcher and Freeman. But he had been waging and winning his own personal war against his own demons. I had questions about the death of Doc Hoppkins, but I knew no one had the answers.

At the Jericho village limits, we hit the first and only roadblock. A rain-drenched trooper took off his gas mask, flagged us down, poked his head in the car and started to give us directions to the high school before he recognized Manion.

"What's the latest?" Manion asked.

"Haven't heard anything for the last ten minutes or so," the officer said. "They had the lights on for a few minutes down at the football field but they went out. Don't know what happened."

"Are you okay?" Manion asked.

"Yeah, outside of the fact that I'm as nervous as a whore at High Mass. From what they're telling us, there is no way to know where the hell that damn cloud is. And I'm hearing from the other outposts that these gas masks aren't doing the job. It's getting pretty spooky out here."

"What's the traffic situation on the north side of the lake?"

"Still all jammed up. CP-D claims he has four to five hundred cars snarled over there, about half of them have already been abandoned and most of the people have started to walk back toward the village."

"Are any of the other routes open?" I asked.

He shook his head.

"Any later word on the helicopters?" Manion asked.

The trooper peeled back the sleeve of his yellow slicker and glanced at his watch. "The first one should be here in another thirty minutes, if they can get the damn lights on so the pilot can locate the football field. Apparently these birds aren't equipped with night vision devices."

We left the man standing in the rain and drove straight to the council building. Manion started to go through town, saw people breaking windows and looting and took a side street. The street in front of the council building where the state police command post had been set up was a jungle of deserted vehicles—cars, campers, pickup trucks and a semi-trailer full of elaborately painted merry-go-round horses. I hustled Cyn out of Manion's station wagon and into the command post. The lemonade lady took one look at her and escorted her to the ladies room.

The command post was now being run by a generator, and we were told that Marlboro was inside the council building on the phone to the governor. A trooper let us pass and we stepped into a smoke-choked room lit by two sparse lights and a few candles. I had a disturbing flashback to a crowded operations room next to a small landing strip in 'Nam and felt sweat trickle down my already soaked back. Even though I had vowed I would never go back, I had; it was still a nightmare.

Peters was limping toward me. He had spotted us when we brought Cyn in. "How is she?"

"Shook up. Chesterton worked her over."

Peters didn't seemed surprised. "Did you see him?"

I shook my head. "He took off before I got there. He took Cyn's car. No telling where he is now."

"What about the rest of the people on that side of the lake?"

I shook my head. "The cloud got there before we did."

Sunday P.M., September 5

As battered as Harrison Peters was, he was still hanging in there. When Marlboro left the room, he took Manion and me aside and told us he still wanted us to see if we could get to the Bartel plant. "As chaotic as everything is around here, the Bartel people in New York have managed to get through to the state police dispatcher in Fort Janes twice within the last hour. They say it's imperative that we locate either Blackmonn or Mueller. If we can't locate them, they want us to send a representative of the Sheriff's department over to the plant to see if we can get those ovens started."

"What the hell are we going to be able to tell them even if we do find a way to get in there?"

"The tough part will be getting inside the plant. Once you're in, you go to the security room on the second level. There is a security screen and lock on the door. They say they can walk you through it if you can get past the first barrier. They have a theory that since they already have Elliott's voice on their security identification and recall tape in New York they can override the computer's reject sequence and clear you on the blue line. Remember blue, it's important."

"Blue," Manion said. "Sounds easy enough. Then they talk us through the correction sequence, right?"

Peters nodded. "They think it will work."

"Still no word on the whereabouts of either Blackmonn or Mueller?" I asked.

Peters shook his head and looked at Manion. "You sure you want in on this one, Doc? It could be dangerous. I wouldn't be asking Elliott here to go, except he's the only one the Bartel people have a voice profile on. And he is also the only one of us that's been inside that damn plant."

"I'm the logical one to go with Elliott. I talk the Bartel people's language." He forced a small smile and looked anxiously around the room. "Besides, as Elliott said earlier, what else is there to do around here for the next couple of hours?"

Peters looked relieved. I could see that he was already turning his attention to the next item on his agenda. As I started to leave, he grabbed my arm. "Elliott," he said, his voice backing up on him. "Good luck."

Manion and I headed for the parking lot behind the council building, and I stopped just long enough to poke my head in the room where the lemonade lady had taken Cyn. The lemonade lady saw me, held her finger up to her lips and informed me that she had given Cyn a sedative.

My banker friend was curled up on a cot, asleep. "Will you need help getting her down to the high school for the evacuation helicopters?"

"I'll manage," the woman said. "Now, get out of here and let her rest."

By the time I got through the tent and out to the curb, Manion was waiting in the Carmi station wagon. I crawled in and began directing him through a maze of back streets. He was driving with the windows down, continually sniffing at the air as he drove. I could hear the glass breaking and shouts of looters as we passed within a block of the business district. At Front Street, he turned right and headed south on a route that would eventually dead end into the lake road leading back past Patton's Pier. We both rolled up our windows as rain began pelting the car again. It was another passing squall line. The windshield wipers were working overtime.

Less than 100 yards after passing the village limits sign, we came across a pickup truck in a ditch. The window on the driver's side was open and the driver's arm was hanging out the window. He had almost made it. The truck, heavily damaged, had veered across the road and plowed into a stone culvert. When Manion slowed, I got out, probed the beam of my flashlight around the interior of the truck's cab, crawled back in the car and shook my head. "Nothing we can do for him. Better keep going."

Manion was cautious. We threaded our way along the twisting road at less than 20 miles an hour. We kept the windows open to detect the vapor cloud, and rain soaked us. It was a route that I had walked dozens of times during the course of the summer, from Patton's place past Graham Hatcher's cottage back to Ginny's, and only then did I realize how few details of my surroundings I could actually remember. Every turn was unfamiliar, every twist in the road another place for the vapor cloud to await its next victim. The rain slackened and we inched our way past the drive to Cyn's place. We were halfway to the Montana Mills road and so far no vapor cloud.

Manion had both hands on the wheel, his eyes fixed on the road ahead. "How much farther?"

"We'll come to a fork in the road about a half mile ahead. The lake road veers to the left, the Montana Mills road to the right. That's the one we want."

At the canvas shop, Manion had to slow. A red Mustang convertible with Illinois license plates was sitting in the middle of the road. The lights were on, the motor running and the driver's door open. The driver hadn't made it more than 10 feet from his car. A rain-soaked, motionless pile of debris was all that remained. Manion maneuvered us around the Mustang and continued on. "It's like a goddamn war zone," he muttered.

When we came to the fork in the road, the police blockade had already been abandoned. The lake road leading to the stone bridge twisted off until it disappeared into the darkness. Manion stopped and I pointed to the right. "That's the one we want."

He sniffed cautiously as I said, "The road loops away from the lake for about a quarter of a mile

and then comes back down until it runs parallel
with the slough."

Manion nodded, wet his finger and held it
out the window. "No breeze. Now there's no
way to tell which way that damn thing may be
drifting."

Over my shoulder I could see repeated flashes
of lightning, and I knew that it was only a matter of minutes until another squall line moved
through.

"The conditions are right for a tornado, you
know. The air is unstable," Manion said, and
I wondered if Dr. Arnold Manion was always
given to such understatements.

I had him slow when we came to the long
curving gravel lane that meandered back to the
Lancer's farm. He knew what I was thinking.
"The question is can you live with yourself if
you don't check on them and you later learn
they were still back there?"

"Probably not," I said.

Manion turned in.

"It's narrow," I said. "It could be a little tricky
if we run into that damn cloud and have to
turn around." He didn't hesitate; he cranked
the station wagon into the Lancer's drive and
started up the tree-lined lane. Through the car
windows we could see little more than a thick
blanket of wet gray. When we pulled into the
yard there was an eerie, empty stillness—no
crickets, no frogs, none of the sounds I had
come to associate with the Jericho summer.
Manion brought the car's headlights around
until they were aimed at the darkened house.

As I opened the door I heard him say, "Be careful."

The man from Carmi waited in the car while I went up to the house. There are a lot of things I remember about that night, and the sensation of being cold is one of them. It was the first time I had felt a chill in weeks. My clothes were soaked, and I felt an uneasy shiver race up the back of my neck. There was the faintest trace of sulphur in the air, and a smothering kind of clinging dampness enveloped all the senses. I turned on my flashlight, played it back and forth across the great wooden porch that extended across the entire front of the ancient two-story house, then started climbing the steps. If the vapor cloud had been there, I remember thinking, the sagging wooden screen door had served as its only barrier.

"Millie!" I shouted. "Millie, are you in there?"

Silence.

"Millie, it's Elliott Wages. I was here earlier today. Are you all right?"

"Better go on in and have a look around," Manion said from the car. "It's late enough that they could already have gone to bed."

I went in, shoving the beam of my flashlight over the threadbare rug in front of me. I called out again, and again there was no answer. The clawing stillness abruptly gave way to a stirring breeze, and the wind toyed with a door somewhere in the house, bumping it against its casing.

"Millie?"

Still no answer.

The Lake

At that point I was beginning to wonder if Peters's nervous little deputy had somehow managed to pull it off. Had he already been there and made arrangements to get George and Millie to safety? The barrier of darkness contributed to my uncertainty. I heard a loud peal of thunder and then the rain again. A car door slammed, and I knew Manion had sought shelter in the Carmi stationwagon.

The floors creaked as the old house bent to the whims of a gust of wind. From the sitting room I moved out into a hallway that lead toward the rear of the house, emerging in the kitchen. There I found a kerosene lantern, groped around until I found some matches and lit it. The flame bounced a pale veil of shimmering light around the room, and I knew that Millie, if she was gone, had left in a hurry. There was an open loaf of bread on the sideboard and a full glass of iced tea sitting next to it. She hadn't been gone long. There was still ice in the glass. The wind stirred the curtains on the window over the kitchen sink, where the rain had been coming in. I shut it just in case. In case what? I thought to myself.

I was certain of something that up until that moment I had been reluctant to admit to myself. Jericho's killer vapor cloud had been there, come and gone. It had left the faint but unmistakable odor of its presence behind along with a thin coat of the black, oily residue I had seen on the barge. The only question in my mind was whether or not George and Millie had gotten out in time.

Holding the kerosene lamp in front of me, I started looking for the stairs to the second floor. The first door lead to a pantry, the second to another hallway. The hall lead to the side entrance. The Mauser was wedged between my belt and the waistband of my trousers. The flashlight was tucked in my back pocket. They were insurance in most cases, but not this time. The old linoleum flooring creaked with every step. I tried another door, which opened into a bathroom. From there I worked my way to the end of the hall and the door leading to the side porch. It was an oversize door, probably made that way to accommodate George's wheelchair. I reached for the knob and heard a noise behind me.

I turned around and saw George Lancer's wheelchair coming straight at me. In it was what was left of the human wreckage Foster Wallace had called a partner in the land deal that had turned out to be nothing more than his personal vendetta against Felix Chesterton.

From a human being who had already paid a terrible price for living, the vapor cloud had extracted one more excruciating toll. He was not yet dead, and in those final awful minutes he was again finding the strength to resist the inevitable. The sound was pathetic, childlike, the kind of pain most men never feel. His mouth was open and his bloated tongue served more to choke him than convey his protest. His eyes were already gone, eaten away. His stroke-immobilized hands actually seemed to be reaching out to me. The chair slammed into me, pitching me back against the door. The door swung open and I was plowed through it, out onto the flooring of the porch. The kerosene lamp flew out of my hand, the globe shattered and flaming kerosene began spreading across the rain-soaked boards, leaving a path of certain destruction. The rain pelted my face as I scrambled to my feet.

There was a pickup truck parked right outside the door. Millie Lancer sat like a sentinel in the driver's seat and I realized what had happened. She had taken George to the side entrance where the ramp was, then gone to get the truck, but the vapor cloud had trapped her just minutes from escape.

There was nothing I could do. The flames quickly consumed the porch and then the body of George Lancer. As they began to scorch the side of the truck and eat their way up the side of the old house, I saw Manion come running around from the front. When he saw what was happening, he grabbed me by the arm and dragged me away from the scene. We stood in the driving rain for several minutes, mesmerized by the horrifying sight of George and Millie Lancer's funeral pyre.

Finally, Manion's voice cut through the sound of the flames. He was urging me toward the car. "Let's get out of here, Elliott. You did everything you possibly could." He looked back at the flames again. "It won't be long till the fire gets to the fuel tank on that truck."

From the road, at the end of the long, winding gravel lane, I turned back to look at the Lancer place. There were angry orange streaks in the black-on-black nightscape. It reminded me of some kind of demented surreal painting. I heard a muted explosion and the color intensified. The inferno was consuming the old house and the rain was doing little to assuage the destruction.

A second explosion came just as Manion was pulling the car back on the blacktop. Neither one of us looked back; we were headed for the Bartel plant.

Outside the security gate to the Bartel plant, we found Peters's harried, diminutive deputy with the thick glasses and the big mission. He had been reduced to a charred mannequin. He was still sitting behind the steering wheel of his Jericho County Sheriff's department cruiser. He had made it as far as the front gate, but no farther.

I got out of the car, circled the patrol car a couple of times and finally worked up the courage to open the door on the passenger's side. I put a handkerchief over my nose and mouth, held my breath and tried the radio. Static. I switched channels. More static.

"Can you get through to Peters?" Manion asked.

I shook my head.

"Too bad. He'd be relieved to know we at least made it this far," Manion said.

The gate was open. Without power, Bartel's state-of-the-art security system was useless. I wondered how Blackmonn planned on explaining its failure to his superiors.

I headed straight for the three cars parked next to the entrance. There were two Oldsmobiles, both with New York plates, and a 450 SL. It was Cyn's car. Manion saw me pull up short.

"What's the matter?"

"Cynthia Wallace's car," I said. "After Chesterton roughed her up he took her car."

"Chesterton?" Manion said. "What would he be doing here?"

That old Wages's sinking feeling about something having gone terribly wrong was starting to gnaw at me. An old friend had once described me as having studied just enough psychology to make me dangerous. "He thinks he understands how people's minds work," she had said. She was right. I knew why Chesterton had headed for the Bartel plant. He had a score to settle. Foster Wallace may have pulled the financial trigger on him, but the Bartel people had given him the gun. This was Chesterton's opportunity to even the score.

Manion opened the door to the 450 and peered in. "Look, Elliott, the keys are still in the ignition." Then he pointed to an ugly red smear on the leather dash. "Looks like blood."

From the looks of things, Cyn had gotten in a few good licks of her own.

I turned and studied Bartel's darkened monument to disaster. "I think I now know why we haven't been able to get through to anyone over here." I started for the door and pulled out the Mauser. Manion's eyes widened, but he didn't ask questions.

Somehow it managed to get even darker inside the plant. Manion pushed the beam of his flashlight along the corridor in front of me. The gray cork walls sucked up the pale wash of light and the sound of Manion's quickened breathing. Without the trail of tiny diode security lamps along the wall, the corridor seemed longer.

"There is a door and a stairway at the end of the hall," I said. "Blackmonn's office is on the second level. The last time I was here he had a schematic of the plant layout on a table beside his desk."

Manion hesitated. "Why hasn't the backup security system kicked in?"

"Because," I said, already convinced that Chesterton was the culprit, "someone came here with the express purpose of making damn sure it didn't."

"Chesterton?"

"Chesterton," I said.

We inched our way to the top of the darkened staircase and stopped. I leaned forward, put my ear against the door and listened. Silence. If Chesterton knew we were inside the complex, he would waste no time setting up an ambush.

I whispered to Manion. "Back down three or four steps and keep a low profile. Stay low when I open the door. Chesterton could be on the other side, waiting for us. If Chesterton opens fire, we don't want to give him any bigger target than we have to."

Manion swallowed hard and sucked in his breath. He was out of his element and he knew it. He backed down, crouched and turned off his flashlight.

I shifted the Mauser to my left hand, took hold of the doorknob with my right and started to turn it. The door opened three or four inches and stopped. I pushed harder but it was blocked. As I strained against the door, I listened for sounds of life from the other side.

Manion inclined his head to one side. "I don't hear anything," he whispered. His voice had a timorous edge to it.

I waited several minutes, braced my shoulder against the door and pushed. Again it stopped. It felt as though something had been wedged against it. I crouched, reached through and felt along the floor between the door and the casing.

"Shine your flashlight down at the bottom of the door," I said.

The splayed beam of Manion's light sliced the darkness and confirmed my suspicions. The wash of light fell on the vacant, hollow face of Blackmonn's assistant. There was a tidy, tiny round hole about the size of a steely marble in the corner of his right eye near the bridge of his nose. The thin trickle of blood had already dried.

It took Manion several seconds to piece together what he was looking at. His hand was shaking and the light quivered. "Who is he?" he stammered.

"Mueller, Blackmonn's assistant."

"Is he dead?"

I put my shoulder against the door and pushed Mueller's body back far enough for us to squeeze through. Manion reached down and picked up Mueller's hand to see if he could detect a pulse. He looked up and shook his head.

"He hasn't been dead long," he said. He rolled Mueller's head to one side and I could see a pool of partially congealed blood on the floor. A large portion of the back of Mueller's head was gone.

"It looks as though we've got two problems now: the vapor cloud and a man with a gun," I said. "Stay alert. Since Cyn's car is still parked outside, five will get you ten Chesterton is still in the building."

When Manion was finally able to take his eyes away from Mueller's body, he began scanning the beam of his flashlight around the alcove. "Are we close to Blackmonn's office?"

"Down the hall, third door on the right. Hold your flashlight at arm's length to your side. Keep as close to the wall as possible. If Chesterton starts shooting, he'll fire at the light."

I could hear Manion's labored breathing as he tried to extend his arm even farther. His voice was barely audible. "Do you think he shot Blackmonn too?"

"I don't like Blackmonn's odds," I said.

We groped our way down the corridor until we came to Blackmonn's office. The door was open. The drawings weren't on the table. Manion started for the file cabinets and I went through the desk drawers. Manion found them, unrolled them and began to trace his finger from one location to another.

"Elliott, in this light I can't be certain I'm reading this drawing correctly. But it appears that most of the system's control equipment is located right here." His finger was pointing to cell 44-S. "If I'm right, it's down one level. This blue line should be the conduit that houses the distribution cable. It appears to lead to a computerized control center—the one marked 46-S. My guess is that's where we'll find the control monitors."

While Manion rolled up the drawings and slipped them under his arm, I checked out the corridor. I was getting more and more nervous about Chesterton.

We worked our way back to the alcove at the top of the stairs. After we passed Mueller's body, we stopped just long enough for me to check behind the other doors opening off the alcove.

We worked our way back down the dark stairs. Several minutes later we were threading our way along the heavy steel grating above the wet bay where the defused RANASUR was moored. We could hear the rain pelting the corrugated steel roofing over the docking area and see occasional flashes of lightning through the skylights. Manion, getting more apprehensive by the minute, had begun assessing the chances of the vapor cloud getting inside the port area.

"According to Blackmonn, this plant has everything: its own power source, its own makeup air system, even its own sewage treatment. The plant is completely self-contained."

"What would Mr. Blackmonn say if he could see his fail-safe system now?" Manion asked with a sneer. "No power, no security and the failure of the ovens to keep the CpP stockpile stable."

"Live by the computer, die by the computer," I started to say, but Manion cut me off with a wave of his hand. He was sniffing the air again. I waited.

The man from Carmi leaned close, his voice muffled. "Smoke. Smell it?" He bent down and sniffed at the air coming out of the louvered plate over the vent opening.

"What kind of smoke?"

"Acrid. Like burnt wiring."

That momentary distraction was all Chesterton needed. The beam from a powerful flashlight stabbed the darkness and glared in our faces.

"Drop your gun over the railing, Wages," he said.

At that moment all I could see was the light. Although he stood on the catwalk just ahead of us, Chesterton was enveloped in darkness. Apparently I hesitated just long enough to make him nervous.

"I said drop it." His voice had elevated an octave. It was flinty and raw.

Manion jerked the beam of his light up, revealing a vague, ill-defined image in the shadows. I didn't need a degree in logic to tell me that Chesterton held all the cards. He confirmed it when I heard the unmistakable metallic click of a hammer being cocked.

"Now, Wages!" Chesterton was making all the sounds of a man who had started coming apart at the seams.

I dropped the Mauser over the railing. It ricocheted off of the hull of the RANASUR and made a sickening splash when it hit the water. I showed Chesterton my empty hands.

The Lake

"What about your friend?" Chesterton demanded.

"Only a flashlight," Manion said.

Chesterton's laugh was hollow. "Excellent. If that's the case, I think it's time I introduced you two to your host. Walk toward me with your hands up."

We did as we were told. Chesterton used the barrel of Peters's Ladysmith to prod us through a door into a room dominated by a large steel console with an exotic maze of electronic controls. A single incandescent bulb plugged into a converter on an emergency power pack illuminated the room.

"Sit down!" Chesterton aimed the beam of his flashlight into the far corner of the room. "Introduce your friend to Mr. Blackmonn, Wages."

Bartel's superintendent was slumped in an untidy heap. His mouth was taped, his hands were tied with several pieces of wiring harness and he looked as though Chesterton had already taken a great deal of his frustration out on him. There were only a few places on his face that weren't covered with bruises. One eye was swollen shut and the other was pleading with me to do something about his predicament.

In the pale light, Chesterton didn't look a whole lot better. I had managed to get in a few good licks on the marina pier, and Cyn had put up a pretty good fight herself. A nasty cut traversed his face from just under his left eye to the side of his neck. There was a sizable lump under his other eye and a couple of random scratches that seemed to further distort his face.

The montage of moody colors gave testimony to just how difficult his night had been.

Despite the fact that he looked rattled, I decided there was no harm in trying to reason with him. "We came here looking for Blackmonn," I said. "There's a malfunction in at least one of the inventory control ovens. According to the Bartel people in New York, the situation is getting critical. Manion and I came here to see what we could do to help."

Chesterton leaned his athletic frame back against the control panel. He forced a laugh that fell apart the moment it escaped his mouth. "Do tell," he said. "And I suppose you expect me to believe that you came here out of the goodness of your heart? Jericho's little helper, right?"

"He's right," Manion said. "The general power failure throughout the area has interrupted the sequencing of the controls in the infrared ovens that monitor the temperature of the CpP storage cells."

The look on Chesterton's face betrayed the fact that he hadn't heard a word Manion said. He kept the barrel of the Ladysmith pointed at me.

Manion tried again. "Unstable CpP is almost certain to result in an explosion. An explosion of any size coupled with that vapor cloud of primary phosgene could result in a disaster of cataclysmic dimensions."

Chesterton continued to ignore the professor. Instead, he turned his attention to Blackmonn. "What no one seems to understand is that none of this would have happened if Foster Wallace hadn't set out to ruin me financially."

"Don't you see, Felix," I said, "you're making the whole village pay for what one man did to you."

Chesterton wheeled, bent down and shoved the barrel of the revolver against my throat. His eyes were glazed.

"No!" he screamed. "It's all lies. First it was Foster Wallace. Then his daughter. Then the whole town. It's a conspiracy to ruin me." Chesterton paused for a moment and looked around the room. "But I would have beaten everybody if I'd been able to pull this off." His voice trailed off again and the momentarily slack mouth curled into a crooked grin. "And you, Wages, what kind of fool do you take me for? Don't you realize that I've got it all figured out? You and Cynthia and Peters rigged up that ridiculous story about that boy being attacked by that so-called giant gar. And that whole thing with Cynthia's boat—that was rigged too."

"Such a creature exists," Manion said evenly. He was struggling to keep his voice under control. "We discovered another one the day before yesterday in the depths of the trench that leads from the slough into Jericho Lake. We have every reason to believe that both of them were mutated life forms resulting from a mix of CpP and phosgene."

"Phosgene, CpP, toxic vapor clouds, giant garfish," Chesterton said, his face no longer contorted. "The stuff of lies and rumors. Didn't your mother tell you, Wages, rumors can ruin a man's life. You said yourself that you destroyed that giant gar. If the gar is dead, why didn't you authorize Marlboro to lift the quarantine?"

"Don't you see?" Manion said. "The mutated life forms are only symptoms. Our concern is the lethal combination of phosgene and CpP."

"Your damn killer fish is dead!" Chesterton screamed. He wheeled and pressed the revolver against Manion's temple. "Why didn't you authorize the reopening of the Jubilee?"

Manion swallowed hard. "If there were two, there could be more. We were just being cautious." He had taken logic as far as he could. He closed his eyes and pursed his lips together.

It was my turn. "Dr. Manion is telling the truth, Felix. We didn't come here looking for you. We came because the Bartel people in New York couldn't get through to Blackmonn or Mueller. They needed someone to see if there was any way the ovens could be fired again."

Chesterton slumped back, leaning his weight against the front panel of the console.

"Look, Felix, your beef isn't with anyone but the Wallaces and the Bartel people. Don't compound the situation. You can put an end to some of this nightmare by simply letting Manion talk to the Bartel people in New York. If you don't, the situation is only going to get worse. Hundreds have already died. Manion thinks that an explosion of the magnitude we're talking about will kill ten times that many."

Chesterton squeezed his eyes shut and stood up. He appeared to be more disoriented than he had when we entered the control room. He was standing too far away from me for me to try anything even if I had a plan, which I didn't. Even though he was unsteady, the Ladysmith tilted the odds too much in his favor.

I tried again. "Give Dr. Manion the phone," I said evenly. "Let him make the call."

Chesterton looked at me and Manion, then began to laugh.

"Here's your damn phone, Wages," he said. He picked the instrument up off of the console and threw it on the floor.

Manion picked it up and looked at me. He was shaking. "Jesus, Elliott, the wires have been cut."

Monday A.M., September 6

Manion set the useless telephone down on the floor and looked at Chesterton. "I don't understand. Why?"

Chesterton twisted his face into a grotesque mask. "Why don't you tell him, Wages. You seem to have figured most of this out. Tell your friend why I can't afford to let him make that phone call."

I had no way of knowing how Felix Chesterton would react if I told Manion how much I knew. It had taken me awhile to put the pieces of the puzzle together, and I still wasn't certain the puzzle was complete.

"Tell him, Wages." Chesterton's voice reverberated like brittle crystal.

"It seems that Mayor Chesterton's trouble began long before this Jubilee. He killed Foster Wallace. And earlier tonight he tried to kill Cynthia Wallace."

"Tried?" Chesterton said.

"Tried. Cyn is alive, Felix. We got to her in time."

I had caught Chesterton off guard. He shook his head and cursed in a low voice. Chesterton's face mirrored his disbelief.

"Manion and I were able to get her to the emergency medical center at the state police command post in Jericho. Peters already has her statement. She'll be evacuated to the hospital in Fort Janes.

"Felix, your vendetta is falling apart. With Cyn still alive, there are at least three people who have figured out what happened the night her father's car went off the road. Killing Blackmonn and and blowing the Bartel facility off the face of the map is pointless. Even if by some slim miracle you think you've figured out a way to survive, you'll be charged with the murder of Foster Wallace."

Chesterton's face again assumed the superficial calm and crooked half grin of a man who was no longer dealing with reality. "Wrong again, Wages, I've got a plan. I've got this all worked out. Now that I have you and your friend here, my scheme actually works better. Don't you see? The Bartel people don't know that I have been sitting here monitoring every one of their conversations with the state police dispatcher. They were just a little too clever for their own good. Their telephone security lines are routed through the command control center. I could hear everything they said. They are victims of their own paranoia, Wages. I came here to get

Blackmonn for backing out on our deal and I got a bonus. You see, I know all about the oven failure and the unstable CpP stockpile.

"I could have defused the situation hours ago. It would have been a simple matter of bypassing the alarm and refiring the standby generator. By now the ovens would be generating enough heat to stabilize the CpP.

"But why let them off the hook? See the poetry in all of this, Wages? Now it's my turn. Now I get even with everyone involved in Foster Wallace's dirty little scheme to ruin me financially. Remember what the Bible says about retribution, Wages? An eye for an eye. Right?

"Like I said, when this Bartel facility blows, Jericho goes with it. That'll teach 'em. No one fucks with Felix Chesterton."

"But you'll die too," Manion said. "Is it worth dying for?"

Chesterton's laugh bordered on the psychotic. "You've got it all wrong, professor. Felix Chesterton doesn't die. Felix Chesterton survives. See this gauge right here?" He pointed to a large digital display on the lower portion of the console. "This is the oven-temperature indicator. I have been watching it very carefully for the last two hours. Do you know what's happening? The temperature has been dropping at the rate of a half degree every forty minutes. When that warning light begins blinking, it will mean that the instability factor of the CpP has reached the critical stage. The situation will have become irreversible.

The Lake

"Mr. Blackmonn's disgusting little colleague was very informative—and very accommodating—that is until he tried to get away and I had to stop him."

I looked at the temperature indicator. If Chesterton was right, I calculated that we had less than 90 minutes.

"What you don't realize," Manion said, "is that as the ambient air inside the oven chambers cools the rate of temperature drop will be accelerated."

"Then I must hurry. Right, professor? If what you say is correct, then I will unfortunately be deprived of the opportunity to do further verbal sparring with you and Mr. Wages."

Chesterton suddenly seemed in control again. He went to a supply cabinet in the corner and removed a spool of plastic-coated wiring, the same kind he had used to tie up Blackmonn.

"You're a fool, Chesterton," I snarled. "If you tie us up like Blackmonn, everyone will know this whole thing, including our deaths, was rigged."

"You don't give me enough credit, Wages." His face tightened and his voice again contorted into a hoary whisper. "I have no intention of leaving anything behind that will arouse suspicion. All anyone will discover is the remains of three charred bodies in the control center of the Montana Mills Bartel facility. It'll look as though the three unfortunates were valiantly trying to take corrective action when the blast occurred. And if they ever identify the bodies, you'll be a hero, Wages. Would you like that?"

Chesterton paused and turned his attention to Blackmonn. He bent over and ripped the tape away from Blackmonn's mouth. The Bartel superintendent made a couple of attempts to talk, but his speech was tangled in an incoherent web. Then Chesterton took out a knife, cut Blackmonn's bindings, stood him up and prodded him over to the side of the room where Manion and I were.

"What makes you think the three of us are going to just stand here while you walk out and leave us to die?" I said.

"Because, Mr. Wages, I have a gun." He brandished the Ladysmith back and forth. "I'm afraid that you and your colleagues will be rendered quite incapable of doing anything about it. Let me demonstrate." He brought the barrel of the revolver down hard, crushing it against the back of Blackmonn's skull. The Bartel superintendent's body pitched forward, landing in front of us.

I figured Chesterton's momentary preoccupation with Blackmonn might be the only chance I was going to get and I made my move. He was off balance. I shoved Manion sideways and Chesterton was suddenly confronted with too many targets.

It was basic stuff. The Wages's defensive warning system told me it was no time to get cute. I lunged for Chesterton and got lucky. My shoulder caught him in the chest and my forearm came up under his throat. Both feet went out from under him and he hit the floor on his back. Before he had the opportunity to react, I hurled all 200-plus pounds of Wages on top of him. My knee came up in his crotch and I went for the throat. His right arm locked around my neck. He pulled me down, rolled me over and the rest was child's play for him.

I remember taking one blow to the pit of my stomach and the barrel of the Ladysmith across the face. A white-hot pain shot deep into my brain stem, and my mouth flooded with the salty hot taste of my own blood. I started choking.

Chesterton was long on strength and short on technique. He pushed himself away and made ready to launch another assault. It was the opening I was looking for. I jerked my knee up and buried a whole lot of muscle and bone in what had once been his handsome face. He let out a choked half scream and I could smell his hot, stale breath. He hit the floor, rolled over, grabbed the blue telephone with his free hand and hurled it at my head. I managed to get an arm up, cleverly deflecting it right into my face.

Chesterton was quick. He landed two more blows before I could clear my vision. I stumbled into him, took a blow to the side of my head and watched helplessly as he arched the butt of the Ladysmith down—until the world exploded.

At that point my world started breaking up into a distressing frame-by-frame time sequence where individual seconds froze to become isolated nightmares of indeterminate duration, passing like hours, but allowing pain to become instantaneously evident at three or four different levels.

I went down. As I did, I saw Manion try to

even up the odds. I had a front-row seat but the skirmish didn't last long. Manion was no match for the muscular Chesterton. The Jericho mayor landed one blow in Manion's throat and it was over. Manion went down gasping for breath.

I was still trying to get my arms and legs to move when I realized that Chesterton was moving in for the kill. This time it was his foot. It landed somewhere in that never-never area between the ear and the temple.

There was an explosion inside my head. The signal went out: go numb, repudiate reality. There was a boom, a roar, a bang, and a pop. My brain broadcasted a distressing evacuation order: dive, dive, dive.

The body is all too aware of what is happening at times like that. An indelible recording is etched into the subconscious. Call it what you will—a breakdown, an omega block, a coda, whatever—but when it happens, the party is over.

The ringing sound in my head lasted for microseconds . . . and then it ceased.

It was later, much later, when I heard Manion's voice. I tried to open my eyes but everything looked greasy. Someone had poured a slimy film over my world. I recognized, or at least thought I did, Manion. His head looked lopsided. And Blackmonn, hunched beside him, staring down at me in the pale illumination of that single light bulb, looked like a man with a bad makeup job. His mouth was where his nose should have been and his eyes were situated on two different planes. I could see Manion's mouth move, but it took an eternity for the words to filter through the mental flotsam.

"Elliott?"

"Don't go out and play with those nasty men," some internal voice warned me. "Stay right here where it's dark and uncomfortable and safe."

"Elliott, can you hear me?"

I tried a nod, but it hurt too much. I tried talking, but my thick, uncontrollable tongue got in the way. Finally I resigned myself to grunting.

Manion shoved the beam of his flashlight into my face and peeled back my eyelid. Apparently he didn't like what he saw because he looked at Blackmonn and shook his head.

Time passed and I was aware of someone stuffing something softer than the steel flooring under my head and trying to comfort me. I listened to muddy voices assessing a bad situation. Everything they said sounded distressing. My reviving powers hadn't checked with the boiler room, and my brain was transmitting instrument settings to a central nervous system that no longer trusted it. Through it all, my lungs were pleading for additional oxygen.

Someone was walking around the room. I figured it was Manion when I heard him say, "Is there any way out of here?"

Blackmonn must have been doing most of his communicating with nonverbal responses because I heard only Manion's voice.

"Do any of these phones work?"

This time I actually heard Blackmonn. He sounded like a man whose lips had been forced

R. Karl Largent

through a meat grinder. "He ripped out most of the wiring. There must have been a short somewhere. There was a fire."

Blackmonn's less-than-eloquent description of what had happened prior to our arrival was lost in the sound of footsteps. There was a rattling sound, perhaps a door, more grunting and more scuffling.

"What about the glass?" Manion asked with faint hope. But Blackmonn informed him that it had been designed to withstand the force of a .45-caliber bullet.

Meanwhile I kept asking myself why I wanted to drag my tortured body into a world with so many problems. The thumb peeled back my eyelid again and I relented. Manion came into focus.

"Elliott?"

I twisted my mouth and forced out something that sounded like a semisnarl. It wasn't much of a response, but it was the best I could do.

"Blackmonn estimates that we have less than an hour to find a way out of here, Elliott. If we don't, we'll be the first to go when the mass of the CpP drops into the critical range."

I rolled my head from side to side to create the impression that there was a vague possibility of life after death and tried to get a grip on Manion's hand.

"Pull me up."

Manion worked his way around to my head and lifted me by the shoulders. By the time he had maneuvered me into a sitting position, I was experiencing a whole new pyrotechnical display.

Everything hurt, but my vision began to clear. I decided to try the old thought-to-mouth maneuver. It turned out to be a one word question: "Chesterton?"

"Gone," Manion said. "When I came to, he was gone and the door was locked. Blackmonn claims all of these doors are equipped with dead bolts, both inside and out."

"The door?" I said weakly.

"Plate steel; security and fire barrier."

Manion had answers, but not the kind I wanted to hear. I looked around our uncompromising little steel cocoon and tried to get my punchboard brain organized into some kind of thinking machine. On the surface it looked as if Chesterton had left us in a no win situation. The walls appeared to be constructed of some kind of high-impact styrene material, and there were no windows except for the heavy plate glass that looked out over the mooring area of the RANASUR.

I tried drawing one knee into position and it worked. I tried the other. Same result. With Manion's help I struggled to my feet. The room took a merry-go-round ride for several seconds and my stomach did a slow, protesting roll.

I wasn't certain the information was going to help us, but I asked, "What the hell happened before we got here?"

Blackmonn's voice was fuzzy, but I was able to get the gist of what he was telling me. "I had just driven into Fort Janes when I heard the weather reports. We always take the precaution of manually activating our emergency power system whenever there are strong electrical storms in the area. So I called the security number here at the plant to make certain it had been activated. There was no answer. I tried getting through to Mueller several times with the same result. The only thing that was left for me to do was come back to the plant."

Blackmonn paused just long enough to struggle through a coughing fit and forced himself to continue.

"The stability of the CpP stockpile has been one of our primary concerns since this facility opened. We are all aware of how critical it is to keep the ovens operating.

"At any rate, Dr. Mueller was pulling into the parking lot when I arrived. We entered the plant together. By that time the power had failed and the security system was down. When I saw the Mercedes in the parking lot I knew something was up. Chesterton was waiting. Somehow he already knew about New York's concern over the power failure. He said corporate had been trying to get through to us and that he had come over to lend us a hand. I believed him. It never occurred to me that he would have any other reason for being here. I had never met the man but I had heard of him. So while I went to check on the computers and see if I could get the alternative power system activated, Mueller and Chesterton headed for the control room to get up-to-date readings on the CpP mass.

"I was returning to my office when I heard Mueller and Chesterton in the corridor ahead of me. I heard a scuffle and then a gunshot.

When I got there. . . ." Blackmonn was shaking so violently he had to pause to get himself under control.

"I suppose you can figure out the rest. He turned the gun on me, brought me to the control room, pistol-whipped me, tied me up, and started tearing out the wiring of the control panel." His story told, Blackmonn could hold back no more, and he began to sob.

"Chesterton came here for the express purpose of making certain that CpP did not get stabilized," I said. "It was his way of getting even with the Bartel people for changing their mind at the last minute and selecting the Montana Mills site instead of the one Chesterton and his pals had gone into hock over."

Blackmonn looked at me. "I know nothing of any site options."

If Chesterton hadn't pasted my lips to my teeth with the butt of his revolver, I might have managed a half grin. There was a perverse kind of irony in all of it.

While Blackmonn unfolded his tale, Manion had been prowling our cubicle looking for a chink in Bartel's security armor. Every 30 seconds or so, he stopped to check the oven temperatures. "How long until the temperature drops into the red zone?"

"I figure we have less than thirty minutes," Blackmonn said. "Give or take five minutes, there is no way to be certain. Sooner or later something will charge it and trigger the explosion."

"What do you mean charge it?" I said.

"Infuse it with energy," Blackmonn said. "A spark, a short, lightning, static charge—it's hard to say."

"Is there any way of minimizing the chance of that happening?"

"The ovens act as a kind of secondary or auxiliary security check. As long as the oven doors remain closed and locked, we're gaining time. Even so," Blackmonn added, "the more the mass cools, the more difficult it will be to keep it stable."

"Did you or Mueller check the oven doors?" I asked.

"I didn't," Blackmonn said, "but in all probability that's the first thing Mueller checked."

I looked at Manion. "I don't like probabilities, Blackmonn."

By our best calculations, we had less than 21 minutes to go until the readout carried us into the red zone. Manion announced the reading and walked to the door as the single incandescent bulb in the power pack flickered twice and failed. He checked his flashlight and quickly turned it off, then slumped to the floor beside me.

In the stillness of that darkened room, which was fast becoming overwhelmed by a sensation of desperation, I noticed a vague, almost imperceptible stirring in the musty mugginess of the enclosed room. "Do you feel what I feel?" I asked.

"I felt something," Manion said. "Could there actually be air moving in here?"

The Lake

In the darkness, I turned to Blackmonn. "How is this room ventilated?"

His voice was still lopsided. "It's all accomplished through the plant-wide environmental control system. It is designed so that if we have to shut the system down for any reason the vent shield plates on the roof open and the wind turbines take over."

"Wind turbines on the roof?" I said.

"The vents are located on the floor at the rear of the console. Like I said, they open automatically when the air reaches a certain density level." As an afterthought Blackmonn added, "Mueller insisted on them when the facility was built."

"God bless Mueller," I said. "How big are they?"

Blackmonn was still confused. "They must be quite small."

I turned toward Manion. "Are you thinking what I'm thinking?"

Manion was already springing into action. "That they might have facade restrictor plates over the orifices?"

"Exactly. And if we can get to them, we might just discover that the contractor used standard ventilating sheet-metal shafts."

I wasn't even through speculating and Manion was already putting his shoulder to the piano-sized console. "It won't budge," he said, wheezing.

"It damn sure will if we all try," I grunted.

Ten minutes later, our three-man effort had managed to move the console just enough for

Manion to slide his slender torso behind the mainframe and snake his hand to the facade plate.

"Give me a screwdriver," he said. "If I can get the plate off I can determine just how much room there is in the vent shaft."

With less than seven minutes to go, I heard the plate rattle to the floor and Manion's partially muffled whistle.

"We're in luck, Elliott. It's coupled about eighteen inches in and goes straight up. I can even hear the rain hitting the weather shield on the wind turbine."

"Can we make it?"

"I think Blackmonn and I can, but it'll be a tight fit for you."

After Manion crawled out from behind the console, the three of us made another attempt to move the console. Finally, Manion decided it would be easier to tip it over. We braced our back against the wall, shoving and straining, and finally it toppled. It worked—we had enough room to get a straight-on access to the opening.

"Let's think this thing through, Elliott. Blackmonn should go first. I'll follow right behind him, that way I can give him a boost. I figure we've got a ten, maybe twelve-foot vertical shaft to scale after we get inside."

"Our luck is changing," Blackmonn said. "The roof is directly above us. The third level drops off after it clears the mooring area."

Manion was still formulating his plan. "When Blackmonn gets to the roof, he can help me out. Between the two of us maybe we can pull you through." While Manion continued to speculate, Blackmonn was already up, uncoiling a spool of electrical wiring and wrapping it around his waist.

Manion handed the flashlight to Blackmonn. "It's up to you now."

Blackmonn, then Manion, inched their way into the shaft, and left me in a world of sobering darkness that seemed to swallow up all sense of reality.

I used my lighter to check the reading on the CpP. If I was computing it correctly, the mass would dropped into the critical range in less than three minutes. It was the first time I ever found myself rooting for an oven door.

The sounds coming from the shaft gave me hope one minute and despair the next. The air was becoming progressively more stale and I realized I was already breathing shallower and faster.

"Keep cool, Elliott," I said, "keep cool. Slow your breathing, conserve your energy."

I sank to my knees and held my face close to the vent, grabbing what little fresh air I could. I listened to the sounds of creaking metal, men straining and Manion struggling to shove Blackmonn to the roof ahead of him.

Finally I heard Manion let out a whoop. "Push up on the shield plate."

I heard a grunt and the clatter of metal. Manion's voice came down the shaft to me. "He made it, Elliott, he made it."

There was more noise coming from the shaft and finally a rush of fresh air.

"Your turn, big boy!" Manion said. "If you can work yourself through that first ninety-degree elbow and stand up, the hard part is behind you."

Manion's words were meant to encourage me, but I knew that even if I could get past the coupling elbow the shaft was likely to be too tight for me to work my way up. Still, it was the only chance I had and I damn sure intended to give it my best shot.

I lay down on the floor, put my hands over my head, reached through, grabbed the elbow and pulled. The hardest part was getting my shoulders through. The burr edge on the hem of the metal clawed away at the meaty part of my arms and gouged out chunks of flesh along the lower part of my back as I shimmied toward the elbow.

I worked my way into a sitting position with my head in the shaft and pushed my back against the back wall of the shaft. The hardest part was still ahead of me. I had to curl my legs back under me with enough clearance for my knees so that I could stand up.

Several times I was convinced that I couldn't go any farther, but each time I managed to relax just enough to inch my legs farther under me. On the fifth try, I made it; one leg was under me and I pulled the other through.

I coiled, shoved and made it a full six inches in the shaft with the first thrust. The galvanized steel walls of the vent seared and abraded raw patches of skin.

The beam of Manion's flashlight cascaded

down on me. Blackmonn had braided strands of wiring into a rope and it hung just inches above my hands.

"We still can't reach you, Elliott. We need another foot or so." There was a note of discouragement in Manion's voice. He knew how much wiring they had to work with. I didn't.

Cold, salty sweat was washing down my face, searching its way into my mouth and eyes. The taste of it was etching my parched throat. I wedged my legs against the metal walls of the shaft and tried to compress my body by exhaling and mentally shrinking the mass as much as possible. The black-on-black world made it all but impossible to tell if I was making any progress.

I exhaled, shivered, slithered, and clawed. After momentary periods of hopelessness and anger and fear, I finally felt something against my hand. Blackmonn's makeshift plastic-coated rope brushed against my fingertips.

Manion's voice sounded closer. "Take your hand and pin the rope to the side of the shaft. Then grab it."

I felt the lifeline slip away from me. I squinted up into the light, and as I did, Blackmonn muttered, "Oh my God! No!"

He moved away from the top of the vent and his face disappeared from my view. All I could see then was the silhouette of Manion behind the light. All I could feel was the reassuring splatter of rain against my face.

I tried to ignore the pain, stretched again and pinned the wire to the side of the shaft. Manion had constructed a loop in the end of it and was able to give me just enough slack so I could get it wrapped it around my hand. I managed to get my other hand up and began pulling. I found a metal hem in the sheet-metal wall and wedged my foot against it.

I slapped my free hand against the side of the shaft and felt the hemmed edge at the top. Manion was pulling and I could feel the plastic wiring sawing into the meaty flesh of my palms. Suddenly I could smell the bitter, acidlike odor of the vapor cloud.

I didn't like my options, but I was damn glad I had been able to maneuver myself into a place where I at least had options. Up and out, or stay put. Either way, Mama Wages's only son could come up a loser. I pushed my head up over the rim of the vent stack and saw the gray, deadly tentacles of the vapor cloud clawing their way over the side of the building. In some places they had already started across the broad expanse of roof.

Blackmonn stood directly in the cloud's path. Manion screamed a warning at him, but the mesmerized man never moved. The cloud of ashen gray and silver mist encompassed him and he screamed. Manion turned away, and I closed my eyes to blot out the image.

When I crawled out of the shaft, the vapor cloud was less than 30 feet from us. "Run!" I shouted.

Manion appeared to be so stunned by Blackmonn's death that he couldn't comprehend what I was saying. I grabbed the flashlight out of his hand, raced to what I hoped was the rear of the building and jabbed the ineffectual beam of light down into the darkness. I couldn't see, but I could hear the rain pelting the surface of the water.

"Over here!" I shouted.

Manion was backing across the roof toward me, retreating in the face of the vapor cloud.

"Jump!" I said. "It's our only chance."

"What's down there?"

"The slough."

"But what if that stuff is down there too?"

"If it is, we'll never know what hit us."

Manion peered over the edge and froze. But from that point on, it was all instinct and very little reasoning. I knew there was no point in staking out our claim on the roof. The slough was our only gamble.

"If you know how to pray, I strongly suggest you get started."

Before Manion could reply one way or the other, I shoved him over the edge. He plunged into the darkness, and I was right behind him.

Monday A.M., September 6

I hit the water flat, butt and back. There was the predictable sucker-punch jolt to the spine followed by the prickly sensation of a thousand needle tips searching their way into every bruised and raw part of my body. When I hit, the air went out of me and triggered the silent protest of stunned sensibilities. Next came an interlude of total confusion and a frantic search for air. All of that, however, was offset by the exhilarating awareness that I was rising to the surface. More than that, I was alive.

I could hear Manion sputtering a litany of half-submerged words, but I couldn't see him. "Over here, Elliott," he said, "in the shallows."

When I started swimming, I realized I was in chin-deep water and began sloshing my way in the direction of Manion's voice. "Are you okay, Professor?"

"I think so. I didn't have the chance to tell you before you shoved me over the edge: I can't swim, but I think I just learned how."

He was standing in chest deep water surrounded by a jungle of cattails and lily pads. His gaunt, unnerved expression was sporadically illuminated by flashes of lightning.

The world was filled with the rhythm of different beats: the pounding of my own pulse, the rain and the long, low protests of deep-throated thunder. I grabbed Manion by the arm and turned him toward the shore. We crawled up on the bank, and both of us had sense enough to test the air before we inhaled deeply.

Manion slumped down on the ground beside me. He was coughing. "What do we do now?"

"We get the hell out of here. The next shift in the wind could whip the damn vapor cloud right back down on us."

While Manion gulped in air, I tried to figure out our next move. The way I saw it, we had used our ration of dumb luck when we leaped from the rear of the building and survived. We had hit water, not solid earth. Any other scenario didn't play out so well. From where I thought we were at the moment, I was convinced we could get back to the car if the vapor cloud didn't get in our way. I figured we were less than 200 yards from the road. All tolled, a lot of ifs, but it was the closest thing I had to a workable plan.

Manion had slumped back in the wet grass with his weight propped on his elbows and his breathing was starting to sound semiregulated.

Suddenly he sat up. "The oven doors," he said. "I forgot about the oven doors."

He was right, but I didn't want to admit it. The oven doors had to be checked. We had to know if Chesterton had opened them. If they were open, they had to be closed. It was the only way to buy additional time.

"We'll have to work our way around to the front of the building and go in through the parking lot entrance," I said. "It's the only way to get back in there."

Out of habit, Manion tried to look at his watch. In the darkness it was a futile gesture. "How long do you think we have?"

"We have to assume the stockpile has already hit critical mass. That probably happened before I was halfway up that vent shaft."

"Then we're officially operating on borrowed time," Manion said.

Not liking the way that sounded, I struggled to my feet, took inventory, and received word back from damage control that all body parts were still functioning. Manion had more of a struggle. He barely made it up, and when he tried to walk, he had a pronounced limp. We stumbled through the darkness until we found the wire fence boundary to George Lancer's place and groped our way toward the road. Manion was groaning softly every step of the way.

By the time we got to the road and worked our way around to the Bartel parking lot, Manion was dragging his right leg. I opened the door to the station wagon and in the dim glow of the car's courtesy lamp saw why. A bloodstained splinter of white bone protruded through the flesh just above his ankle.

"Must have sprained it or something," he said.

At that juncture I didn't see any reason for telling him anything different. He had enough to worry about.

"It hurts like hell, Elliott."

"I've seen worse." I lied. I hadn't. Everything from the ankle down appeared to be shattered. "You stay here. I'll go back in the complex and make certain those oven doors are shut. I'll be right back." What I neglected to tell Manion was that I had my fingers crossed. Even finding the ovens was going to be a chore.

"I better go with you. You may need help."

It didn't seem to be the time or place to tell the man from Carmi that I would be a hell of a lot better off going solo. "No, you stay here. If I'm not back in twenty minutes, crawl behind the wheel and head for the evacuation point. Marlboro and Peters will need to know we couldn't get the CpP stabilized."

Manion didn't protest. His leg was hurting him too much. I left him propped in the passenger's seat and started for the plant. Cyn's car was gone, which meant that Chesterton was off only God knew where.

I threaded my way through the darkened corridors, formulating my plan as I went. I had no idea where the ovens were located. So I had to follow one of two courses of action. I could go back to Blackmonn's office and hope there was a second set of drawings. Or I could head for the control room where Chesterton had taken us, because Manion was carrying the first set when we were discovered by Chesterton.

I opted for Blackmonn's office. But halfway up the stairs to the third level, I smelled the vapor. I froze and sniffed the air. At that point I wasn't able to determine whether it was in the stairwell with me or waiting at the top of the landing.

"Think it through, Elliott," I said, "think it through."

I took another step and the odor seemed stronger. When I backed down a step the odor didn't dissipate. In the darkness I began to conjure up images of some malevolent creature bent on destroying me and me alone, as if it had a personal vendetta.

I took out my lighter, well aware that I could be wasting time and sealing my own doom, and lit it. It flickered for a moment and went out, but in that brief instant, I realized what was happening. The stairwell was serviced by the ventilation system—the odor was coming from the vent opening.

Why the hell hadn't I thought of it? The makeup air system had shut down; the wind turbines had taken over. The vapor cloud was on the roof—the wind turbines were on the roof. That meant the vapor cloud could be anywhere in the building.

I tried to reason out my next move, well aware that I had damn few options. I started back up the staircase, paused just long enough to tie my handkerchief over my nose and mouth and inched the door open. There was a strong odor of bitter sulphur and things dying. I worked my way past Mueller's body and hit something with my foot. Momentarily, at least, my luck had changed. It was Mueller's flashlight, the one he had been carrying when Chesterton decided the little man was expendable. I picked it up, turned it on and surveyed my surroundings. The vapor cloud was everywhere, hovering no more than three feet above the floor like a low-hanging deck of stratus. I decided I could make it if I stayed low to the ground.

I made it to Blackmonn's office, clawed through several file drawers and finally found what I was looking for. It was sheer Wages luck. There it was, a drawing of cell 1-B-5. It even gave me the sequence code to fire the chambers of the individual ovens. Hope escalated.

From the drawings, I realized that the ovens were down one level, adjacent to the RANASUR mooring area. I knew where to go—all I had to do was figure out how to get there.

I got down on my hands and knees and crawled back out into the corridor. The smell of the vapor cloud was stronger. I plastered myself against the plate steel flooring and tested the air again. The vapor tentacles were searching lower and lower. At that point I couldn't shake the feeling that it had all come down to a confrontation between a mindless killer and the fool who had the unmitigated gall to defy it.

The corridor leading back to the stairway was closed. It belonged to the vapor cloud. I was out of options. The only thing I could do was go out to the catwalks suspended above the bay and attempt to get to the lower level by shimmying down one of the girders that supported the roof over the mooring area.

I remember thinking it was a good thing I was operating in the dark. I hate heights, but without light, I couldn't see how far down I had to go. I realized that one miscue could result in a 30-foot plunge that would splatter my remains all over Bartel's four hundred million dollar problem child. One near suicide leap into space was enough for one day, and I had already managed to survive that one.

Mueller's flashlight wasn't much help. I noted that the batteries were getting weak, studied the configuration of the vertical and support beams for several seconds and stuffed it in my pocket. I waited just long enough to regulate my breathing and began inching my way out over the edge of the catwalk. It was necessary to swing my legs out, hang by my hands and swing back until I could get my legs wrapped around one of the steel I-beams supporting the roof. As I loosened my grip on the catwalk, I realized that I still hadn't taken a breath.

Through the skylights over the mooring area came a continuous display of lightning and an unending volley of thunder. The storm and the vapor cloud were playing mind games with me. Ghostly afterimages filled me with a debilitating doubt and visions of the killer cloud lurked in every corner of my mind.

There is no way of knowing how long it took, but the repeated carbinelike cracking of thunder that rattled the skylights and shook the building made it seem like an eternity.

I slipped, somehow managed to get one leg hooked over a horizontal support beam and steadied myself. My arms ached and the burr along the extruded edges of the beam cut into the fleshy part of my hands. At one point everything went gray and I thought I was losing consciousness; I had been holding my breath again. To compensate, I inhaled, kicked out, and got a foothold in one of the cross members. Gaining my equilibrium, I waited until the sensation passed.

Finally my foot came into contact with what I knew had to be the handrail on the catwalk of the 1-B level. I jockeyed my body around to the side of the I-beam, lowered myself until there was something firm and flat under my feet and loosened my death grip.

I took out the flashlight, danced the failing beam up and down the grid and watched the pale yellow stream of light grow dimmer. I shut it off, knowing I would have to save what little light there was left to check the ovens. The problem was I had to check each room until I found the right one because of the darkness.

The first one turned out to be a maintenance room, the second was locked. At the third, the sulphur-acid odor grew stronger when I opened the door, and I dropped to the floor to protect myself. It was the room with the ovens.

I took out the light. It lasted just long enough for me to see the silver-gray barrier between me and the ovens. I had just run out of options and luck. Mueller had lived long enough to give

Chesterton all the information he needed. The oven doors were wide open—not just one, but every one in all three chambers.

The citizens of Jericho were the big losers. I hadn't been able to buy any additional time. If anything, I had wasted it. Any hope of protecting Bartel's CpP stockpile from a random energy spark was gone. The explosion could come at any time. There was no way around it.

It took me awhile to resign myself to the fact that the fight was over. I had played out the string. All that was left was to get back to the car and to drive Manion to the evacuation site. Marlboro and Peters had to know. In a gesture designed more to give vent to my frustrations than accomplish anything, I hurled the useless flashlight at the oven. There was a dull thud, then a clanging sound as it clattered to the floor.

I crawled back out on the grid in front of 1-B-5 and decided that the quickest way out was through the wet bay where the disabled RANASUR was moored. I lowered my body over the side, hit the water and began to grope my way with one hand while I treaded water with the other. I found the slough inlet, took a deep breath, ducked and swam through it. I came up on the other side, exhaled and took a cautious breath of air. I experienced a wave of elation when I discovered it wasn't fouled and uttered a quick prayer.

Papa Wages always said we should take time to celebrate small victories. I wasn't so sure that one was small, but I celebrated anyway. I was still alive.

The Lake

* * *

When I got to the car, I gave Manion a cap-sule version of the situation with the ovens. He listened and speculated that it was just a matter of time. He theorized that the cooling CpP combined with the deadly phosgene vapor cloud would result in a blast not unlike that of a miniature nuclear explosion. His cold, aca-demic assessment sent chills down my back. As he spoke, the rain intensified again, pelting the windshield with small grains of hail. Tracer bullets of lightning streaked across the sky.

"The Bartel plant is equivalent to ground zero. Jericho is no more than ten to twelve miles from what will be the epicenter of the blast. That's much too close, Elliott. Very few will survive. Those who aren't killed in the initial shock will be victimized by the toxic fumes from the spent CpP and phosgene."

"Are you saying it won't do any good to try to seal the building off?"

Manion's assessment was growing more sober by the moment. "It will have very little effect on the final toll. The value will come, for those that make the effort, in knowing that they tried."

At that point, Manion closed his eyes in an effort to seal out the pain. "We made a valiant effort, didn't we, Elliott? I mean, we really did do everything humanly possible, didn't we?"

"We gave it our best shot." I said. "It's too damn bad we didn't get there before Chesterton. We might have had a better chance."

I could have saved my breath. He had lost consciousness.

R. Karl Largent

*   *   *

The scene at the old Jericho high school was
right out of a Dali painting. The parking lot of
the old complex sat adjacent to the lake. The
lake itself disappeared in the darkness. Only the
lightning illuminated it. When it did, I could see
the silver-gray killer cloud no more than 30 or
40 yards offshore. Time and space and human
emotion had welded it into a sculpture of warped
unreality.

Those who remained, mostly men and a handful of women, had been assembled in the old
gymnasium. The only lighting was provided by
two incompetent 60-watt light bulbs powered
by a hand-cranked generator. Three men were
taking turns keeping it going.

I found two of Peters's auxiliary deputies and
convinced them that I needed help getting
Manion into the building. Neither of them was
eager to step beyond the supposed safety of the
door. One of the men produced a stretcher and
we were able to get Manion to the medical area.
Then I went looking for Peters.

The sheriff was parceling out rolls of furnace
tape and instructing the people to seal off anything that looked like a place where the vapor
cloud could enter the building. He saw me,
turned the task over to one of his deputies and
limped toward me.

"What happened?" His crooked half grin betrayed his expectations.

"We were too late."

His face sagged. "Too late?"

The Lake

I nodded. At that particular moment there didn't seem to be any reason to burden him with all the gruesome details. "Manion thinks the plant could blow at any minute. What's the latest here?"

"Well," Peters said, "you can see for yourself." His gray empty eyes scanned the gymnasium. "This is where I went to school, Elliott. I know this old gym like I know every lake in this county. The bleachers hold about three thousand people. I'd judge them to be about half full. Most of the people don't realize how bad the situation is."

"Where is Marlboro? He needs to be brought up-to-date on the situation over at the Bartel plant."

"Last time I saw him he was trying to get a communications center established on the second floor in the old observatory. He's got people trying to keep an eye on the vapor cloud. You were out there, how close is it?"

"Everyplace but here," I said. "It's sitting thirty or forty yards offshore. What about the evacuation flights?"

"They called 'em off, too risky. When the last line of squalls hit, the Air Guard commander ordered the helicopters to return to their base."

"Were they able to get any more gas masks?" Peters shook his head. "Not enough to help."

"What are we telling the people at this point?"

"Marlboro has been leveling with them—at least those he can get to settle down long enough to listen. He's been telling them that it's a poison gas cloud that results from leaking barrels at the bottom of the lake and that it's being shifted around by the winds in the squall lines. He's been assuring them that if we can hold out until morning and the storms quit, then there is a good chance that the sun will diminish the vapor cloud. If those things happen, he tells them there is a good chance we can get out of this alive."

I wondered what Marlboro would tell them when he learned about the ovens. "And what about Cyn? Was she evacuated?"

Peters shook his head. "We tried to get her on the last flight, but she wouldn't leave until she knew you were safe."

"Where is she?"

"Last time I saw her, she was with a crew that was trying to tape up the windows in the old school library. It's in the annex wing leading back to the schoolhouse proper."

At that very moment I was wondering if this was the way it was for Gordon in the final hours at Khartoum—no way out and no place to retreat. If we were going to survive until dawn, the cloud of deadly phosgene had to be held at bay and Divine Providence had to intervene to keep Bartel's CpP stockpile from detonating. Both were long shots.

I confiscated a flashlight from Peters and headed for the library to find Cyn. For a guy who had chosen to ride out life's storms single masted, seeing and touching the woman who had made my Jericho summer had suddenly become very important.

She was alone in the library, looking small and vulnerable, an altogether different Cynthia Wallace. Her face was swollen and bruised. The enticing Wallace smile was gone and the flirtatious green eyes were little more than glassy slits in a mask that made her almost unrecognizable. She saw me, began to tremble and reached out. Her defenses collapsed and the tears broke through. The worst part was I knew that we had only a few precious minutes before I had to get word to Marlboro.

"Stay with me," she pleaded.

We sat down in the darkened library, still holding on to each other and she put her head on my shoulder. Then her whole body sagged with exhaustion. Within minutes she had spiraled into a deep sleep.

I don't know how long it was until Peters found us, but it was the sheriff who was shaking me.

"Elliott, wake up. We've got a new problem. That last squall line roared through here like a freight train. There was some damage to the gymnasium and we lost part of the roof. We've got to evacuate the people."

"Evacuate 'em? Where?"

"We're herding them into individual classrooms."

Monday A.M., September 6

I left Cyn in the old library and went with Peters. It took us the better part of 30 minutes to get the people out of the gymnasium and situated in classrooms.

From there, Peters and I went to the old observatory to find Marlboro. One of the officers was trying to patch us through to the Bartel people in New York.

"I think I finally got through, sir," the officer said. He handed the telephone to Marlboro.

Marlboro took the phone, wedged it between his ear and shoulder and reached for his clipboard. "Who am I talking to?" he demanded.

"Dr. Steven Bentley. I'm the technical director on the RANASUR Project. What's the situation, Captain?"

Marlboro started to explain, hesitated, then handed me the telephone.

"Elliott Wages here, Dr. Bentley. Dr. Manion

and I have just returned from your Montana Mills facility. The storms have knocked out all the power, and the temperatures in all three ovens have reached the critical zone. We made one last effort to buy some additional time by securing the oven doors, but the toxic vapor cloud has already taken over your entire facility."

There was a prolonged silence on Bentley's end of the line. When he spoke, much of his early confidence was gone. "Are you telling me there is no hope of getting back into the facility, closing the oven doors and firing the ovens?"

"No hope," I said flatly.

There was another delay on Bentley's part. Finally he said, "Fortunately, Mr. Wages, our systems monitor is still working. The temperature in unit one is 129.4, unit two is 128.9, and unit three is 127.7. Unfortunately, unit number three is where the largest store of CFUS-POLCON-PRIEMON is maintained."

"What do you mean, largest store? How much of this stuff are we talking about?"

"The weight of the CpP stockpile is unimportant, Mr. Wages. It is sufficient for you and your colleagues to know that there is more than enough CpP in the third oven alone to create an explosion of cataclysmic proportions."

"Any estimate on how long we have before it blows?"

"Our experiments indicate that once a mass of CpP, of any size, reaches a temperature of less than 125.0 it becomes unmanageable."

"You didn't answer my question, Bentley, how long do we have?"

"The mass in unit three is losing heat at the rate of two-tenths degree every seventeen minutes. My guess would be that you have less than an hour to implement any last-minute safety procedures that haven't already been implemented."

I asked Bentley how the open oven doors affected the situation.

"It's difficult to say. We're running models through our computers now. Unfortunately we have no file information on the contribution of a trace gas composed of phosgene and diluted CpP and its subsequent introduction to an unstable CpP mass. And the open oven doors create another variable. In addition to permitting a more rapid heat loss, they increase the probability of random energy being introduced in the form of static electricity. Based on everything we know about it, the CFUS-POLCON-PRIEMON is already astatic enough to discharge at any moment. When you add the unstable air factor with the frequent passage of squall lines, you have a worst-case scenario."

"Is there anything you can do to help us?"

There was another pause. "I'm afraid not, Mr. Wages. My colleagues inform me that when the CpP reaches a base permutable temperature of 125.0 degrees, the chain reaction is irreversible."

There was nothing else to say. I didn't even acknowledge Bentley's last input. I handed the phone to Marlboro, got up and walked to the observatory windows.

"How long?" Peters asked.

"An hour, maybe less," I said.

"What the hell do we do now?" Peters sighed. "Do we tell these people they're on their own and let them run for it?"

"What about the roads?"

"Impassable," Marlboro said. "Littered with abandoned cars, trucks and RVs. A handful might get through but that's about it."

Peters unwrapped a cigar, bit off the end and lit it. "If we go out there, the damn vapor cloud gets us. If we stay here, the explosion gets us. Sure as hell ain't much of a choice."

"You know this old school, Harrison," I said. "Is there any place we haven't utilized yet? A place that might hold up to the explosion?"

Peters tried to think of such a place. "The old boiler room might hold up," he said. "It was built back in the forties. The walls are made of solid concrete, thicker than hell."

"How many people will it hold?" Marlboro demanded.

"Not many," Peters said. "Maybe twenty—a few more if we really crammed 'em in."

Marlboro turned to his communications man. "Find some way to get Manion up here. We need to know what happens when the CpP explodes and sets off the phosgene cloud. We know there will be fallout, but how long will it last?"

Peters looked at the captain. "It doesn't make any sense to cram those people in that old boiler room if they end up starving to death waiting for the fallout to clear."

I had just started for the door to help Peters find Manion when I saw Rudy Perrymore running down the hall toward us. His face was flushed and he was out of breath.

"Sheriff," he said, panting heavily, "I just saw Mayor Chesterton. He's got Ms. Wallace. He's holding a gun on her. He took her out the door that leads to the parking lot."

I started for the door with Marlboro right behind me. We bolted down the hall and down the stairs to the first floor. By the time I got to the door of the library, Marlboro had fallen behind. Out in the parking lot I could see Chesterton. He was forcing Cynthia into the 450.

I shouted and Chesterton fired. He was off target. The bullet tore into the decaying brick wall several feet to my right. By the time he fired his second shot, I was threading my way through the tangle of cars in the parking lot.

By the time I got there, Chesterton had crawled behind the steering wheel of the SL. I could see Cyn slumped in the other seat, her head tilted to one side.

Chesterton jammed the Mercedes into reverse and the tires squealed until it ploughed backwards into a pickup truck. He shifted into first, tires again screeching, and the once sleek convertible slid sideways. It sideswiped a minivan and catapulted out over the curbing, spinning onto the grassy area leading down to the lake.

I was still chasing them when Chesterton got the SL under control, wheeled around and aimed straight for me. I was staring at two glaring headlights getting closer by the second. There was very little time to react. I faked left and lunged right, but the front fender on the driver's side caught me. A glancing blow spun me around, knocked me off balance and left me sprawled helpless on the grass.

I looked up just in time to see Marlboro drop to one knee, steady his revolver, aim and fire. The windshield of the SL exploded. The car spun into a one-hundred-and-eighty-degree turn and careened wildly across the grass toward the water. It slammed into the end of the pier, catapulted up on its nose and came down in five feet of water with the passenger's side submerged.

I don't know how long it took me to get there, but it seemed like an eternity. Chesterton managed to push his door open and crawl out. He brandished the Ladysmith in one hand and held on to the door with the other. He was dazed and dangerous.

Plowing into the chest deep water, I grabbed Chesterton, pulled him off the car and down into the water with me. He pitched forward, his weight landing on top of me, taking us both underwater. A wet, black world closed in around me and I couldn't breathe. I shoved, kicked and clawed until I was able to work my way free and push him aside. My head rose above the surface just in time to avoid the inevitable explosion in my lungs.

Chesterton came up at the same time. He was coughing and sputtering, struggling to gain his equilibrium. It would have been easy to finish him off right then and there, but I had to get to Cyn.

I braced my foot on the transmission housing, crawled up on the driver's side and leaned down into the driving compartment of the SL. Cyn's face had been rammed against the dashboard when the car collided with the pier, and she was hunched forward with her face underwater.

I reached down, grabbed her hair, and pulled her head out of the water just as Chesterton fired. The bullet tore into the meaty part of my thigh and I let go. Cynthia slumped to one side, her head wedged between the driver's and passenger's seats, and I tumbled back into the water.

Chesterton fired two more shots, neither of which hit their target. Then I heard the welcome metallic click of the firing pin striking an empty chamber.

I could see Marlboro on the beach. His face covered with blood, Chesterton circled me. Marlboro couldn't shoot because I stood between him and Chesterton. As we stood there, the rain stopped, but sporadic flashes of lightning still streaked across the sky.

"I should have finished you off back at the Bartel place!" Chesterton screamed. His voice was filled with rage.

He lunged, buried his shoulder in my midsection and knocked me backwards. I felt his hands coil around my throat as we both went under. When the butt of his hand slammed into my face, my jaw went sideways and my mouth flew open. Chesterton knew what he was doing. I felt the sudden, terrifying rush of water as it filled my nostrils and mouth. I started to choke, held my breath as long as I could, then realized that Chesterton had tightened his grip. I couldn't have breathed if I had tried. I flailed away with both fists, but I couldn't get any force behind my blows.

Chesterton was holding all the trump cards. He was on top of me and he had a death grip on my throat. We were struggling in a surreal underwater world illuminated by the submerged headlights of the SL. I could feel both the will to fight back and the strength to do it slowly ebbing out of me. I kept struggling, trying to pry his hands away from my throat—and then I saw the gar.

It came out of the black shadows like some great prehistoric creature that defied description. Its body was bloated and etched with lesions and its eyes had a shallow dead look.

The gar circled us once, then again. I felt its rough, armorlike hide rub away the flesh on my forearm as I struggled with Chesterton. For a moment, it retreated into the blackness. But when the creature returned, its lethal mouth, lined with rows of razor-sharp teeth, was poised for attack.

It rammed into Chesterton, spearing him in the side, gouging out a huge chunk of flesh, instantly polluting the water with a thick black-red fluid that blotted out the image of both the man and the beast. Chesterton released his grip on my throat and he began to thrash about in the water.

Free of Chesterton, I clawed my way to the surface, my lungs again near the point of bursting. I gulped in oxygen and tried to brace myself for the beast's attack. There was no reason to assume that the gar was going to be discriminating in who it attacked next.

The creature released Chesterton for a moment, then struck again. Chesterton's head came out of the water. He gasped for air, but the giant gar raced in for the kill, its great mouth tearing away Chesterton's throat. Cyn's former lover tried to scream, but there was no sound. The churning water had become the battleground for two killers, each in his death throes.

I backed toward the beach into the shallows, only then realizing that Marlboro was right behind me. He had sliced through the convertible's fabric top and pulled Cyn to safety.

As we watched, Chesterton's mutilated body bobbed to the surface one final time and the giant gar circled him twice before pulling him under. The water churned for a moment and then slowly became tranquil again.

I looked at Marlboro and then at Cyn. He had his arm around her, holding her up. She was dazed but aware of what was happening. The three of us stood staring at the water. Finally, Cyn turned away and began to sob.

When I managed to get my wits about me, I said, "How is she?"

"Can't tell," Marlboro said, "but at least we know she's alive."

"Good, then let's get the hell out of here."

"Where to?" Marlboro asked.

"To the boiler room."

The last thing I saw as we entered the building was the ominous silver-gray cloud of phosgene. It was moving closer to the old high school.

The Lake

* * *

The CpP in the Bartel Montana Mills plant reached critical mass sometime during the early morning hours of Labor Day, Monday, September 6.

At 4:51 A.M., exactly 37 minutes after Harrison Peters, Arnold Manion, Cynthia Wallace, Marlboro and I, along with 27 others, had barricaded ourselves into the old boiler room, the explosion occurred.

Some 20 hours later, on the dawn of Tuesday, the seventh day of September, Harrison Peters carefully donned a gas mask and limped outside to inspect the damage. The phosgene-saturated air over Jericho Lake had cleared.

When he returned, he said the three most beautiful words I have ever heard.

"It's all over."

Epilogue

Cuts, bruises, even gunshot wounds heal rather quickly. The trauma of emotional scars takes longer.

Thanks to my old friend Ginny Fordice I had a place to recuperate—the small cottage behind her home in Maine. By the time the first snow fell, I felt good enough to start work again on my overdue manuscript. I finished it during the holidays and fired it off to my publisher in New York, relieved to have the task behind me. In retrospect, I have done better work.

Ginny Fordice took extensive notes as I recounted the events that led up to the Jericho disaster. As for her losses, she was philosophical about them. She assured me that while she had fond memories of Jericho Lake she was just as happy to have the insurance money.

And then, the following spring, I received a phone call from Arnold Manion. It was he who suggested the reunion.

The Lake

So, one year to the day that the Jericho story culminated in that cataclysmic explosion, we stood near the site of the old high school. And we reflected.

Names were recalled: Hatcher, Freeman, Patton, Leonard, Rudy Perrymore, Cletus Mackey, Mrs. Fern, Basketcase, George and Millie Lancer—and even Felix Chesterton.

Manion walked with a cane. Harrison Peters smoked a cigar. Marlboro stared at the rubble.

"Doesn't seem possible," he said.

I looked back at the car. Cyn had refused to join us. "I know what it looks like," she said. "I see it every night in my sleep. The nightmares never stop."

In closing my journal, I have but a few final notes to add. By official estimates, 1,741 people died. But the real numbers will never be known. Two weeks to the day after the disaster, the government declared the area off-limits and constructed a 12-foot-high chain-link fence around the 12-square miles that constituted the epicenter of the blast. The government investigation continues to this day.

And finally, this, from *The Wall Street Journal*. Curiously, both items appeared in the same issue: *Government Bans Further Experiments In Development Of CpP*. And this item: *Bartel Files Bankruptcy*.

Too little, too late.

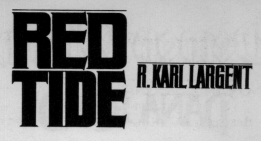

RED TIDE
R. KARL LARGENT

"A writer to watch!" —*Publishers Weekly*

COUNTDOWN: 72 HOURS

Aboard a yacht on the peaceful Caribbean, a secret meeting between the leaders of the U.S. and the former Soviet Union is set to take place. Protected by the most sophisticated technology known to man, they will have nothing to fear— if one of their own isn't a traitor.

OBJECTIVE: DESTROY THE
NEW WORLD ORDER

In a tangled battle of nerves and wits, Commander T.C. Bogner has to use his high-tech equipment to defeat a ruthless and cunning foe. If he fails, the ultimate machines of war will plunge the world into nuclear holocaust.

_3366-6 $4.99 US/$5.99 CAN

Demon Within

DANA REED

Bestselling Author of *The Gatekeeper*

Hoping to escape the nightmare of her past, Samantha Croft moves to New York City. There she is drawn, as if by fate, to an old apartment building—where a new nightmare awaits her. No one can stop it, no one even believes it exists. But Samantha feels its evil presence lurking in the dim hallways, hungering for her body, craving her soul....

_3382-8 $4.50 US/$5.50 CAN

HELL ~O~ WEEN

DAVID ROBBINS

On Halloween night, two buddies decide to play a cruel trick on the class brain...but the joke is on them.

They only want to scare their enemy to death...but their prank goes awry and one of their friends ends up dead, her body ripped to pieces.

Soon seven teenagers are frantically fighting to save themselves from unthinkably gruesome ends...but something born in the pits of hell is after them—and they have no hope of escape.

_3335-6 $4.50 US/$5.50 CAN